THE CONTAGION OF LOSS

Helen Ryan

Copyright © 2019 Helen Ryan

All rights reserved, including the right to reproduce this book, or portions thereof in any form. No part of this text may be reproduced, transmitted, downloaded, decompiled, reverse engineered, or stored, in any form or introduced into any information storage and retrieval system, in any form or by any means, whether electronic or mechanical without the express written permission of the author.

This is a work of fiction. Names and characters are the product of the author's imagination and any resemblance to actual persons, living or dead, is entirely coincidental.

The views expressed in this work are solely those of the author and do not necessarily reflect the views of the publisher, and the publisher hereby disclaims any responsibility for them.

ISBN: 978-0-244-16763-9

PublishNation
www.publishnation.co.uk

CHAPTER 1

Fuse

In the end, you see, if justice is not done some will not choose to live peaceably. Bear this in mind before dispensing mercy or seeking closure or, simply, advising that peace will follow if we forgive. Injustice magnifies loss, forging a dangerous path and leaving a trail of contagion in its wake.

~ ~ ~

Before Sara left home on the morning she learned that Kimberly, her sister, had been assaulted, she reminded herself to water the impatiens which Martin had given her the week before. It was already wilting. Martin, the only son of her aunt Tabitha, had told her to plant it out in one of her window boxes sooner rather than later, but she hadn't. She would do so, she insisted to herself, just as soon as she got back that evening.

The next time she noticed the plant, two days later, it was dead: beyond retrieval. She had binned it, trying not to imagine the disappointment in Martin's face when he peered into the corners of the flat, searching for a glimpse of its vibrant pink petals. Anyway, by then she was already on her way from one continent to another, travelling across vast seas and over horizons to a different land, where that sweet, hopeful plant would appear, hopelessly, out of place.

The call had come through on Sara's mobile around lunchtime that day. It was Kim herself, calling from the hospital. At the beginning of their conversation, she sounded calm but it took only a few questions from Sara for Kim's composure, always fragile, to fracture. Two minutes in and she was at full throttle, ranting and saying she was discharging herself. Sara could hear a nurse in the background, telling her to stop shouting and to get back into bed. When this had no effect on Kim, the nurse requested to speak to Sara.

"What for?" Kim snapped.

The nurse changed tactics then, abandoning the briskness demanded of her role and pleading with her instead.

"Please," she said. "Let me speak to your sister. You're getting upset." There was sympathy in her voice, thought Sara, alongside the weariness.

"Kim, hand me over to the nurse. Please."

Kim had relented, and Sara was able to establish why she was in hospital. She had been brought in the previous night by ambulance after some sort of altercation at a party in a block of flats in Greenford. It had not yet been established whether it was during or after she had been assaulted that she had fallen down a flight of stairs. Whatever had occurred, the incident had been serious enough to warrant the paramedics involving the police. Sara was told that Kim needed X rays to check her ribs, a scan to establish whether there was any internal damage. There were cuts and bruises to her face which suggested she had been hit.

"What happened?" asked Sara.

"We don't really know the details. An ambulance was called when she was discovered unconscious at the bottom of some stairs. Your sister was a bit – well, worse for wear when she was brought in."

Drunk, thought Sara. Bloody drunk. Why didn't she just say so?

"She mustn't discharge herself," the nurse went on. "It's potentially dangerous. We need to check her over properly and we've not had the opportunity to do that yet."

The comment provoked another explosion from Kim.

"Yes, you have. You bloody well have."

Sara could imagine her face, ugly with rage, as she spat out the words. There would still be alcohol on her breath, even twelve hours on from her last drink. Its smell would wash over the medics as they made note of the fact in Kim's notes.

"Let me speak with her again," Sara said to the nurse.

"They've been messing me around all morning. I just want to get the hell out of here."

"You heard what the nurse said, Kim. Just stay until they've done what they need to do. Otherwise you'll only be back again and then you might have to stay in longer."

Sara knew she was wasting her words. Kim would go. Kim would do as she wanted to. She might as well admit it to the nurse so that she could get on with helping someone who might welcome the attention.

"I need a fag. I'll be ok."

"Kim!"

Sara put her phone back in her bag and then took it out again immediately and texted Martin *call me when you can.* She'd have preferred to have spoken with George – preferred to have *heard* his deep voice speaking measured words - but it was getting on for 1.45. He'd be back in class, or on his way.

Sara had two visits scheduled for that afternoon. The office had discussed whether she should go alone to the first one but Patsy was on leave and there was no one else *available* as the senior practitioner, Gloria Bostock, had put it. Looking around the office, Sara doubted that this was really the case but her colleagues' heads were bent over their computers or else they were staring intently at screens. Certainly, there were no volunteers for a trip out to the Grenadier estate in Greenford to meet John Wright and his eleven year old son, Stevo. Stevo was missing from school without explanation and described by his teachers, on the few days he had attended, as *appearing malnourished*.

"I've no reason to think the Dad's trouble," Mrs Bostock had said to her. "He's just inadequate. Mum abandoned them a year ago and never visits."

The inaptly named Gloria had imparted this information without affording Sara one single glance. She nodded when Sara assured her that she had read the file but she didn't look away from her screen or apologise for being distracted. Sara could see she was typing up a statement for court. Her anxiety was reflected in the beads of moisture which had settled on her top lip. Sara's usual contact with her boss was a brief acknowledgment as Gloria scurried up and down the office corridors, her ill-fitting shoes clacking on the scratched wooden floors, strands of wispy hair escaping from her sloppily tied ponytail. Once, Sara had seen her weeping quietly in her car at around 6 one Friday evening. She had been the last to leave the office and the place was empty except for Gloria in her Smart car. Looking up from her tissue, Gloria had waved cheerily and Sara had waved back. As she'd walked home that evening, Sara wondered why she hadn't gone over and talked to her. It would have taken five minutes of her time: just five minutes to acknowledge Gloria Bostock's sadness. It would have had no impact on Sara's evening, taken nothing from her, and perhaps made Gloria's weekend a little better.

As it happened, George called her that afternoon before Martin did. She heard the buzz of her mobile in her coat pocket just as she approached Stevo Wright in the under eights playground half a mile from the estate where he lived. His father had been relatively polite, invited her into his flat and become very emotional when she'd asked about Stevo, saying he was *losing him* and he didn't know what to do. They'd gone out in her car to look for him and his father pointed out his son, sitting on the fifth step of the slide in his black hoodie.

"You go and speak to him," John Wright said and she did as he suggested which turned out to be a mistake as, when she looked back, she saw him leave the car and start walking back in the direction of his home.

A couple of older boys were occupying a bench on the far side of the playground, smoking weed. Sara could smell it from where she stood at the bottom of the steps looking up at Stevo.

"What d'you want, Missus? I ain't done nothing."

Sara was surprised at the boy's defensiveness. It suggested he'd been expecting her to visit. Before she could respond he jumped down, landing at her feet, startling her. She stood back quickly, just in case he wanted to exhibit some bravado in front of the two onlookers although she didn't really believe he'd hurt her. He was small for his age and, close up, she could see the dark circles under his watchful blue eyes. She was about to speak when he sprinted off, adopting a similar route to his father. No doubt he'd seen him.

"Stevo, wait! I just want to talk to you."

But when he didn't turn around, Sara decided against further intervention. As she watched the slight, hooded figure disappearing into the distance, her phone began to buzz again.

"Hi."

"Where are you?"

"I'll call you back when I get to my car. I'm about to get soaked."

Sara put up her hood as a sudden wind announced the arrival of rain. The stoners on the bench sat on, cupping the shared spliff between them as if sheltering a baby bird.

Back in her car, Sara called George, munching her way through a bag of crisps which she might have shared with Stevo had he bothered to stay around long enough.

"Christ. Poor Kim. Which hospital?"

"Ealing. Anyway, I bet she left after speaking to me. She'll be at home now – or in the pub. I'll have to go round this evening."

"Do you want me to come?"

Sweet George. No doubt it was the last thing he wanted after a day trying to encourage Year 9 to read the poems of Ted Hughes.

"If you can bear it."

"Of course."

"I'm due at the Family Centre. Supervising a contact session. I'll see you back at the flat."

Sara locked herself in the car and got out her laptop to record her encounter with the Wright family. She called the Family Centre manager to check whether the mother and father had turned up for their contact which was due to start in ten minutes. Only the mother, Sandy, was there. The father had not been seen by anyone since the previous afternoon when he said he was *popping out for some fags*. Sandy was being defensive on his behalf, saying she didn't believe he'd resumed his crack cocaine habit but seemed unable to put forward any other plausible explanation for his absence. It was *disheartening*, said Mildred, the manager. His two little boys would be disappointed not to see their father.

The boys, Ned and Toby, both chubby, both wearing glasses, had the sweetest faces that Sara had ever seen, she told George later in the car as they were travelling over to Kim's flat in Greenford. It had been a constructive contact. Sandy had interacted well with them and prepared *a nutritionally balanced* meal. She appeared more relaxed without the father's anger flying around, cast like a net over anyone who dared stray into his sightlines. Sara told Sandy this as they were leaving, saying she would be writing a positive report. A rare smile appeared on Sandy's face. She hugged Sara, her bony chest pressing into her, asking her if she knew when the boys would be returned home. When Sara said it was *too early* to talk about Ned and Toby coming home, Sandy began to cry, her voice breaking at first and then a couple of sobs, like sniffs, escaped from her. Sara had given her a lift home then, back to the Grenadier estate, because the rain was lashing down with a ferocity to flood the streets. An extra thirty minutes in gridlocked traffic was preferable to the image of a drenched Sandy, waiting forlornly at the bus stop, missing her beloved boys.

Kim's flat was on the ground floor of a terraced house fronting the A40. The traffic pounded past her front window most hours of the day and night. Even in the bedroom at the back, where the noise lessened, the vibrations of the lorries and the buses punctuated Kim's sleep. Sara rarely visited without remarking, either internally or to whomever she was with, that she wished Kim could move somewhere which might induce relaxation rather than anxiety. But Kim was in rent arrears and there was no prospect of arranging an exchange or requesting the local authority for a transfer. She'd been on the verge of eviction more than once. It was only her parents who kept the bailiffs at bay: favouring the provision of money, in light of its predictable benefits, over other more creative and risky actions. Sara had once called Kim's housing officer, knowing full well the woman wouldn't speak to her, but wanting to try – just in case this one was less worried about data protection and all that stuff. The stuff that stopped people like Sara helping people like Kim.

"She needs to be further away from the off licence, for a start—" Sara had said, before she was told, not unkindly, that the officer couldn't comment but that she would call on Kim in the next few weeks.

Kim's flat was five doors down from the little convenience shop selling alcohol and open from 8 in the morning to 11 at night. The Asian family who ran it were nervous of Kim and her moods.

"Scared of their own shadows, that lot," Kim told Sara, on a cheerless grey Saturday last December when she and George called round to make one last attempt at persuading her to spend Christmas day with them. She'd not been in when they arrived. From the door-step they had watched Kim exit the shop, carrying her afternoon's quota of cans. The pink scar on her upper lip, which extended to her nose, stretched with the grin she gave them as she searched for the key in the pocket of her jeans with her spare hand.

"Ever since I got a bit mouthy with them when they refused to give me a can to tide me over when I was skint. Treated me like shit, as if they didn't know me. One of your best customers I reminded them."

Inside the flat that day, Sara and George had gone into the living room where Kim, flopping down on her black, mock leather recliner had opened a can of Strongbow cider, even though it was not yet lunchtime. The remaining cans from the pack had been dropped at her feet, an arm's stretch away.

Sara had left George to make conversation with her sister, disappearing into the kitchen to unload the bag of shopping she'd brought before scrubbing out a couple of mugs for their tea. They had to be spotless, otherwise she would become irritated at the sight of George alternately inspecting and then rubbing at the rim of his cup as he drank.

"What are you up to?" Kim had called out eventually, even though Sara's visits usually followed the same pattern. From the kitchen, Sara heard Kim laughing, no doubt amused at George's inability to hide his discomfort, disgust even, at the filth surrounding him. The carpet, impregnated with five years' worth of dirt, would be littered with the detritus from that week's takeaways. George, having asked permission, would now be wrestling with one of the sash windows, preferring to risk some permanent lung damage from the traffic fumes rather than endure the smell of curry and cigarette smoke which lingered throughout the flat.

"At least the cat's gone," Sara observed on their way back to the car, anxious to find some reason, however minor, not to surrender to the despair which attached its tentacles to her as Kim's front door closed behind them.

Their parents, Emily and Steve Turner, had stopped visiting Kim altogether in the last year. Sara was in no doubt why they'd moved away in the first place: an ill-concealed attempt to put just the right amount of distance between them and their first born so that the journey there and back could not be comfortably undertaken in the course of a day. And whilst, when they confessed that the family home had been placed on the market, Sara had adopted her deadpan face - the one she'd worked on for the last seven years in a job derided by much of the public - inside she seethed.

"*Their* choice demands *my* sacrifice," she had declared to George, who didn't comment, but couldn't quite dispel the image of Emily Turner's face which popped into his head whenever her name cropped up. She had the look of a defendant watching the jury return to the courtroom having reached their verdict: a woman at the mercy of others. Any agency she'd had over her own future had been relinquished many years ago.

When Sara made the same complaint to Martin, he'd diffused her anger by suggesting that she would come to value their choice when it came to a holiday destination in years to come.

"Not quite my point."

"Clean air whenever you want it," he'd insisted, rocking so far backwards in his chair that Sara expected him to land flat on his back on the next tilt.

"They just couldn't wait to get as far as possible from her and her problems. I'm surprised they didn't emigrate."

"*Or* – they wanted a house by the sea. A quiet retirement."

"Bollocks."

"Ok. They made her worse anyway. You said so – all the time they lived here. You said you had to cope with them as well as her. So now, you've just got Kim. Be grateful."

"Do you always have to find a silver lining?"

"It's the way I see things."

"You mean lying to yourself most of the time?"

"It's called *balance.*"

"Thank you, Sigmund. Let me know when you buy the couch."

That was Martin for you: endlessly upbeat. He worked in a garden centre for little more than the minimum wage. In his spare time, he crafted boxes out of wood or strong cardboard which he sold over the internet making a modest profit. Martin's boxes were compact and sweet – like Martin himself who was barely five feet eight, dark and wiry, with a head of extraordinary curly black hair and red lips. So as not to be mistaken for a girl, he had a little goatee beard which Sara pulled when she wanted to steal his attention away from his precious boxes.

No two of Martin's boxes were the same – even when one sold immediately and there were emails galore asking when he might have more available. The money was welcome, necessary even, but he wasn't corrupted by it. The boxes were square or oblong, some with drawers on each side, which pushed against one another so that one was always open with something appealing inside, on show – like a tiny man or mouse or a replica of a cream rose in bloom lying in velvet. Some boxes featured a painted lid; often urban scenes, like Lowrys, with little people scurrying along streets in the rain with their collars up or clutching umbrellas. They were curiously old fashioned as if their creator had inherited the memory of some distant ancestor and was compelled to replicate his history.

Martin rented a room in the house of one of his colleagues from the garden centre. He had a single bed and a work table in one corner. A stack of shelves on top of the table, propped up against the wall, held all his materials. An essential item was an electric glue gun which fascinated Sara.

"Do you ever feel inclined to sniff it, you know like when you've had a bad day or something?"

"I don't have bad days. We have quiet days at the garden centre and busy days and we have very, very quiet days and very, very busy days and…."

"Yes. I've got it," Sara interrupted.

Martin did it on purpose. He listened to her with a serious expression on his face but rarely felt the need, or so it seemed, to talk seriously about himself. His emotions were all catered for in the tender care he gave to his plants and the boxes he created. If he longed to love a woman, or a man for that matter, such longing did not reveal itself to others.

~ ~ ~

"Have you spoken with her again since this morning?" asked George, as they turned on to the A40 from the Greenford roundabout. It was coming up to eight and still raining. He had wanted to check this rather important fact before they'd embarked on the journey but had, politely, allowed Sara to narrate the details of her afternoon's encounter with the bespectacled, cherubic brothers, before doing so.

"You are *sure* she's left the hospital?"

"Yes, sorry, I meant to say. She texted me shortly after you and I had spoken to say she was home. She asked me to bring some painkillers as she hadn't got any and she was in agony."

"What's our strategy?"

"I'll see how she is. But I might try to persuade her to let us drive her back to the hospital tonight."

George nodded.

"I'll try to find a parking space," he said, turning left into a side road and pulling up.

"No," Sara said, putting her hand on his knee. "Let's go in together. I can't bear being alone with her, not tonight. God knows what sort of a state she's in."

George glanced in his side mirror and they made a familiar tour of the local streets looking for a gap.

Fifteen minutes later, they were waiting for Kim to answer the door. When there was no response, Sara put her finger on the bell and left it there for a good ten seconds.

"Call her," suggested George.

As Sara was looking for her mobile, they heard Kim shout from inside her flat.

"Give us a moment, for God's sake."

The door opened. There was no light in Kim's tiny porchway, the bulb hadn't been replaced. But the glow from the streetlamps was sufficient to give George and Sara their first intimation of the seriousness of Kim's injuries.

"Oh, Kim," whispered Sara, putting her arms around her sister.

"Ow! Be careful, sis." Kim pushed her away gently and Sara released her, apologising.

"Let's get you back to your chair," said Sara, carefully placing her hand under Kim's elbow. Kim could barely walk. With Sara's help, she hobbled her way back to her recliner and lowered herself down, wincing with almost every movement.

She lay back, breathing heavily. Sara put her hand on Kim's forehead, pushing the limp strands of her fair hair away from her eyes, the left of which was ringed with a livid black bruise, streaked with purple. On the same side, her eyebrow was encrusted with dried blood from the two-centimetre cut above it.

"Her ring caught me," explained Kim, as she watched Sara scrutinising her face. "She punched me right smack in my eye and her ring cut me."

"Has it been cleaned?" asked Sara.

"Yes. The nurse did it. Anyway, it looks worse than it is. It's the pain in my chest that's bad. Hurts like hell even when I breathe." Kim paused, putting her hands on either side of her thin chest, just under her breasts. "It's my ribs. I've fucking cracked them."

"I brought you some Nurofen," said Sara, kneeling down by Kim's side. George was now sitting on the sofa, watching them, seeing, even in the room's dim and dusty light, the shine of tears in Sara's eyes.

"Good girl. Can I have a couple?"

As Sara started her interrogation of how long it had been since Kim had last taken anything, Kim squirmed in pain as she tried to get comfortable

"Just give them to me, will you?" she said. "I don't need the lecture."

George jumped up, eager to intervene before the scene unravelled in front of him. Kim didn't have a fuse: she could spontaneously combust at the hint of provocation.

"I'll get some water."

In the kitchen, as he was running the tap, Sara appeared beside him.

"My God, she's in a terrible state. We can't leave her here, alone."

"She should be in hospital. We can take her there now."

"You suggest it. She might listen to you."

"What are you two plotting?" asked Kim, as they came back into the living room.

"Have you had your ribs X-rayed?" asked George. "Have you had any sort of a scan?"

Sara handed Kim two tablets and the glass of water.

Kim shook her head, gulping down the water and then lying back in her chair. She closed her eyes.

"I think you need to go back to hospital," said George, gently. "I think it's important. You can't know what damage there is inside without a scan."

"When did you get your medical degree?" asked Kim.

Sara remained silent. *If we don't play this next five minutes exactly right*, she thought, *we've had it*. Once Kim had adopted a position, she stuck to it. It was another crucial element in the art of self-destruction and Kim was mistress of it: a perfectionist.

"The Nurofen will kick in soon and I'll be fine," she said, opening her eyes and looking at George.

"The drugs are painkillers. You may need some other treatment," George went on.

"I'll be fine."

Sara couldn't help herself. "Kim, please."

"Stop hassling me. I just need some rest. Leave the tablets, will you?"

"One of us will stay with you at the hospital," Sara said, knowing as she said it that she could not possibly be absent from work the following day, given the commitments she had.

"Or you could come back with us and we can keep an eye on you," offered George.

Kim closed her eyes again and shook her head.

"I can't leave you here like this," Sara said, looking down at Kim's ravaged face.

Apart from her scar, which wasn't *that* bad, Kim had an ok face. She'd said that to Kim, once, years ago now, in the garden of their old house. They'd had lunch with their parents and were then outside as Kim wanted to smoke. It had been apparent to them all that day that Kim's drinking was becoming a problem. Before they'd sat down to the meal, she had been jokey and chatty, even when their father questioned her about her finances and what she was doing about getting a new job. But after a few rapidly downed beers and then a couple of glasses of red wine with the beef, Kim had begun picking away at her parents' lives, measuring her comments to see how well she was scoring. With every hit, reflected in her mother's twitchy glances around the table, Kim would celebrate with another mouthful of wine. As her mother began clearing the table, anxious to bring the meal to an end, Kim had leant over to grab the wine bottle.

"No, Kim," her father said, moving the bottle away from her.

When she'd stood up in order to extend her reach, her father had become angry.

"No, Kim! I said no. That's enough. You're drunk."

Kim left the table then, saying "Jesus, I'm out of here."

A couple of minutes later she was back.

"I'm going out for a fag and I won't be back," she announced to her parents and then, fixing her gaze directly on her younger sister, "You coming with me, Sara?"

Sara, twenty at the time and back from her first year at University, had looked at both her parents and her mother had nodded her consent at her. It wasn't that she needed permission, she just didn't want to inflict more wounds on them. Kim, on the other hand, was eager to do precisely that by taking Sara away.

It was a summer's afternoon; August. There had been a discussion about whether they should eat in the garden but their father had vetoed the idea. On the bench under the apple tree, Kim began rolling a cigarette.

"Do you have to be so cruel?" Sara asked her.

Kim laughed.

"Come on. They get on your nerves just as much. I'm just more honest than you."

Sara had forced a smile and decided to let it go. Kim's green eyes had a familiar glassy look to them. Drink had her in its grip. Changing the subject, she enquired about Kim's love life.

Kim admitted to her then that her relationship with Tony had just ended. They'd not been together long but Sara knew Kim had been very keen. Tony was a seasoned drinker, the worst possible partner for Kim. He'd not had the courtesy to end it in a civil manner, just stood her up. When she went looking for him, she'd found him in a pub with another woman and there'd been an embarrassing scene.

"It's my face," said Kim.

"Hey, that's nonsense. You've got an ok face. Beautiful eyes."

"No. I'm a freak." And Kim had touched her scar with her index finger, tracing the pink line which ran from her lip to her nose where the cleft had been repaired.

It was that day, nearly a decade ago, in a garden now belonging to some other family, which Sara recalled as she put her head down on Kim's lap, letting the tears spill out over her sister's stained and smelly tracksuit bottoms.

"I'm not leaving you like this," she repeated. "I mean it. You'll have to kick me out if you want me to go."

"Hey, come on," said George, staying where he was, dragging his nails across the back of one hand.

But he knew that Sara's tears signalled defeat and they left a few minutes later, without Kim.

"We never even asked her what happened," commented Sara, on the drive home to Ealing. She had stopped crying, making a huge effort to recover and substitute a feeling of annoyance towards Kim rather than the pity she felt on seeing her sister's suffering.

"You can call her in the morning and we can go back tomorrow night after work," said George, stifling a yawn.

"I suppose I should call my parents."

"Tonight?"

"No, perhaps not. It'll only mean a sleepless night for Mum. Tomorrow."

George glanced over at Sara. The tips of two of her fingers were in her mouth.

"Stop biting your nails," he said. "She's a tough cookie, your Kim. We've just got to play the long game with her."

Sara turned to look at him, taking his left hand from the steering wheel and squeezing it in gratitude.

CHAPTER TWO

Punchbag

That same evening, Sara texted Kim whilst George was in the bathroom brushing his teeth.

Hope the pain has eased. Call me if you need me. I'll leave my phone on. Xx

Nothing came back.

They were both preoccupied at breakfast. It being September, George was still adjusting to revised timetables and a new sixth form course. His commute was far longer than Sara's and he was already late in leaving.

"Look," said Sara, as he bent down to peck her on the lips before leaving, "Don't worry about tonight. You stay in. Martin will come over to Kim's with me."

"If you're sure, that would be helpful."

She hadn't actually asked Martin if he would but since he didn't have a social life he was usually available at short notice. Anyway, Kim was much more relaxed with Martin. She didn't have to be on good behaviour. She could be as angry and difficult and unreasonable as she liked. Martin would always come back.

"George is tied up. Can we go over on the bike?" she asked, taking a break from the tedious detail involved in recording Sandy's contact session.

"Ok," said Martin. "I'll pick you up around 7, traffic permitting. I'll text when I get there."

He didn't get much of the story from Sara. When he started to ask about Kim, she interrupted, telling him *you'll find out, soon enough.*

Sara called Kim periodically throughout the day. In mid-afternoon, Kim eventually answered.

"At last. How are you?"

"In agony," Kim replied. "Every time I turn, I feel as if a knife is twisting in me."

"For God's sake, Kim, you *have* to go back to the hospital. Martin and I are coming over this evening and we'll take you."

Sara was marginally comforted when Kim did not argue with her but such comfort as she felt dissipated when Kim asked her whether she'd be *a darling* and bring some cans with her.

"Or wine," she said, "if it's easier."

"Do you think you should mix the painkillers and alcohol?"

"Perfect combination," replied Kim, giving a sudden intake of breath. "Christ."

"Are you ok?"

"I will be when I get a drink."

"Kim…"

"Don't give me any grief, Sara, not today."

"Ok."

Kim usually drank cider. It had rotted her teeth with its sugar content. Nevertheless, Sara did as she was bidden and visited the off licence on her way home, picking up two packs of cider: eight cans. She put them in her rucksack along with some cheese and tomatoes. She was engaged in googling *internal injuries* when Martin texted *here* from his bike outside. She could hear the engine running as she ran down the stairs to the front door. Dan, the grumpy old guy who lived in the downstairs flat emerged from his door when he heard her, asking some question about the recycling boxes. The red one – was it for plastics? – had gone missing. Did she have it? Sara assured him that she did not and disappeared quickly before she became engaged in a discussion about where it could have gone. Impulsively, as she was shutting the door, she told him that if it couldn't be located she'd get on to the garbage people about a replacement. Dan mumbled something uncomplimentary about the council as he returned to his flat. Whatever he said, Sara noted that the words *thank you* were absent from it.

As she approached Martin, in his leathers, he handed her a helmet which matched his own and they sped off, Sara hanging on to him as the sudden velocity of their departure almost unseated her. Martin liked speed. It was a strange anomaly in his calm and, almost, stolid character. He'd taken up with motorbikes at the age of 17, changing machines regularly when his finances allowed. Currently he was riding a Harley Sportster Iron 883. Sara's mother was appalled at the thought of Sara and Martin winding in and out of the London traffic but had no support from her sister, Tabitha. Tabitha was quite happy to travel pillion with her son and often summoned him to take her shopping or pick her up after a boozy night out with friends.

The trip took a quarter of the time it had taken Sara and George on the previous evening. Martin was just about able to squeeze his bike into the gap between the front window and the wall of the property, so there was no time wasted looking for a parking space either.

"Hey up!" said Martin to Kim, as she opened the door to them. They were standing side by side, clutching their helmets in the crook of their right arms. Roughly the same height and build, and both dark, they looked like twins. Kim's spirit rose a degree at the sight of them.

"Jesus," said Martin as they followed Kim into the kitchen where the harsh florescent light exposed her facial injuries in all their colourful detail. Kim had always been slight but the self-neglect which accompanied her drinking habit had resulted in some weight loss over the years. Dressed in a shapeless grey tee shirt and black jeans, she now looked almost emaciated. Her thin, dark blonde hair was unwashed, hanging in greasy strands around her injured face. She eased herself down onto the only kitchen chair, the bone in her jaw working as she gritted her teeth.

"Not a pretty sight," she said.

"What exactly happened, Kim?" asked Martin, coming straight out with the question that Sara had seemed unable to frame twenty-four hours earlier.

Kim sighed and immediately turned to Sara, asking if she'd brought the booze with her. Sara slipped her rucksack down off her shoulders onto the only space on the small, collapsible kitchen table which was not taken up with some unwashed crockery or tins. As she did so, the table tipped and a pan, containing the dregs of a can of baked beans, clattered to the floor. Kim did not respond, delving into Sara's bag whilst Sara retrieved the pan and then began a search for a cloth with which to clear up the trail of orange bean juice. It was already leaking into the grout between the tiles. Martin looked on as Kim pulled on the ring of one of the cans and began drinking. It was more like *pouring* than drinking, he thought. Kim held the can an inch from her lips and tipped its contents into her mouth, swallowing noisily.

"Let's go into the other room," said Kim, bringing the can down from her mouth so quickly that some of the precious liquid dribbled on to her jumper. "Marty, can you carry the rest of the pack in for me."

Martin glanced back at Sara as he watched Kim moving slowly towards the kitchen door, one hand clamped to her right-hand side, the other clutching her can of cider. But Sara was bent down, mopping the floor. As he helped Kim into her chair, leaning on the back so that the footrest would flip up,

Sara shouted from the kitchen asking if Kim wanted a cheese toastie.

Kim shook her head at Martin and he relayed the answer to Sara.

"I had some beans a while ago and I've not much of an appetite," she explained.

"Well? Are you going to tell us?" persisted Martin.

"What's the point? I can remember how it started but not much more."

"Who? What? Try starting from the beginning."

Martin smiled at her, even though he had to force himself to keep his eyes focused on her as she talked. The bruising around her eye, on its way to completely closing, had now extended towards her cheekbone and that side of her face was swollen. It had the effect of distorting all her expressions.

"Is it painful to speak?" he asked, as Sara joined them from the kitchen. She handed Martin a cup of tea.

"Is there no coffee?" he asked.

"Just drink it," said Sara, pushing at him with her elbow so that there was room for her on the sofa.

"Not really," said Kim, in answer to Martin's question. "It's my chest that's causing me gyp."

Sara put her hand on Martin's arm, a gesture to let him know she wanted to speak before he did, before they got side tracked and Kim became angry – as she might, if forced to recount her side of the story.

"Listen, Kim, let's go to the hospital now. We can Uber it, together. Martin can follow us on his bike. I'll stay with you until you're seen. Promise." She looked pleadingly at her sister.

Kim drained her can and nodded at Martin to pass her another from the pack he'd placed on the table. Martin obliged, pulling the ring and handing it to her.

Kim ignored Sara's plea, concentrating on the cider.

"I met these guys outside the shop on Sunday evening. They were just hanging around and one of them asked me for a fag and we got talking. They said they knew of a party going on at the flats and I could come with them if I wanted. To be honest, I knew they only invited me because I had some cans with me. But I had nothing on and I quite liked one of them so I went. It was the usual sort of thing, a lot of people, a lot of weed. Then this couple – I'd seen them around but didn't know them - started on at me saying I'd been drinking *their* vodka. The woman, a mouthy cow, kept waving the empty bottle in front of my face and yelling at me, asking me what I was going to do about it. In the end, I got so pissed off with her that I grabbed the bottle and pushed her away. She slipped and went down onto the floor. Her fella came at me then, punching me. Then she gets up and smacks me in the eye."

Kim stopped talking abruptly, her eyes reddening as she battled with her tears. She placed a finger tip on the cut she was describing in confirmation of what she'd said had happened.

"And then the guy threatened me. He said something like – *I suggest you get the fuck out of here now before I do you some real damage* -. So, I left although I don't remember much after that. I just remember being carried out of the building on a stretcher. I was found at the bottom of some stairs, out cold, apparently."

"Who found you?" cut in Sara.

"Someone who'd been at the party, I think, because it was them who told the paramedics I'd been assaulted by those two fucking maniacs."

"Christ, did they push you down the stairs?"

"I don't think so but I don't really remember much after they'd hit me."

"Were you drunk?"

Kim gave a half smile as if to say *what a bloody stupid question*. Instead of answering, she shrugged.

"Oh, Kim," breathed Sara.

Kim glared at her, immediately taking offence at what she interpreted as criticism in Sara's words.

"What? Don't start, Sara. For fuck's sake."

"Have the police been in touch with you?" asked Martin quickly. He was practised at spotting the signs of impending discord between the sisters and even, on occasions, able to intercept it.

"They came to the hospital but I couldn't talk. I was being sick at the time. My head hurt."

"And have they been back in touch with you?"

Kim shrugged. "I don't know if they've got my number."

Martin was shaking his head, disbelievingly. As he brought his tea to his lips, his grip slipped a little and he placed a hand on either side of the mug to steady himself.

"You need to get checked out. Properly," said Sara, not caring any longer if she was irritating Kim by her persistence. "You could be bleeding inside."

"I'll be ok," said Kim, gulping loudly. "Stop fussing, Sara, for God's sake. I'm feeling better already. Cheers."

She held up the second can to them and finished it off. As if to goad Sara, she reached over to pick up a third, opening it with a flourish. The cider sprayed out. Martin felt it on his face, like a gentle mist. In normal circumstances, he would have made some mild, if sarcastic, remark but experience told him that it would be unwise to enter into this particular battle of wills. He secured his decision with a few sips of tea.

Sara exploded then. She slammed her mug down on the table and jumped up, startling Martin.

"Stop being so bloody stubborn, Kim. For once, *just fucking once*, take some advice from someone."

Martin, abandoning his earlier resolve, tried to speak but Sara overrode him.

"What is so difficult about allowing someone – someone who knows better than *you* do – to check you out? Is it the drink? You're now so dependent that the idea of having an evening without it is too terrible to contemplate? Because if that's the case, hospital is probably the best bloody place for you at the moment. Drinking won't help you, Kim. Look where it's got you. Christ almighty."

If Kim had been able to get up and walk out of the room, she would have done and Sara knew that. But she did the next best thing. She fumbled around in her chair for the remote control to the television and, within seconds, the room was filled with the sound of a reporter, previously undercover at a chicken farm in the Midlands but now challenging the manager with regard to animal welfare standards and sell by dates.

"Is that your answer?" asked Sara.

"Yes, my final answer," replied Kim, her eyes fixed on the television, although the three of them knew that she could not possibly have any real interest in the subject of poultry production. "And I don't want to call a friend or ask the audience." She stopped speaking and looked up at Sara with a smile laden with sarcasm. "If that's ok with you, of course."

Sara turned abruptly and headed for the door, grabbing her jacket and slinging her rucksack over her shoulder as she did so.

"Come on, Martin," she ordered.

Martin stayed where he was, studying his tea, wondering if he could possibly retrieve matters.

"Sara, wait up. What's the rush?" was all he came up with. But Sara had left the room and Kim would not make eye contact with him.

"Kim?" he tried again, reaching over, putting his hand on her arm. "She's just concerned about you. Let us help you."

"I'll be ok, Marty. And I'm tired now so it's ok, you can go with her. I won't hold it against you."

"This is madness, Kim," he said, standing up.

"No change there, then."

In the hall, Sara was waiting for him. He gave her a weak smile, which was not returned, and, silently, they donned their helmets and departed, approximately seventeen minutes after they had arrived.

~ ~ ~

As the evening went on, tiredness eroded Sara's resolve to keep Kim from her thoughts. She wanted so much to remain angry with her, to blame Kim for her own misfortune. It would mean she could feel justified in walking out on her. But if Sara abandoned her, Kim would have no one. That was what kept her getting up again every time she became the focus of Kim's fury and was used as her punchbag because, simply by being there - when no one else could be bothered or could tolerate it - she was an easy target. Sara would withdraw occasionally, *letting her stew* as she would say to Martin, but then the apology arrived, by text usually

Sorry x -

And Sara would relent and forgive and make some excuse for her to George, who did not feel obligated to pass judgment on other people's behaviour and, anyway, over the years, he had adapted to the pattern of the sisters' relationship.

"I think I'll ring Mum," Sara informed George, getting out of bed even though she hadn't been in it for more than a few minutes.

"Isn't it a bit late?"

It didn't chime with what Sara had said the previous evening about the right time to call.

"I know. I should have called them earlier. But they need to know."

Sara pulled on her dressing gown, telling George she might be some time and she'd make the call from the living room.

Tucking her legs under her on the sofa, Sara stared at her mobile, considering exactly what she was going to say to the parent who answered her call. She hoped it would be her mother because her father's response would annoy her in its predictability. If he felt any concern for Kim, which Sara doubted, he would not express it in those terms. Kim was his major irritant. Sara could not recall a time when he had treated her otherwise. When Sara followed her sister into the family, the damage to Kim had already been done. She was a resentful little girl who had learned, even as a babe in arms, that the world, which included her father, did not act fairly. She had been born imperfect and she was punished for it. If he could avoid it, her father would not look at her directly which meant that Kim, the child, devised all manner of tricks to make him do so and when it didn't work, when she could no longer suppress her belief that he just didn't like her, she turned away and stopped trying to please.

When she was little, Sara had wondered why Kim loved fairy tales so much. She had a little library of them on top of her desk, stacked between two heavy horse head bookends. She enjoyed reading them to Sara and, sometimes, even acted them out using voices and dressing up clothes, making the tales as scary and horrible as she could, taking pleasure in seeing Sara's face become pale with fear when Rumplestiltskin threatened to steal the princess's baby unless she was able to guess his name. Sara knew now why the black and white world of Grimm's fairy tales appealed to Kim. She wanted the equation of good and bad to balance. It wasn't enough for the good to be saved: the bad had to suffer in the process.

Her father answered the landline call but then immediately passed the phone to his wife.

"Hold on. I'll get your mother."

Emily whispered her greeting to Sara, her tone hesitant and hushed, indicating that she knew already that no good news could possibly be relayed at such a late hour.

"It's Kim," said Sara. "She's been attacked and is in a bad way. Obviously, I thought you should know."

Into the sound of her mother's anxious breathing, Sara related what Kim had told her and Martin as succinctly as she could, reassuring her that she had done what she could to persuade Kim to seek some medical treatment. She even confessed to her angry outburst.

"It was futile. She wouldn't listen to me, to either of us. You might try speaking to her. Not that I think you can do much more than I did. But call her anyway," suggested Sara. But Emily was already calling out to her husband, asking him to talk to Sara. She had lost the ability to bear such news alone.

Much to her annoyance, Sara was forced to repeat the whole account to her father, who had his own incapacity issues: he was unable to make a response that did not signify, to anyone he thought might be listening, a rational mind uncluttered by an excess of emotion.

"Well, if she won't behave sensibly, she's only got herself to blame. Her own worst enemy, as usual."

"Is that it?" snapped Sara.

"Well, what else do you expect me to say?"

"Glad I called you."

"Don't take it out on your mother and me, Sara."

"Just pass the phone back to Mum. Please."

"What d'you think might help?" asked Emily. In the background, Sara heard her father's heavy tread and then the close of a door.

"I've no idea. Just call her, that's all. She needs some support."

"Ok, darling. Shall I call now?"

When Sara didn't immediately offer her opinion, Emily continued.

"I'm only asking because you saw her last and you'll know what's best…." she trailed off.

"Whatever, Mum. It's late. I'm off to bed. Speak tomorrow, ok?"

There was another short silence.

"Ok, darling. Well, thanks for calling. I'll ring her in the morning, I think."

She shouldn't have bothered to call, she told herself standing at the bedroom door, watching the rise and fall of George's sleeping form. Why did she expect them to jump in the car and drive the 240 miles from Cornwall just because that was what she would have done in these circumstances? Because *she* would not have presumed that it was perfectly ok to let her carry the weight of Kim's situation entirely on her own. *She* would have enquired further. *She* would have known how lonely it must feel to be making that call at midnight.

She reached into her dressing gown pocket for her mobile.

Kim how are you?
And then
Please let me know
And then
I'm sorry we argued

~ ~ ~

Back in his room, Martin was varnishing one of his wooden boxes. He had been experimenting with various designs on the theme of 1930s motor vehicles. Some had caused him more trouble than others. And whilst he had derived enjoyment from the task, he wasn't sure now that it had been successful. Perhaps he should have added some other detail to the scenes, such as a chauffeur or a family or even a couple of hunting dogs. He had his ear phones in and was listening to Five Live, surprised to realise that it was almost midnight.

At ten that evening, he'd stopped what he was doing and put on his jacket, intending to bike back over to Kim's and see how she was doing. He wouldn't have stormed out like Sara did had he been on his own. He would have sat it out until she came around and started talking to him again. He would have endured the programme on chickens, making such banal comments that Kim would have eventually given in - even if it was only to swear at him. But he'd taken his jacket off within a minute of putting it on, changing his mind when he recalled the way she'd looked when she opened the door to them. The thought of seeing those bruises and cuts again, of watching her struggle to speak, the extent of her pain reflected in her one good eye, was too much to bear. He contemplated *Whatsapping* Sara, asking her if she wanted to try another visit to Kim's the following evening. He would have bet a dozen of his best boxes that she would have regretted her decision to leave Kim within an hour of arriving home. She'd now be lying in bed, trying to sleep, her muscles taut with anxiety.

We can try again tomorrow. Don't worry. M x

The reply came back within seconds.

Thanks. I'll call you when I can x

Sleep brought Martin a resilience he had lacked the previous evening. He wasn't due at the garden centre until the afternoon. As the light leaked away from the evenings, heralding that summer was nearing its end, his hours had been reduced accordingly. He'd bike over to Kim's, see how she was and then call Sara - surprising her with the good news that he and Kim were together and that all was ok.

That was the theory.

CHAPTER THREE

Cadence

There was a gap in the net curtains in Kim's front room, where part of the rail had collapsed, but Martin couldn't see through the window as it was thick with dirt from the road. It was a bright morning so the fact that there was no light visible from inside the house did not surprise him and, anyway, it was only 11am. Kim was probably still sleeping. He had deliberately not alerted her to his intention as she may well have refused the visit. This way, his already standing on the doorstep, she had little real option but to let him in. This plan had been developed whilst he was eating his Weetabix earlier that morning. It now appeared flawed.

   He could hear that the bell was working and when it produced no result, Martin bent down to peer through the letter box. The postman had been. A couple of manilla envelopes were lying on the puckered red lino of the hall floor. Bills, no doubt: letters requesting Kim to contact some official about the rent arrears or reminding her that the electricity account remained outstanding. He was reluctant to start banging on the door as he might disturb someone. Kim had mentioned that there was a tenant in the upstairs flat although he had never actually seen anyone. Putting his mouth as near as he dared to the discoloured metal of the letter box, he called Kim's name a few times. He knew it was a token gesture. His barely raised voice would not raise even the lightest sleeper from their slumbers.

He called Kim's mobile number for the third time in five minutes, even putting his ear to the box to see if he could hear it ringing. At least then he'd know she was in the flat. But the noise from the steady stream of traffic passing within fifteen feet of him obliterated all other sounds. As he was considering whether to text Sara, the door opened and a middle-aged lady peered out at him, her eyes squinting suspiciously through heavy framed glasses.

"Hello. Please, who do you want?" she asked. There was an accent, although not a pronounced one.

Martin explained.

"So, I'm just calling round to check on her – you know – make sure she's ok," he finished off. And then he threw in a smile, one of his most charming ones. He saw the lady looking at his mouth and knew that she was admiring his straight, white teeth, set in his full lips. When, as a teenager, he'd complained to his mother that he looked like a girl, she had attempted to reassure him of his masculinity by saying that he was lucky - *most girls love pretty boys.* Studies had been made of this phenomenon, she said. Martin had gained no comfort from this observation; indeed, his mother had merely confirmed his own belief. He grew the goatee beard just as soon as his hormones allowed him to. But, as the decade had gone by, he had come to realise that he could disarm most women within seconds of talking to them. All he needed to do was to guide their eyes to his sensual mouth and they would buy anything, tell him anything, trust him with anything. There were times when the ensuing *over* confiding in him produced embarrassment or irritation, but, on occasions like this, he was grateful for the short cut his looks afforded him.

"You had better come in," the lady said, her tone now soft and concerned. "I do not see her much. I hear her singing sometimes and I hear music - but I have only spoken once or twice to her."

The reference to Kim's singing evoked in Martin a memory of being at a karaoke evening with Kim, Sara and a group of Sara's student mates when Sara was in her final year at university in London. He had gone along, innocent of Sara's intention to set him up with one of her friends. She failed but, fortunately, that was the night she first met George and she was so distracted that he managed to escape from the clutches of his blind date, a mere half an hour after meeting her, to join Kim at the bar. Although only twenty-five, Kim's capacity for drink was already beginning to define her. Despite Sara and Martin's best efforts, they could not prevent her from grabbing the microphone from someone and insisting that she wanted to sing "Don't Cry for me Argentina".

"They won't even have that song," Sara had said, as Kim wriggled past the two of them and began climbing up on the stage before the last singer had even finished murdering "I Will Survive" in a dangerously high key. She made no enquiries, just started singing a cappella, stripping the room of its rowdiness immediately with her sweet, melodious voice and tentative vibrato. Glancing over at Sara, feeling it only fair that they acknowledge, albeit privately, how wrong they had been, Martin had been moved at seeing both joy and pride in his cousin's expression.

To claps and cheers, Kim jumped down from the stage after her performance and ran through the throng to re-join Martin at the bar. A couple of people came over to congratulate her but she seemed concerned only with ordering two more pints of cider before time was called.

"Her voice should have saved her," he remarked, many times in the years that followed, when it became apparent to those who loved Kim that she was on a mission to destroy herself. He was thinking the same then, as he stood in the cramped hallway, whilst also remembering that Kim's flat had its own separate entrance and he had no key.

"Thanks so much," he said. The lady watched as Martin started knocking on Kim's door.

"She's not in, perhaps?"

"She might be asleep."

The lady frowned. Martin decided he may as well get to the point.

"Or she may be too ill to get to the door."

"Should you call an ambulance?"

"I don't really know what to do for the best."

"Wait," she said, turning away and heading for the stairs. "Wait a moment. I have an idea."

Martin resumed his knocking, a little louder this time.

Within minutes, his befriender was back clutching a thin bladed knife and her hand bag. Martin stepped away from the door, taken aback by her confidence. She manipulated the knife into the lock and when this didn't achieve anything, she plucked a credit card from the purse and started trying to flick the lock open with it. Martin peered over her shoulder, fascinated, until she asked him to move away as he was blocking her light.

"This is not a very strong lock," she observed after a few moments. "This should be easy."

As if she had cast a spell with those words, there was a click and she pushed the door open.

"You want me to come in with you?" she asked.

Martin swallowed. He felt unprepared for whatever experience awaited him. But it didn't seem reasonable to take up any more of this lady's time. He was worried too that Kim might react badly to him forcing his way in and become angry. It was better he faced her alone.

"No, thanks. I can take it from here. You've been very kind."

She nodded and he waited where he was until he heard her door closing on the floor above. Even then, he didn't move from the threshold. There was some quality to the sound of the silence within the flat which frightened him: he sensed he was alone.

"Kim?" he called out. "Kim?"

He walked slowly into the living room.

Kim was lying in her chair, head to one side, her face almost obscured by her hair. On the floor around the base of the chair, empty cans were scattered and there were some open packets of pills on the coffee table.

Standing stock still, Martin repeated her name. He could detect no sign from her chest that she was breathing. Stumbling a little, he ran back out of the flat and tore up the stairs. The lady opened the door before he had chance to knock, as if she had known he would return.

Martin tried to control himself but he couldn't stop the sobs which exploded from him.

"We need an ambulance. She's not breathing."

The lady picked up her mobile from the table near the door and ran past him, back down the stairs. Martin stayed where he was, wiping his face with the cuff on his leather jacket. Then he could hear her voice on the phone, high pitched and anxious. Perhaps her accent was causing some problems. Martin knew he should go down and assist but he didn't want to go anywhere near Kim again. He wanted to get on his bike. He fingered the keys in his pocket, pushing the serrated metal edges into his fingers.

But *he* could understand her. She was saying that Kim was dead.

"She is dead, I think. She is cold like ice. She is not breathing."

Martin closed his eyes. His balance wavered and he stretched out a hand to the wall to steady himself. Then he felt someone gently guiding him into an unfamiliar living room, full of bright colours and soft cushions. The lady pushed him down into a sofa and patted his arm.

"I will make you some tea," she said. "The ambulance is on its way." She disappeared into the kitchen and he heard the tap gushing and then the sound of her gulping water. Martin looked around him, wondering how he could just sit there drinking tea when Kim was dead, or dying. He should have attempted some sort of first aid, he thought, instead of behaving like a hysterical child. He got to his feet just as she came back in carrying two mugs of tea. He got a proper look at her then. She was in her forties, slim, in blue jeans and a short, knitted cardigan. Her hair was thick, shoulder length and dark brown. The starkness of the large glasses clashed with the fragile features of her face. There was an elegance to her.

"I need to tell people," Martin said, moving toward the door of the room.

"You must sit down and drink your tea," she ordered. "You have had a bad shock."

She pulled him back to the sofa and then sat next to him. His hands trembled as he took the mug from her. He could feel the tears beginning to slide down his face.

"How long will they be?" he asked. She pulled a tissue from her sleeve and passed it to him.

"They gave me no time. Just said soon. I think I should stand at the door, outside, so that they see me. You stay here. I will take them in to her… her room."

"Kim. Her name is Kim Turner."

"Right. Kim. And your name?"

"I'm Martin MacTaggart. I'm Kim's cousin."

"I'm Marie. Marie Chambon."

"They'll want details," said Martin. "I'd better come down with you."

"I will bring them up here – if you prefer?"

Martin nodded. The tissue was disintegrating in his hands. He wiped his left hand on his jeans.

A few minutes later, they both heard a siren and Marie got up, patting Martin's knee as she did so.

He heard them entering the building and then their voices. It sounded like two men. Marie did not appear to be saying much. Then they appeared at the door, Marie and one of the para medics.

"He needs some details from you, Martin."

Martin looked up at the young man standing in front of him. Even as a professional, he looked like you'd expect someone to look on confirming a death: apologetic that he was ruling out any last vestige of hope.

"She's dead," said Martin, stating the fact in the hope it would cut short the conversation which would inevitably follow.

The man nodded.

"I'm sorry. Yes - for some hours. We've called the police. They'll need to investigate before she can be moved. Kim. I understand her name is Kim."

Martin dropped his head onto his chest and, cupping his face, gave vent to his anguish.

Marie put her arm around his shoulders.

The man waited for a few seconds and then carried on speaking to Marie.

"The police will want to interview him and later arrange for the body to be removed to the hospital mortuary where, in due course, formal identification will need to take place. There'll be a post mortem."

By the time the police arrived, Martin had composed himself and was able to provide them with some background information on Kim. When Martin mentioned the assault on Kim, one of the officers left the room saying he'd make a call to check out the details with one of his colleagues back at the station. They said they may need a formal statement from him in due course but were mainly concerned with establishing Kim's next of kin so that they could be informed of Kim's death.

Martin gave them Sara's number and the name of the school where she worked. From what he could understand, they would visit her immediately to deliver the shocking news in person and to establish contact details for her parents.

Even if he had been allowed to contact Sara before the police got to her, he knew it was a task beyond him. He felt like he'd been attacked himself, that if he looked down there would be spatters of blood on Marie's rug. He couldn't move.

"You wait here until they have gone," she suggested. "I am not due in work until this evening so it is no problem."

Her soft voice relaxing him a little, Martin thanked her and then felt the tears spilling from his eyes again.

"I'm really sorry," he murmured.

Marie shook her head.

"No worries, Martin. This is a very sad day for you. I am sorry for your loss."

"She should have been in hospital. She wouldn't go. I came over to try to persuade her." He knew he was repeating himself - and for his own benefit, not hers.

"Then you did what you could to save her, I am sure."

"We came over last night, you see. But it was no good..."

He trailed off, exhausted by his own words.

"I can see you are a good man, Martin. It is written in your face, even in your hands."

Martin looked down at his hands, wondering what she meant. He rubbed each thumb over the tips of his fingers, trying to dislodge the sparkling speckles of glue which clung to them.

"You work with your hands?" she asked, smiling.

He nodded and told her about his boxes.

"Hence the glue," he said, holding his hands out in front of him so that she could see what he meant. "An occupational hazard. Sticky fingertips."

They were both aware of the necessity of distraction as the muffled sounds of people moving around downstairs floated upwards. There was the odd shout from the road, occasionally a siren.

Marie made more tea and offered food. Martin had some toast, surprised at how hungry he felt. Marie was French, teaching the language part time at a couple of places, including the Institut Francais in Kensington. The flat was owned by a friend of a colleague of hers and she was there only temporarily, which was just as well, she said. She disliked the busy road and felt unsafe in the area.

"This is not how I expected London to be," she admitted, having established that she would not be offending Martin by criticising the A40 in Greenford.

"Your English is perfect," Martin told her, wondering why he felt the need to comment, what relevance it had to anything.

At 1pm, almost on the dot, Martin's mobile vibrated in his pocket. He fished it out, reluctantly. It was Sara. Did she know yet? He let it go to voicemail.

They talked on, ranging from subject to subject. She didn't ask him any questions about Kim, didn't enquire further into what had happened to her. Occasionally, Martin would break off from what he was saying, remembering why he was there and who was downstairs, lying dead in a chair. The panic would rise like bile in his throat and he would swallow, self-consciously, embarrassed at exposing someone he'd only just met to the intensity of his emotions.

He apologised repeatedly, saying he was sorry for taking up her whole day and putting her through such an ordeal. Marie simply smiled and offered even more tea although, at one point, Martin became sufficiently confident in her company to request coffee. He got a biscuit then, too. *A Florentine*, she called it. It was brittle and covered in nuts. He would never eat one again.

They were to be forever associated with that long, strange afternoon.

No-one let them know when the formalities had been dealt with and Kim's body removed to the hospital mortuary. It just became quieter and Marie said she thought she had heard the front door being banged shut. She nipped down the stairs and returned to say *yes, the coast is clear*. She described the yellow and black tape on the door of Kim's flat – *police do not enter* – preparing Martin for when he walked past it on his way out.

"I will walk down with you?" she offered, as she helped Martin into his leather jacket.

"No. It's ok. I'll be fine. Thank you for letting me stay here. I appreciate it."

As he looked at her, he could feel a pressure building up in his chest which, if released, would fell him. Marie engulfed him in her arms and whispered something to him in French, which he struggled to understand at the time although, later, when her words came back to him, he decided it was something along the lines of *you will survive this*.

In the weeks which followed, the aftermath, Martin would recall his hours with Marie, her embrace and her words: drawing comfort from her prophecy. But there was one night when his doubts were so deep that he rode back over to that terraced house fronting the A40, at some ludicrous speed, to tell her. It was winter by then. Besieged by images from *that day* with Kim, he stood on the doorstep and rang the bell to Marie's flat, convinced she would forgive him his surprise visit. But Marie did not come to rescue him from his conscience and his fears.

No one answered.

~ ~ ~

And whilst Martin was speeding along the A40 in the opposite direction to home, because he just wanted to be on the road and in control of something, and because he knew that *that* evening, and the evening after that, and on and on as far as his imagination would take him, would verge on the intolerable, Sara was in the back of a police car. The officers had insisted that they drive her home and wait with her until George arrived back from school. They hadn't questioned her much, just confirmed the address of her parents and said two of their colleagues would be visiting them immediately. She'd been told about Martin finding Kim's body earlier that day and they'd referred briefly to a post mortem being conducted.

"Where is he now?" she had enquired, perplexed as to why Martin wasn't there with them. "Is he at the hospital?"

She was seized with an overwhelming urge to know where he was. When the officers explained that they had only spoken with him briefly when he *was in the flat upstairs*, Sara was confused and tried to call him from the backseat of the vehicle, scrabbling in her bag to find her mobile. When he didn't answer and she just heard his cheery voicemail, *don't panic, caller – I'll get right back to you* - she began to cry, softly. The woman police officer had looked back from the front passenger seat.

"It's not long now, love. You'll soon be home. He's probably there already, waiting for you."

It was an hour before George returned. Sara spent much of the time in the bathroom, lying on the cold tiled floor. At one point she moved her head from the floor to the bath mat to take advantage of its fluffy texture. When the lady constable knocked on the door, Sara assumed it was to ask her if she was alright but, no, they were probably used to people locking themselves away to grieve in private, she asked if she could use the toilet. There again, perhaps the request was just a ruse to check on her, whilst pretending not to.

When George arrived back, he joined Sara on the sofa and they sat, huddled together, survivors, his face white, hers a blotchy, swollen pink. A leaflet about the post mortem process and the role of the Coroner was left on the coffee table and phone numbers were exchanged. The family would need to identify Kim's body at some point in the next 24 hours. *Best to get that bit over with as soon as possible,* they were advised. At the door, they said again that their colleagues from the CID would be in touch. Sara knew from an earlier conversation that enquiries about the assault on Kim had been ongoing. Now she had died, seemingly from those same injuries, the police's enquiries would intensify.

Martin arrived a few minutes later.

"Where have you been?" asked Sara, as if it mattered.

"Nowhere," he said. Sara turned away and George ushered Martin into the living room.

"Come and sit down, mate."

But Martin and Sara remained standing, looking at each other, searching the face they knew almost as well as their own, for some explanation as to how they had reached this day.

"Do you want to be left alone?" asked George, hovering somewhere near the door, unable to decide what was appropriate.

But his question was ignored. So he left anyway, murmuring about making some coffee.

Martin stepped closer to Sara and reached for her hands.

"Christ, I'm so sorry," he said, his voice ragged.

"Tell me," she whispered. "Tell me what happened."

"Nothing. I went over there around 11 and found her. It must have happened in the night, I guess."

Sara let out a moan and threw herself downwards toward the sofa, almost tripping as she did so.

"The police will have been round to Mum and Dad's by now but I haven't spoken to them yet. How am I going to do that? *How*?" She looked at Martin beseechingly. Martin sat down in the armchair, covering his eyes with his hands so that the sight of her distress was blotted out for a few seconds.

"Shall I speak to Mum and ask her to call them?" he asked, resurfacing.

Sara shook her head.

"No. Perhaps I should go down to see them, this evening. Bring them back to London so…"

She faltered on the ending of her sentence, gulping in air like a climber struggling against altitude.

"So they can see her."

Martin got up and went to sit next to her on the sofa. He thought of Marie's words, the translation suddenly forming in his head after so many hours delay. *Vous survivrez a cette.*

When George came back into the room, with three mugs of coffee, Martin and Sara were locked together, seeming almost like lovers – save for the cadence of their sobs which seeped from them suggesting grief, not passion.

He was hesitant, not sure if he should stay, putting the mugs down so clumsily on the coffee table that they clinked against each other, inappropriately musical, their contents splashing out over the card left by one of the police officers. Aware that George was there, Martin and Sara pulled apart.

"Thanks," said Martin, reaching for his coffee. He handed a mug to Sara.

"My parents," repeated Sara to George. "We need to bring them to London."

George nodded.

"Perhaps we should go down there this evening. Can you take tomorrow off?"

"Of course," George replied. "I'll telephone the Head now. They'll just have to cope."

Taking his coffee with him, George disappeared back into the kitchen to make the call. Sara and Martin sat on in silence for a minute, listening to George explaining why he wouldn't be in school the next day.

"I shouldn't have left her," said Sara. "I just shouldn't have left her."

"You didn't do this to her, Sara. Someone else did. You did – *we* - we did our best."

Martin didn't mention that he had put his jacket on the night before and then changed his mind about going over to Kim's. He wasn't going to torment himself by playing that purposeless game of *what if.* Nor was he going to encourage Sara in that direction.

Madness was already peering through the keyhole looking for a place at the table. Best not invite him in.

CHAPTER 4

Strangers

It took Sara and George four hours and thirty eight minutes to drive to Polperro in Cornwall, which time included a stop for petrol and caffeine at a bleak outpost of a service station somewhere off the A30.

In the years that followed, when Sara was able to talk about what happened on the day that Kim died, she would say that the first call she made to her parents was oddly unemotional. She knew the police had told them. This was confirmed by the officers who'd attended her.

As she knew he would, her father answered.

"Dad, it's me. You've heard."

"Yes, Sara. I have."

He was stoical, calm.

"George and I will come tonight, to bring you and Mum back to London."

"Yes. Thank you. What time do you think you'll be here?"

"I'm not sure. Before midnight, I hope."

Neither suggested delaying things until the morning. It was a matter of instinct for Sara to go to them, to believe that they should be with each other as soon as possible. However dysfunctional, most families prefer to share their immediate grief with each other.

"Tell Mum I'm on my way. I'll be with her soon."

After she'd rung off, she sat where she was for a few moments. She was practised at suspending her emotions, not feeling too much in the moment, dealing with it when she was alone or, more usually, when she was with Martin or George – when she would sound off to them angrily about one of her clients, already lost, because help was only available when the damage had been done and, by then, it was too late.

But in those few seconds after the call, Kim returned to her, in clear focus: she could see her face and watch her scar as its shape changed when she smiled.

"I have lost my sister," she said starkly to George when he came back into the living room, saying he was ready to go.

Occasionally, on the journey to Polperro, Sara cried, allowing her pain to consume her. Perhaps, she thought, if she could discharge some of the shock and misery before she met with her parents, she might be able to carry the three of them through the next twenty four hours – or just the next twelve. Twelve hours would suffice. See them. Take them back to London. Go to the hospital. *See her. See her. See her.*

George drove on, uncomplainingly. Occasionally, he would remove his hand from the steering wheel and place it on Sara's knee. Marginally, inside, he preferred this to talking. Concentrating on the drive whilst also filtering his words so that they struck the right balance – between the compassionate and the platitudinous – was beyond him. He felt wired, his mind unable to stand still: running on, like leaping from rock to rock over a fast moving stream, to when Sara's parents would open the door, to when he saw their stricken faces, to driving back to London, to sitting in the hospital waiting to be called in for the identification process. Forced into a tragedy for which he felt inadequate, panic trickled through him. More than once he crunched the gears and then muttered an apology to Sara, as if the interruption might be interpreted as insensitive.

He'd thought of Martin too whilst he'd been driving, going back to his little room, alone, spending the rest of the evening hunched over his desk working on his little boxes. Initially, when he had first met Sara, the relationship between her and Martin had baffled him. He had never known cousins spend so much time together. There were in jokes, from which he was excluded and, occasionally, he would glimpse an expression on Martin's face that he had seen on Sara's. Sara had a few friends, unlike Martin, who was a self-confessed loner, but none rivalled Martin. George assumed things would change when he and Sara became closer and they started talking about living together after finishing university, but he was mistaken. One of the factors in choosing their shared flat was its proximity to where Martin was living. If she and George decided to go out for a drink during the course of a Friday or Saturday evening, Martin would be informed so that he could join them if he so wished. It was fortunate that George was not a possessive man and fortunate too that his calm disposition meant that he engaged his brain before opening his mouth. He wasn't given to impulsiveness, or conflict, so he never challenged Sara about Martin, never made any snide comments about him, or them. In fact, he came to value Martin. He considered him to be a straightforward, decent bloke with a dry sense of humour who understood Sara in a manner which bordered on the uncanny. And if, on the odd occasion, he wondered whether there was some *co-dependent* element to their relationship, he would banish such a thought believing it simply reflected a tiny bit of jealousy on his part. The reality was, that if he wanted a life with Sara then he had to accept Martin's presence in it, in a way similar to accepting a best friend who was a girl.

"We were brought up together," she had told him, casually, just after she had introduced Martin to him on that karaoke night, when they had both seemed to be fretting, to him unnecessarily, over Kim wanting to sing. "Our mothers are sisters and they got pregnant within four months of each other. My older sister, Kim, was a bit of a handful so I was often left with Martin and my aunt. Sometimes, for whole weekends. We spent most of the school holidays together too, whether at his or mine, or away somewhere."

"Are you close to his mother, your aunt?" he had asked her.

"No, not really. She's laid back and can be quite good fun – unlike my mum – but I wouldn't say we're close. I wouldn't confide in her. She and Martin are very close, though. He's loyal to her. In the same way he's loyal to me."

That September evening, they had all left the flat together, silently, George and Sara to make the long drive southwards and Martin to his bike. George had noticed that Martin's hands shook when he clipped his helmet on.

"Drive safely, mate," he said.

He'd gone before George had even switched on the ignition.

The Turner's retirement home was a large bungalow on one of the top roads above the fishing village. Sara's mother called it *the best of both* house. Facing one way in their kitchen was a water colour picture of a craggy, green hillside dotted with quaint cottages. Through a second large window was a view of the harbour with its bobbing boats and a glittering sea beyond, beckoning. It was a steepish climb up and down to the town but there were benches on the way where they could rest and commiserate with fellow travellers who also struggled against the gradient.

As George pulled into the driveway, the light in the porch was joined by others from within. A wooden shutter was tilted open and Sara glimpsed part of her mother's face behind it, as if peering from a prison cell. Within seconds, it closed again. Sara blew her nose hard and smoothed down her hair, flicking her tongue over her dry lips. Whilst George was looking at her, she cast round for her water.

"Here," he said, handing her an opened plastic bottle. She took a couple of quick sips.

The air had its own character here. It swept down deep into the lungs as if keen to do battle with the muck that had accumulated from all those years of urban living. Sara breathed deeply, gathering oxygen for the dive that lay ahead. At the pale blue door of the bungalow, two people stood waiting, already diminished, she decided, by the shock and the dread. *They look older*, she thought. *Please*, she begged silently, *please, please, freeze this minute*, so that I can escape.

As Sara and George approached them, hand in hand, her mother disappeared from view, whatever courage she had mustered to greet them having deserted her when faced with the reality of seeing her younger daughter.

Her father remained. The skin on his face appeared to have collapsed into his neck. He looked grey with fatigue.

Sara and George followed him into the living room, now harshly lit, every light blazing, making them blink at one another after the soft and comforting darkness of the outside world.

"Where did Mum go?" Sara asked, when she realised she wasn't in the room.

She didn't wait for her father's reply. She ran up the stairs to her mother's room and knocked on the door before entering. Her mother was lying on the bed, holding something. When she saw Sara, she gasped and let out a long wail which took up occupation in the room, rendering words redundant. Sara enclosed her mother into her arms, her own composure abandoned. The photograph frame her mother was clutching dug painfully into Sara's ribs and she moved apart from her to take it. It was a photograph of Kim as a young girl of around ten, holding on to a rope swing and laughing. There was a joyful innocence in her expression which Sara could not remember ever knowing.

Downstairs, George was searching his mind, as if flicking through a text book, trying to locate a page which might guide him through these moments alone with Sara's father. Steve had yet to say anything. On Sara's departure, he had sat down heavily in one of the armchairs and stared into the middle distance. George left the room and returned with a couple of glasses of water.

"I'm so sorry, Steve," he said, offering one of the glasses to him. Steve looked at him, nodded and took the water, gulping at it.

"Something stronger would be nice," he said.

George went over to the drinks cabinet and looked through the bottles.

"Anything in particular?" he asked.

"The brandy. The glasses are in the kitchen."

George went back out to the kitchen, returning with a whisky glass. He was dispatched again to rectify his faux pas, wondering why, on such an occasion, it mattered how the liquor was absorbed – whether by tea cup, pint glass or bucket – provided it entered Steve's system.

He poured Steve a generous measure and sat opposite him, relieved to have found some activity to fill the time until Sara re-joined them. They had both heard Emily's wail on seeing her daughter; agony so palpable, it was as if the feeling had been delivered to them on the back of some black winged creature flying down the stairs from the room above.

After twenty minutes or so, Sara and her mother entered the living room. By this time, Steve was on his third double brandy and his eyes were red, his cheeks flushed. As he saw them, he stood unsteadily.

"That girl. That girl. This was always going to happen, wasn't it?"

No-one answered him. Let him rant, thought Sara. What does it matter any longer?

"We should leave soon," said Sara, looking over at her father. "So that we can go to the hospital tomorrow, today, you know…" She was reaching the limit of her resilience. She could not complete the sentence, knowing she would falter on her sister's name. *Do not think of her*, she had told herself. *Keep her away, far away – just for the time being.*

"Tonight? Is that a good idea?" he responded, turning to George, seeking out a male ally to agree with him.

"Sara and I can share the driving," ventured George, sipping at the water which he had meant to give to Sara's mother.

Steve got up and left the room, abruptly, not saying where he was going. They heard the door of the downstairs cloakroom shut, the key turning in the lock, the flush of the toilet followed by the sound of running water.

Emily sat down, white faced, on the sofa.

"Mum, go and pack a bag and let's go," said Sara, stroking her mother's arm. "None of this will be easy, I know. But we have each other and…" Once more she trailed off.

"Where's your father gone to?" Her voice was hoarse.

"He's in the downstairs cloakroom, I think."

"Why don't we wait until the morning?"

"Because there's no point. None of us will sleep, anyway. And there will be more traffic on the roads."

Emily nodded and slowly rose from the sofa.

"I'm going to find your father," she said.

Sara and George looked at one another as she left the room and then George came over to her and sitting down, looped his arm around her.

"That's one of the worst bits nearly over," he whispered. "You were – are – amazingly strong. I'm not sure I could have maintained my balance the way you have done."

Sara looked sideways at him and, for the first time since learning of Kim's death, she smiled, faintly. It was a very "George" thing to say – to make such an observation. An observation which, at its heart, was designed to leave her in no doubt as to his support.

His heart gave a sudden leap when he saw her smile. *Whatever is lost, we are still here.*

Back in the hall, Sara's parents were holding one another. Steve's reserve had collapsed now that the brandy had washed through his system, weakening his defences.

Fifteen minutes later, George was stowing some luggage in the boot of his car and saying he would drive the first hundred miles or so. Then Sara could take over. Sara's parents sat in the back together, clutching each other's hands, still in their coats despite the temperature. Sara looked back at them from the passenger seat.

"See if you can sleep," she said. "It will help a little. And there's nothing we can do until we get back to London."

"I've bought a flask of coffee with me," said her mother. "Let me know if either of you want any on the journey. I've brought digestives too. Plain ones."

If Kim had been with her, Sara thought, the sisters would have struggled to contain their giggling at this remark. Kim would have made some sarcastic comment - *Gosh, Mama, I hope you haven't forgotten the Kendall Mint Cake* - and her father would have retorted that she *just might be grateful* for her mother's thoughtfulness in due course, *Miss Clever Pants* - the latter phrase bringing about another, more intense, fit of laughter from them both. But George was not Kim. With his eyes fixed firmly on the road ahead, he murmured his gratitude to Emily. And as soon as Sara had had this thought, Kim was back. Sara understood too, at that moment, that her own grief would not just lie in her regret that Kim had not been happier in her life, that her addiction had triumphed, that, somewhere along the way, they had all allowed her to give up. No, mixed with all that, and hurting much the same, would be the better parts of Kim – the callous humour and the savage wit. Her voice. The voice which should have saved her. Sara dipped her chin down and tears escaped into her mouth.

On the M4, they stopped for a toilet break and Sara took over the driving, glad of the concentration which was needed and anxious to give George a break.

"May I put some music on?" she enquired of her parents.

"Nothing raucous," replied her father. Kim would have made the most of that remark as well, skipping through the radio stations, the music blaring:

"Is that too raucous? How about this one?" On and on, wearing them all down with her inability to *just let things go*, as her mother would have said - for the sake of *a bit of peace and quiet,* her father would have added. In the mirror, Sara glanced at her father's face.

"Well, you've got your peace and quiet now, haven't you?" she wanted to say to him. "So just stop issuing fucking orders. We're all equal tonight."

George tuned the radio to Classic FM and they were rewarded with a perky little advertisement about life insurance before Erik Satie's Gnossienne No.1 was played which, in its quiet simplicity, was soothing.

When it had finished, Sara asked George if he had ever played the piece. George had played the piano from an early age, taught by his mother who had been a music tutor.

"Yes," he replied. "It's much more difficult than it sounds – like most of Satie."

"We should get a piano," she said.

"We haven't got the room."

"Then we should make room," Sara said.

From the back of the car came the soft but unmistakable sound of someone crying. Sara didn't need to check in her mirror to know it was her mother. She could hear her father too, whispering words of comfort to her: hushing her.

The sun was yet to lighten the sky when they reached Ealing. There was even a chill to the air, hinting that autumn would arrive soon. George said he would bring in the bags whilst Sara made them all some tea, assuring Sara's parents that they would be sleeping in the only bedroom. He and Sara would make do with the sofa bed in the lounge.

In the kitchen, they spoke in low voices.

"They'll have some privacy in there," said George, watching Sara pour the boiling water from the kettle into a teapot he had not been aware they owned until that moment. She was laying out a tray like a lady from a bygone age, anxious to impress the neighbours. He half expected her to produce a tiered cake stand to complete the tableau.

"Do you want anything to eat?" she asked.

"Eggs or toast maybe? Shall I ask them?"

She nodded wearily, wishing they were on their own and she could behave as she wished, selfishly. Put on the television and watch the morning's news in the hope she might doze off, her head on George's shoulder, feeling the warmth of his living body, familiar and comfortable, next to hers. She waited, carefully re-arranging the items on the tray, as if she might have to describe exactly where the cups were in relation to the milk jug at some later point that day.

"No," said George, coming back into the kitchen, "they only want tea, nothing to eat. They've gone to lie down for a couple of hours. Can you eat anything? I'm starving."

Sara picked up the tray and walked to the bedroom. She had been prepared to knock but the door was ajar and she walked in. Her parents were stretched out on the bed with their eyes closed, their footwear placed neatly at each side: her mother's a pair of beige leather low heeled shoes, her father's a highly polished pair of black leather ones. She hadn't noticed he was wearing them when they'd left Polperro. But she saw now that they were shoes suitable for a funeral. The curtains were already drawn and both bedside lights were on. They looked as if they had decided on a suicide pact. Only the note was missing. She placed the tray on the makeshift dressing table, announcing into the silent room that the tea *was brewing*. As if anyone cares, she thought, whether the tea is brewing, or stewing, or not there at all. These little routines are simply here to occupy us in our misery: ritual is comforting and provides respite from *feeling* so much. And so much of our lives are spent, wasted even, in seeking control, having been peddled the lie from such an early age that little in life is random. *We make our own luck, Kim.*

Sara said nothing to her parents about going to see Kim at the hospital mortuary. She decided that she would tackle that when they'd rested although she knew that Kim's body would need to be identified at some point during that day. She had meant to call Martin, as she had promised. Not only would his mother, Tabitha, be a source of strength for her mother, it would also relieve Sara of some of the burden of coping with her parents' grief. The grief would probably be relatively straightforward, she thought. It would be its common counterpart, *guilt,* which might present the greater challenge. During the three years they had lived above pretty Polperro, the barrier her parents had erected between themselves and Kim had grown higher. Once they had adjusted to living a predictable life, one not punctuated with the tribulations of her chaotic lifestyle, they felt unable to risk any return to those stormy shores. They weren't just getting older: they had no appetite for the negotiation that was necessary. How soon would it be until her mother concluded that their abandonment of Kim was a possible factor in her death? All those arguments between them, the ones that had slowly diminished when they moved away, would return. Except that now Kim was dead, the guilt would polarise their earlier positions. Grief would only temporarily obscure it. When guilt returned, locking horns with futility, it would do so with a bitterness that might destroy them.

~ ~ ~

"It's me," said Sara. It was eight o'clock. Martin would be up and eating his Weetabix.

"How is everything?" His voice was faint as if he was speaking into a strong wind blowing over the sea.

"Where are you?"

"With Mum. In the flat."

"She knows then?"

"Yes," he replied, his voice becoming a little stronger. She imagined him moving rooms, probably going outside into her aunt's courtyard garden, which Martin had designed for her. She wondered if the pink and white Oleanders would still be flowering. She had been there with him in the spring a couple of years ago when he'd planted them. Unable to transport them from the garden centre on his bike, she'd agreed to help. They'd taken her car, Martin sitting in the back with the plants, like an overprotective parent, warning Sara to take the corners more smoothly. Sara had guffawed at the hypocrisy of this request. Martin had never taken a corner *smoothly* in his biking life. They'd made a second journey with two stone pedestal urns. His mother wanted a traditional look: low box hedges and a conservative colour scheme. Martin did not try to influence her. He was content to make her happy and excited at the prospect of creating a garden. In the centre of the courtyard was a swan, its wings outstretched, poised and ready to fly, made of bronze and costing more than the rest of the entire project. Sara's father had been appalled.

"More money than sense, your sister," he had maintained to his wife on the day of the garden's official opening. And yet, a very similar bronze statue had appeared on the bungalow's back lawn in Polperro a year later. It was of a dog, a golden retriever, life size, sitting erect and alert, and, Tabitha was certain, costing a good deal more than *my swan*.

Sara had guessed correctly. Martin was outside, over by the swan, his hand on one of its cold metal wings, the phone tucked between his shoulder and his ear.

"I've been here since late last night," he confessed. "I...I couldn't face going back to my room. I suppose you're back now. How are they?"

"Shattered. As you'd expect them to be."

There was a brief lull in their conversation.

"I think Mum would like to come over to you, to see Emily. Do you think that's a good idea?"

"Yes. Although I suppose I ought to ask them."

"Ok. When are you going to the hospital? After that might be the best time."

They agreed on this and rang off, not needing to explore each other's emotions.

It was too early to contact the police about the identification process. Or was it the coroner's office she needed to contact? Sara could not remember what she had been advised and she fumbled around amidst the newspapers and documents on the coffee table looking for the leaflets.

"Just ring the police station on the number they gave you and clarify it," said George, who had finished his breakfast. He looked at her, the deep circles under her large brown eyes, the still swollen eyelids from all the crying, and wondered when he had last seen her cry.

"Or I can phone if you want," he added, pushing back a strand of hair from her face, the gesture an excuse to touch her.

In the end, there was little discussion about who or who might not want to see Kim. Sara contacted the coroner and arranged a time in the afternoon, simply informing her parents of when they would be leaving. George said he would drive them to the hospital. When there, outside the room where Kim lay, they were given various warnings about what to expect, such that Emily felt unwell and George, who remained in his car in the carpark, was summoned to collect her. He suggested that the two of them went to the cafeteria to wait for Sara and her father but Emily baulked at the idea of spending any further time within the hospital and, instead, they tramped around its grounds.

"They said I should be prepared for her to look different, some skin discolouration on her face. And I wouldn't be allowed to touch her and that someone would be present in the room with us, the whole time. I wanted to say goodbye to her, George, but I don't want to remember her like that."

George nodded.

"I understand," he said. "I'd probably feel the same. I'm not sure I would have gone in either."

Emily grasped his arm in gratitude and a sob hiccoughed out of her.

"It's ok," he said, gently, putting his arm around her. They were standing by a rose bed in the late afternoon sun. Emily leant in to him and gave vent to her misery.

When they returned to the car park, Sara and her father were standing on opposite sides of the car like strangers who had nothing in common and were tired of making small-talk. A look of relief swept over Steve's face as they approached, glad to see that his wife was still upright but equally relieved that they could now depart. No-one asked about their experience. Conversation on the journey home was limited to the traffic conditions. Back in the flat, Sara's parents immediately retired to their bedroom and remained there for most of the evening, only emerging to have something to eat.

"Let's leave it for today," Steve said, as he ate his fish and chips which George had gone out for. "Your mother's exhausted. We can talk in the morning." Emily picked at her food as he said this, not looking up when she was mentioned. Sara knew she should try to comfort her mother, briefly wondering when she had become inured to being spoken about as if she were not there. But there was a wall around Sara. She had been building it all afternoon, brick by brick, and she couldn't risk it being breached. It was her current *modus operandi*. She stuck to the mundane and the functional - the food and the bedding and who wanted to have a shower or a bath and did anyone want to watch television?

Sara recounted to George later that evening, once they were alone in the living room, that her father had been rude to the Coroner's assistant who had been present throughout the visit. He had questioned her aggressively, even though it was clear to Sara that the poor woman wasn't in a position to tell them anything more than they already knew. The post mortem would take place later that same day and they would be assigned a liaison officer who would keep them informed of the outcome.

"Dad kept saying – *and when are the people responsible for my daughter's death going to be arrested? What's happening about that?* The assistant had tried to explain the difference between the coroner's role and that of the police, saying that he needed to speak to the police. But he wouldn't listen. Kept on and on – *someone should be made to pay for this.* As if it wasn't bad enough that we'd both just seen Kim, lying there, looking so…so unlike Kim, so horrible. So *absent.*"

"What about the funeral?" asked George.

"We can't plan that until after the post mortem and the body's released. You know, I hate that. The way people suddenly stop using someone's name when they're dead, calling them *the body*. It's still her – what's left of her. All that's left of her. Let's dignify her by continuing to call her by her name. Anyway, I can't contemplate the funeral at the moment so it's just as well we're not having to."

Sara remembered her conversation with Martin then. Before she climbed into the small, lumpy sofa bed with George that evening, she texted him, apologising. She would ask her mother to call Tabitha in the morning.

Emptied out, she was grateful that she slept for a few hours before awaking and going over the events of the last forty-eight hours. The sadness felt like flames licking her body: lashed to a stake with the fire increasing in intensity around her. She could not untie herself nor was there any prospect of her being untied.

George went off to work early the next morning. Sara had been granted some compassionate leave and would not need to go back in until *she felt ready* as Gloria Bostock had said. Sara explained that she would need to meet with the police at some point and provide a statement concerning the visit Martin and she had made to Kim's the night of, or before, her death. She mentioned that her parents were staying with her and that she needed to be around for them. She started to explain to Gloria how she had tried to persuade Kim to go back to the hospital but Gloria had interrupted, saying she did not need to explain herself or her actions. What had happened was *a terrible, terrible, tragedy* and they were all thinking about her. That same morning, when the doorbell went, Sara assumed it was the police, even though they hadn't made an appointment, but it was a delivery driver holding an enormous bouquet of flowers sent by Gloria and the rest of the team at the office. After she shut the door, Sara contemplated the flowers trying to feel grateful. Surely, people sent flowers in celebration of events, not in commiseration? She took them into the kitchen and left them next to the sink. If Martin brought his mother over later that day, he'd deal with them for her.

"You could have at least stood them in some water," he said. He and Tabitha had arrived around midday and Tabitha was sitting in the living room with Sara's parents. Martin and

Sara, after an exchange of glances, had escaped to the kitchen. Tabitha was doing her best to be practical and supportive but it was horribly apparent that Steve was becoming irritated with her. He had cut himself shaving and scrappy bits of toilet paper were stuck to his chin. There were deep grey pouches under his eyes, which watered incessantly. Every now and again, he would release an explosive sneeze, making them all jump. He was having an allergic reaction to something in the flat although none of them had bothered to comment on it. Emily sat stiff and silent. She had hardly spoken a word since the hospital visit. The difference between the sisters was striking. Tabitha, her blonde-streaked hair tied neatly with a wooden clip at the nape of her slender neck, was smartly dressed in black trousers, black ankle boots and a close-fitting tunic in soft shades of orange, which blended perfectly with her honey coloured skin. Emily looked as if she had spent the night on the streets. She was wearing a midi length skirt, which Tabitha was sure she'd had since the 1980s, but had not bothered with any tights. A network of blue veins ran like rivers through her alabaster legs. On her feet were slippers, brought from home, perhaps in the hope that they would comfort her in the trials that lay ahead. They were a faded pink with a ruff of grubby fur around the edges. As Martin and Sara left the room, Tabitha picked up her sister's hand and was stroking it.

"I couldn't be bothered with them," Sara said, looking at the white lilies and roses for the first time.

"I can put them in a jug or two if you don't have a vase," said Martin, opening one of the cupboards as he did so. "Assuming you have any jugs, that is," he added, casting her a look which wanted to be a smile. Sara was not known for her culinary skills. She had given up smoking a year before, three days after she had turned twenty-nine, assuring everyone that she wanted to change her lifestyle. She had taken up jogging until she'd had an unpleasant encounter with a flasher on

Ealing Common. George had suggested she join a running club, where there would be safety in numbers, but it smacked of over commitment for her and she gave up instead. George was not interested. Work itself was enough of a battle for him, he said, without adding unnecessary obligations into his daily schedule. It had been Sara's intention that they would eat more healthily. She would cook at the weekends and freeze vegetable casseroles and crust-less quiches for defrosting in the week but it never happened. Despite the fact that, over the year, her taste-buds underwent some form of renewal, she couldn't summon much enthusiasm for a Saturday afternoon or Sunday morning spent in the kitchen. Eating was a means to an end, she told Martin, whose approach was not dissimilar in terms of his relationship with food.

Sara gave voice to her earlier thought about why the office had considered it appropriate to send flowers to her.

"Flowers signify hope, I suppose," he said, although his tone didn't suggest he believed it to be true.

"And where is hope in all this mess?" she had asked him. "There is nothing to hope *for*. We have lost her."

"Don't," said Martin, who was already beginning to discover that he achieved nothing in simply being a bystander. "Don't despair. Please."

She went over to him then and kissed him on the cheek.

"Thank Christ you're here," she said. She sat down on one of the kitchen chairs and looked on, indifferently, as he hunted through the cupboards without any assistance from her. Eventually, he pulled out an unattractive glass vase from under the sink.

"This will do," he said.

Sara smiled.

"I forgot I had that," she commented.

"I'm not surprised. It's hideous," he remarked and, filling it up with water, he started to cut the cellophane from around the bouquet. When he next looked at Sara, her head was on her arms and he could tell she was crying. A great wave of hopelessness descended on him as he watched her shaking shoulders. There was no guidance for these times they were enduring, he thought. His instinct was all he had and he'd no faith in it that day, standing by the sink in Sara's kitchen, a perfect white rose in his hand. A thorn scratched him as he laid it back down and went over to sit beside her.

Eventually she looked up at him with mournful eyes.

"It just comes back to me, every so often, that I will never, ever see or talk to her again."

"I know," Martin said.

"I wish I could go back to the beginning of the week. Go back and get it right. Persuade her. Why did I give up so easily?"

"You didn't. You never did. We weren't to know."

He recalled again his impulse on the night of their visit when he had put on his jacket, ready to bike back over and try again, on his own, in his own way. Sara was right, they *had* given up too easily.

He went back to trimming the stems of the roses and the lilies, putting them in the vase, arranging them and then rearranging them. Whilst Sara sat at the table watching him, or seeming to, he concentrated on the task as if it had significance. And in the stillness of that moment, she felt connected, briefly, to something other than the horror of her loss.

CHAPTER 5

Seed

The police visited Sara and her parents on the day after Martin's visit. The post mortem had already been carried out, they informed her, and the preliminary results of the pathologist were now with the Coroner's office. They were likely to call Sara that same day to convey those findings although it would be some weeks before a final written report was available. However, the police had been informed and had already started their investigations.

The pathologist concluded that Kim had died from a ruptured chest cavity caused by three displaced ribs. Around two litres of blood had accumulated around her heart which stopped working. There may have been other factors at work at the time of her death: her consumption of alcohol for one. This would be clarified in due course when the outcome of the toxicology tests was known.

Sara remembered the cans she had brought over to Kim at her request. Had she really drunk all eight of them?

Two police officers were present. There was detective superintendent Gary Cowley who explained his role as the Senior Investigating Officer and did most of the talking and his side kick, Brian, whose chief function, at that juncture, appeared to be to stand at the door of the living room, surveying them all with a studiedly serious expression. If any of the family returned his gaze, he just nodded and transferred his attention to his boss. They were also to be assigned a family liaison officer who would, apparently, support them through the rigours of the investigative process including any court hearings.

Emily was unable to contribute to any of the discussion and retired to the bedroom less than ten minutes after they had arrived. It was Sara and her father who listened and asked questions. Steve appeared strengthened by the news that the police investigation was now properly underway and that there appeared to be no question that his daughter, immediately prior to her death, had been viciously attacked *by those two thugs*. He said more than once that he looked forward to the day when they would be *behind bars, where he hoped they would rot*. His voice shook with anger when he uttered these words. Superintendent Cowley did not respond directly to these statements. He was appropriately judicious in the terminology he used. Years of experience had taught him that making promises – *don't worry, Sir, we'll get them* – so beloved in television dramas – was unwise. Criminal litigation was full of surprises: many of them unwelcome. He had learnt that justice and the law were not always compatible bedfellows. The family wanted the former whereas he had only the tools in the latter category available to him. If they coincided, then well and good but such was not always attainable. Tell them the facts, he had been advised during his training – what investigations you're making, why and when. Confine the conjecture, so far as possible, to the station and your colleagues.

DS Cowley wanted a full statement from Sara and said that Brian would remain behind after he'd gone to take it down on his laptop. She didn't need to come to the station to provide it, unless she'd prefer to. Initially, Sara couldn't envisage a situation where visiting the police station would be preferable. When Brian suggested that they go into the kitchen to talk, she realised that they were conscious of her parents being around and how this might upset them and, even, prevent Sara from providing the essential details.

"We need everything you can remember," said Brian, facing her over the kitchen table.

"I haven't got descriptions of who attacked her, if that's what you mean. I'm not going to be able to help you identify them. How are you going to find them?"

She had wanted to ask DS Cowley this, somewhat significant, question when he'd been talking to them earlier but he had given her the definite impression that he was reluctant to provide any real detail at that stage of the investigation.

"We know where she was on the night of the attack. We've taken a statement from the person who found Kim at the foot of the stairs and someone else who confirmed that she had been assaulted at the party and had left alone in a bad state. We're looking into who else was there, identifying further witnesses. From you I want to know exactly what she said happened and how she appeared."

"Will that be useful – repeating what she said happened? I could say anything, couldn't I?"

DC Brian Barnett looked at her.

"What you say may corroborate the accounts of other witnesses."

"Of course. I just wondered, that's all."

She and DC Barnett were together for over two hours. It was an intense process. As she spoke, repeating as much as she could of the account Kim had given to her and Martin about the incident at the party, she felt a quiet rage taking root in her. *This seed will grow*, she thought to herself as she recalled Kim's battered face and imagined her staggering her way, alone, out of the party, desperate to get away from her attackers. *Every time I think of it. Every time I remember her voice telling me. Every time. I can feel it growing a little bit more.*

"How could people just stand there and watch her being battered? She left the place on her own, bleeding. Why didn't someone help her?" Sara asked him, more by way of comment than question.

"The details aren't clear," Barnett said. "We don't know the facts yet."

"We know the outcome, though," said Sara.

Towards the end of the interview, they got on to Kim's problem with alcohol. He seemed keen to explore this and Sara inferred from his close questioning that the police were attaching some significance to it, although in precisely what respect she didn't know and didn't ask. She remembered Kim's anger toward her when she asked if she had been drunk. She recalled the shrug of her shoulders.

"She had been drinking alcohol obviously and she said there was weed at the party. That's all I know, all she told me," clarified Sara.

"I understand she had a longstanding problem with alcohol. Is that the case?"

Sara wondered where he had got this information from. Had Martin volunteered it?

She hesitated for a few seconds but then decided that if she wasn't totally honest about Kim's problems, it may well have the effect of undermining other parts of her evidence.

"Yes."

"Would you describe her as an alcoholic?"

"I don't know."

"She hadn't been in work for a long time, had she?"

"No. I can't remember when she was last employed but it was a few years ago."

Sara could have expanded on this but declined to do more than just answer the question Barnett was asking. It made her wonder what it would be like to be on the witness stand and cross examined.

"Will I have to give evidence?" she asked.

"We don't even know if this will go to court," Barnett replied. "It's too soon to say."

Kim had left school shortly after she'd entered sixth form. Sara was around 13 at the time and remembered the rows at home which ensued from Kim's decision. She hadn't told her parents that she'd dropped out. Her mother learnt of the fact one day when the school telephoned to ask if Kim would be coming back. She had been absent for over three weeks.

Kim had pink, spiky hair then and wore ugly heavy boots, like Doc Martins – except they weren't because she couldn't afford them. Her father said he could *hardly bear to look* at her. He tried to ban her from going into Sara's bedroom, where she would sit on Sara's bed and talk about her boyfriends, the tattoo she was going to get when she was older and how many spliffs she'd smoked that day. He maintained she was distracting Sara from her homework and keeping her up at night.

"I don't want you following suit," he would say to Sara, on the days she couldn't escape from him because he'd insist on driving her to school. "That young lady is the worst possible role model. Who knows why she turned out that way, I don't." It was as if he were commenting on someone he didn't know well, speculating about her as he might about a neighbour's daughter. There was no *connection*.

Occasionally, as she got older, Sara would take issue with him, arguing in defence of her sister, who could be tedious and difficult but then, suddenly, inexplicably, assume a different persona: someone with bounce and light, exposing the best bits of herself.

"It's as if, every so often, she performs a psychological striptease," Martin said. "And decides to shed the dark stuff to reveal a lighter hearted self underneath."

Martin frequently surprised Sara with his insight, which was what made him an interesting companion. He was one of the world's *observers,* that rare breed who stand on the side lines rather than playing in the match or chanting in the crowd. She wasn't sure what had made him an observer, whether its genesis was shyness or a lack of confidence but, forced to analyse it, she would say that neither characteristic applied to him. Martin was secure in his identity and didn't look to others for affirmation. But more significantly, he was born with an instinct for knowing, and then doing, what made him happy. Kim never knew it, thought Sara. Like most of us, she only managed to identify what did not bring her happiness - which is not the same at all.

When DC Barnett eventually left, it was mid-afternoon. Emily and Steve returned from a walk just as Sara was looking at a missed call on her mobile. There was a voice mail from someone called Paul, identifying himself as their family liaison officer and asking when it might be convenient to pay them a visit. Sara explained this to her parents as they were taking off their coats in the living room. Emily did not appear to have regained her voice and disappeared back into the bedroom leaving Sara in mid-sentence.

Her father sat down on the sofa, pulling at his chin.

"She's not really coping with any of this," he said, ignoring Sara's question about needing to agree a time for the liaison officer to visit.

When Sara did not respond, he looked over at her.

"Did you hear what I said?"

Sara looked back at him and nodded.

"Yes."

"I think I should take her back home."

"If that's what you both want. I doubt the funeral will take place for some time."

She waited briefly to see if he would ask after her own welfare and whether it was okay to leave her to cope with the police and the coroner, and all the rest of the effluent which she would feel forced to wade through during the next few days. When he didn't she got up, feeling she was going to cry and not wanting a witness.

"Yes, I think it's best you do go back home," she said. "The flat's too small for the four of us."

"Right, I'll go and speak with your mother. I'll look at the train timetables."

He went back into the bedroom and Sara heard their voices in conversation and then a piteous whimpering. She went over to the bedroom door and knocked.

"Mum? Can I come in?"

The door opened a few inches and her father's face peered out at her.

"It's ok, Sara. I've got it, she'll be ok in a little while."

Sara pushed past him, into the room. Her mother was sitting on the side of the bed, her arms by her side, her head bent, an anguished sound leaking from her.

Sara put her arms around her, struggling to find any words of comfort. Her earlier thoughts reappeared. There was nothing to hope for. Wherever these days took them, it would never be where they wanted to go. The best would be when they were over, when there was nothing else to endure save for the fact that Kim was dead. An unalterable fact.

"Leave us for a moment, will you, Dad?" Sara asked her father.

Her father obliged, closing the door behind him, wordlessly. A minute elapsed during which neither of them spoke.

"I didn't call her, Sara," Emily said, sitting more upright and blowing her nose. "Remember, after you telephoned to tell us she was badly hurt. You said I should. But I didn't. I didn't speak to her before she died. And she died alone and in such pain. I can't bear it. I've been trying to remember the last time I spoke to her and I can't. I can't. She was alone. My poor girl. My poor girl."

Sara tried to respond but Emily had only stopped to take a breath between the sobs.

"I decided to wait until the morning and, even then, I hoped you'd call me, telling me she was ok or that she'd gone back into hospital. And now, I don't know why I thought it was alright to do that. I don't understand myself."

As she was speaking, Steve re-entered the room, saying that the family liaison officer, Paul, had just left another message but on the landline, this time. He'd either been listening at the door or overheard his wife's confession.

"Because we weren't told how serious it was, Emily. That's why you didn't call her. You didn't know they were life threatening injuries. We weren't told."

Sara stared at him from the bed.

"What are you saying, Dad?"

"I'm saying if we'd known, if you'd have explained it in more detail, we would have come down immediately. And I would have insisted she went back into hospital even if I had to drag her there myself. And perhaps – I'm not saying definitely – just perhaps, we might not be here now. In this – this situation."

"Is this not enough for you, Dad? Is it not enough that Kim is dead? That she was *murdered* and not only are we going to have to bury her, my sister, your daughter, but there'll probably be a trial as well with the press and everything and this will all take a long, long time and who knows how the fuck it will end? That's what we've all got in store. But no. You want to add a bit more to it. You want to blame me into the bargain. Blame me because you can't bear to face up to just what a fucking shit father you were to her."

Sara was on her feet now.

"Please, Sara," her mother murmured. "Please."

"No, I won't shut up. Don't you dare attach any blame to me. I'm the one that cared for her whilst you and Mum swanned off to your precious life by the sea. Have you ever asked yourself where her problems started from in the first place? Would you like to go into that now, Dad, given how much you enjoy the blame game?"

"You're overwrought, Sara. You've had a difficult day. We all have. I'm not blaming you. You've jumped to that conclusion. I'm sure you did your best."

"Oh fuck off, Dad."

Sara walked past her father, out of the room, slamming the door as she did so. She was shaking with anger and her eyes stung with tears. She fetched her jacket and bag and left the flat. With any luck, they'd get an early train or go to a hotel. She couldn't bear the idea of spending any more time with her father and was already formulating her words to George – *no, I'm not going to forgive him* – along with the excuses George would make for him and his exhortations that she should think of her mother. And she knew that Martin would feel the same but say it in a different way – which he did.

Martin's rented room was fifteen minutes' walk away. She didn't call or text him, she just hoped he'd be in although she knew he went biking on a Friday evening. He was part of some weird biking fraternity which tore up and down the M4, a solid mass of *easy riders*. It was the closest Martin got to a social circle. She half ran and half walked to where he lived, the exercise burning off some of her fury alongside the ever-present misery. By the time she rang the doorbell, hoping that Martin would answer and that she wouldn't have to engage with his landlady who could never shut up, she was wild haired and sweating.

The day was not going to change its pattern to accommodate Sara. The lady owner answered the door, delighted at the prospect of some company.

"Sara! My, you look a bit hot. Did you jog here? You're lucky. He's been staying with his mother for a few days. He only just got back."

Marjorie Twist was in her sixties, portly with a particularly chubby face which incorporated a treble chin. Except for its decrepitude, the semi-detached house was unremarkable. The bathroom which Martin shared with her had not been updated for a few decades. The kitchen, similarly, could have been used as a film location for a 1950s drama. The garden, however, was like walking into a Provencal paradise, full of palms and olive trees and Cordylines. At dusk, lights appeared at intervals around the garden transforming it into a different space, creating shadows, changing colours. Mrs Twist had made full use of the few perks available to her through her employment at the garden centre. Martin helped her out. His rent was low for London and it was his way of acknowledging it. Anyway, Mrs Twist loved Martin who listened to her and sat with her on spring and summer afternoons at the little stone table at the back of the garden. She had a son who was an accountant and of whom she was immensely proud but he didn't *listen* the way Martin did. And he never helped in the garden. Martin knew when plants needed to be pruned and was content to discuss the bulb planting scheme for as long as was necessary. He devised a method of preventing the squirrels from eating the tulip bulbs which Mrs Twist said he should patent.

Mrs Twist beamed at Sara. Clearly, Martin had not shared the news about Kim.

"Come in, come in. Can I make you a cold drink or would you prefer tea?"

Sara stepped into the hall. On the hall table there was a metal jug with scarlet dahlias in it.

"Is he in his room?"

He appeared then. Running down the stairs to greet her, Sara could not prevent her relief at seeing him turning into tears. She dabbed at her face with a tissue whilst, simultaneously, attempting an explanation of why she was there.

"Oh my word," said Mrs Twist. "What on earth has happened?"

"Shall we go out?" Martin asked Sara. "Hold on, I'll just get my keys."

Mrs Twist surveyed Sara while they awaited Martin's return, appearing more concerned than embarrassed by Sara's display of emotion.

"You can stay here and sit in the garden if you like, dear," she said.

Sara muttered her thanks and fixed her eyes on the stairs.

As they walked to The White Horse, Sara told Martin of the post mortem results and her meeting with DC Barnett. She could hardly believe that they were walking down a street in the late afternoon on a day in September talking about an investigation into her sister's murder.

Later, they got onto Sara's row with her father.

"He's such a bastard," she declared, gulping at her beer. She knew Martin wouldn't object to the description. Such were the differences between him and Steve Turner, they could have been born on different planets. During her lifetime, Sara had often noticed the look of perplexity which passed over one or other's face when they were forced into conversation at family get togethers. Their relationship was not helped by Martin's mother, who did not attempt to disguise her disapproval of Steve's dominance over his wife.

"It's his way of coping, assuaging his own guilt," said Martin, who was drinking coke through a straw and tilting his chair back. "Probably his only method of facing the reality of what has happened."

"By blaming me?"

"By saying he hadn't known the extent of her injuries. He wants to believe that he would have acted differently had he done so."

"Letting himself off the hook, then?"

"We all do, Sara. Either by forgetting or distorting. It's a self-defence thing, I think."

"And I should allow him that?"

Martin nodded. "Probably. For the moment."

Sara asked him if he had mentioned Kim's problem with alcohol when he had spoken with the police at Kim's flat.

"I really don't remember much of what I said that day," he said. "I was in shock. When I got up the following morning, I was sick. It was really weird. Kim's drinking was not a secret, Sara. The police would find that out eventually."

She thought back to the nurse at the hospital saying that when Kim was brought in she seemed *worse for wear*. She nodded, patting Martin on the arm, just in case he thought she was being critical.

"Do you want to come for a ride?" he said. "I fancy getting out on the bike somewhere."

"Where?"

"Let's go over to Cookham, by the river. You like it there."

"I'm not sure I'm capable of liking anything at the moment."

"Ok. It's a different place to be sad in, then."

Sara looked at him. He appeared the same as usual. The whites of his eyes were clear and his skin was brown and smooth from all the hours he'd spent outside at the garden centre over the summer. He didn't even look tired.

"What?" he said, as she continued to look at him. "A bad idea?"

"No," she replied, not quite managing a smile. "A great idea. Let's go and never come back."

~ ~ ~

The weather blessed them that evening, sending sun and warmth and a light breeze which sounded like soft rain as it found its way through the trees. Sara had texted George, telling him where she was and feeling guilty about allowing him to come home to her parents. But George would understand and, anyway, there was a faint chance her parents would be gone by the time he returned to the flat.

In Cookham, leaving the bike in the car park, they tramped the muddy path through the marshy meadows, heading for the Thames which appeared like a mirage, a shiny ribbon, in the distance. Leaving London, so quickly, had felt like freedom but, being a Friday, the traffic was heavy and Sara could sense Martin's frustration that he didn't have the clear fast run he had wanted. Martin was commenting on the abundance of Red Kites in the area, circling above them, portents of doom, using their forked tails to steer.

Inevitably, as they perched on some spread-eagled, protruding tree roots at the edge of the river, they came back to their loss.

"I feel so heavy," said Sara. "The weight of it all, pressing down on me. And I'm starting to get flash backs. Sudden images of her appear in my head. Her expression when she looked up at me before we left on Monday evening, when she refused to go back to the hospital, with that smashed-in eye and the bruising. Or when I went to the mortuary. I keep walking back into that room and seeing her covered body from the door. I knew she was dead but seeing her and then leaving felt like an abandonment of her. And that made me remember her life and wonder how often she felt abandoned. I don't know how to get rid of those thoughts."

"Hopefully they'll fade," said Martin. "They'll be replaced by earlier memories, happier ones."

Sara turned to look at him.

"Oh, *please,*" she said, scornfully.

"Come on, there were some happier times."

"Maybe. A long time back. Before the incident in the park, perhaps. But since then, I rarely saw her happy. I saw her pretending to be happy, when she was drunk."

Martin said nothing more. *The incident in the park*, he thought. Occasionally, on a summer evening, when the light came through the trees at a certain angle, he would recall the account his mother had given him of what had occurred. The shock of learning what Kim, someone he thought he knew, was capable of had traumatised him.

Sara leant against him and closed her eyes. She could hear the river running over the stones and some bird singing lustily nearby. They sat on without talking until Sara said she was getting cold and perhaps they should go home.

"I thought we were never going back," said Martin, pulling Sara to her feet. He extracted an old scarf from his jacket pocket and offered it to her. Wrapping it round her neck, she started jumping up and down to warm herself.

Speeding along the M4, Sara pressed her head into Martin's leathery back and wished they could ride forever. Around them as the light faded, the drivers switched on their headlights.

Meanwhile, a weary George arrived home. An uplifting session with Year 10, who had persuaded him that they needed to act out certain scenes from Dr Jeykll and Mr Hyde, had been followed by a dispiriting staff meeting with the Head. More cuts were on the horizon. After Sara's text, he'd been gearing himself up for an hour or so on his own with her parents. The relief he felt, when he saw that their bed had been stripped of its sheets and heard the whirr of the washing machine, was matched with a guilty elation. He celebrated by taking a beer from the fridge and switching on the television. As he was untying his shoelaces, in preparation for a stretch on the sofa, the landline rang. Inclined to ignore it, he plumped up the cushions and slipped them under his head. The line stopped ringing and then, almost immediately, it started again. This time the caller decided to leave a message.

"George, it's me," came his father's voice. "Just heard the news about Sara's sister. From Frank. Truly shocking. Don't know what else to say. I wanted Sara to know how sorry I am. Her parents must be ...well, in bits."

George was unable to bear hearing his father struggling through his condolences.

"Hi, Dad."

"George. You *are* there. Just saying…"

"Yes. I know. About Kim. It's been a bloody hard week."

CHAPTER 6

Shade-less

Despite it being a Saturday, Paul Burley, the family liaison officer assigned to them, visited Sara after lunch. He was a tall gangly man in his late forties who maintained eye contact throughout their conversation in a manner which Sara found unnerving. His gaze never wavered.

She explained that her parents had returned to Cornwall, a fact which surprised him, saying he'd hoped to meet them and help them understand the nature and process of the investigation into Kim's death. Sara knew from her research into his role that this was not the only reason he was disappointed that her parents were not there. His was as much an investigative role as it was a supportive one. Any intelligence he gained from his contact with the family would be passed on to the DS Cowley.

Paul Burley was an experienced FLO. This was evident from the moment he introduced himself. He pre-empted most of Sara's questions, seemingly demonstrating that he knew exactly what was important to her at that moment. He said the inquest was likely to be adjourned after a short hearing and not concluded until after any criminal proceedings. This made Sara think that Kim's attackers had already been identified.

Paul didn't say whether they had or they hadn't. "We're still interviewing witnesses. We haven't made any arrests yet. I will let you know immediately, if we do."

He went on to talk about the press interest and advised her not to speak to anyone without discussing it with him first. He made some disparaging comments about reporters and journalists who were expert at making people *trust them*. He appeared confident that trust wouldn't be an issue between him and Sara.

"What about Kim's funeral?" she asked, at last able to raise a question which had not already been dealt with.

"You'll need to liaise with the Coroner's office about that. You may have to wait a while."

Sara said she would let her parents know and Paul left, assuring her he would be in touch and that she should call him if she needed to. He smiled, for the first time and briefly, at the door as she saw him out. She decided she liked him. His unfussy, unemotional style suited her. He hadn't commented when she blinked away some tears after he made reference to Kim's injuries; hadn't rushed to find her a tissue or asked her if she wanted a glass of water. He'd carried on regardless which, curiously, seemed respectful of her grief rather than dismissive of it. And he didn't presume a relationship which was not there.

Time weighed heavily on Sara that weekend. She thought of calling her parents, her conscience stabbing away at her whenever she thought of her mother. Her father would be engaged in any activity which prevented him from dwelling on his daughter's death: cleaning tools, chopping wood, repainting the inside of his shed. Her mother would be neither eating nor sleeping. And even if she could speak, she would not voice her distress to her husband knowing that he would likely advise her that *nothing's going to bring her back now, Emily*. They would sit at the kitchen table opposite each other at meal times. *Please try to eat something, Emily*, at lunchtime. And at dinner time, *eat something, Emily, for God's sake*. Pouring himself another glass of wine, his face would flush with anger when she put her hand over her own glass, shaking her head. Frustration and fury held him close, keeping despair at the gate - for the time being. For Emily, in the rubble of her house, it had already feasted on her and she was hollow.

On the Monday, after a restless night, Sara waited until the alarm went off and then told a bleary-eyed George that she was going to call Paul Burley to ask whether Kim's flat was still a crime scene. If it wasn't, she intended to go over there later that morning.

George propped himself up on one elbow and looked down at her. His black hair stood up in spiky points from his scalp.

"Are you sure that's a good idea, Sara? It's too soon. It will just…" He faltered. "Just make you feel worse."

"I have a really strong urge to be where she last was," she said. "I'm not asking you to come, obviously. I'll take a cab over there. Don't worry about me."

"What about Martin? Perhaps he'll take you on the bike."

Sara shook her head.

"I don't want to bother him again. Anyway, I think it might be better if I'm there on my own."

George hugged her hard before he left for work, extracting a promise that she would call him if she needed to.

By noon, having established she could go, Sara was letting herself into Kim's flat with a set of keys which Kim had given her when she first moved in. She'd remembered them during the night, when the thought of going over to Kim's had first occurred to her. On a key ring bearing the initial *K*, they had been located in one of the kitchen drawers after a frantic search.

Sara was unsure what she needed to take with her. She doubted Kim had any black bags or cleaning products. And then she wondered whether she was really going to embark on a spring clean of the place. Her real intention was to gather up all Kim's personal effects before the Housing Association repossessed the place and discarded them. She didn't want strangers touching Kim's things, examining them wearing rubber gloves and overalls, making faces as they picked up the clothes that would be strewn around her bedroom. She wanted to be the one to touch the places that Kim had last touched: to take her hair from her hairbrush and squeeze it in her fingers, a part of her left behind.

She had entered that flat so many times previously and almost reeled at the smell which greeted her. Grease and cigarette smoke usually. This time the odour had a new pungency although she couldn't place the overriding source of it. Perhaps it was connected to the team of personnel who'd been called out to examine the place following the discovery of Kim's body: plastics and powders. Sara walked slowly through the four small rooms which had comprised Kim's accommodation for the last few years of her life. It had been Kim's refuge rather than her home, she thought. There were no pictures on the walls or rug in the bedroom, no blind on the kitchen window. Even colour itself was missing. There were off whites and muddy greys, although hanging on a hook behind the bathroom door, there was a blue hooded sweater which Sara had given her for her birthday that year. She picked it up and tied it around her waist. She'd planned on buying Kim a jacket but her mother had said, *no, let me do that*. She couldn't think of anything else, she said. Kim was difficult to buy for, most gifts being regarded as charity- *because I'm on benefits, you think you have to buy me something useful.*

She started in the bedroom. The bedclothes were in a heap on the floor. It looked as though the mattress had been removed in the search undertaken by the police. Various pieces of clothing were strewn around, bras and knickers and jeans. Sara gathered it all up, stuffing it into one of black bags she'd brought with her, occasionally looking into Kim's pockets just in case there was a personal item in there which she should save. In the wardrobe, all the hangers but one were empty. The space was taken up by boxes of books and CDs which their parents had passed on to Kim when they moved out of the family home. Rifling through a couple of the boxes, wondering whether she should just let it all go to a charity shop, she came across Kim's fairy tale collection and the horse head book ends. In the inside of the front covers Kim had stuck in book plates with her name and address printed neatly on them. Picking up Hansel and Gretel, she tried to imagine Kim reading to her when they were children, tried to recall her voice, but nothing came. There was just a ringing in her ears and the sound of the relentless traffic outside.

In the kitchen, she found a radio and switched it on for company whilst she cleaned out the fridge, which wasn't difficult as there was so little in it. The cupboards were largely empty too. She filled up another bin bag and left it by the front door so that she wouldn't forget to sling it into one of the wheelie bins when she was leaving.

She hesitated at the door of the living room, looking over at Kim's black recliner. Death is often shown in empty chairs, usually accompanied by an item embodying the person gone - an emblem of some sort, glasses or walking stick for the old, a toy or dummy for the young. For Kim, all Sara could see was the remote control. No doubt much had been removed for analysis, such as her tobacco pouch and the cans. On the table by the chair was Kim's bag. It had been emptied out and lay like a dead and unloved thing upside down. She lowered herself into the chair and, lying back, picked up Kim's bag and hugged it to her chest. She looked around her. This is where she lay that night. This is what she saw. A peeling ceiling and a shade-less light: a television screen peopled with strangers in a room devoid of company.

Glancing down at the table, Sara noticed a small passport sized photo underneath the receipts and tissues. She reached over and picked it up, blowing the bits of tobacco from the two faces which overlapped one another in the photo booth. It must have been in the bottom of Kim's bag and ended up on the table when whoever it was emptied it out.

She didn't recognize the girl with Kim. She had a Mohican style haircut and a plethora of facial piercings. She was pulling a face and Kim was laughing. As she was scrutinising the girl's features, she thought back to the incident in the park and the gang of girls who had been involved. She could have been one of them. It was strange that Kim had kept the photo. As far as Sara was aware, Kim had not had contact with any of them since the court hearing following the incident. Over the years, they'd all learnt not to refer to it in front of her. Kim had struggled with coming to terms with her own behaviour and refused help when it had been offered by her probation officer. Her stubbornness had won out then too, thought Sara. She tore the girl's face from the photo - keeping Kim's intact - and rolled it into a tiny ball which she flicked back onto the table.

She was looking at her sister's happy face when her mobile rang. It was Paul Burley, telling her they had made two arrests. The man and woman were in the process of being interviewed. He would keep her informed of progress.

She didn't do much after that. She hadn't asked Paul for any details of the two people now in police custody. She knew they were a man and woman but that was the only information she had on them. She would see them in due course should she want to, standing in the dock, *your blood on their hands*, she whispered to herself, still looking at Kim's face. *Bastards.* She sounded deranged, even to herself.

She looked away from the photograph and out of the window to the familiar blur of traffic thundering past. She would order an Uber and go home, back to the flat and George, where she would be reminded that there was a world other than the one which Kim had inhabited. A world where lots of good things happen.

CHAPTER 7

Witness

Seven days on from her death, Gail Flood and Gary Timms were both charged with the manslaughter of Kim Turner. It was reported in a couple of newspapers and splashed over social media. A local reporter, Ms Cox, turned up at the convenience store where Kim had bought her supplies of alcohol. She learned nothing. The Singh family, showing a loyalty to Kim undeserved in her dealings with them, declined to provide even the most perfunctory of information. They asked Ms Cox to *please, Madam, either buy something or leave.* A few of Kim's old school friends got in touch with Sara, via Facebook, saying they were shocked to read about Kim's death and hoped she would let them know the date and time of the funeral. Sara acknowledged their messages but didn't engage further with them.

Paul Burley said he would like to visit her parents and Sara agreed that it was a good idea. The arrests of Flood and Timms had provided her with an excuse to call them. She and her father were civil with each other and brief apologies were exchanged. They both recognized that confining themselves to the factual was the least damaging manner of communication. When Sara asked to speak to her mother, she was told that she was lying down and that he would ask her to call Sara back when she was up and about. When no call came, Sara turned to Martin's mother. Tabitha was blunt.

"She's not coping, Sara. I'm really worried about her. Stuck down there with just your father for company."

As Tabitha had anticipated, Sara agreed with her.

"I know. When did you last speak to her?"

"A few days ago, when she returned from your place. Since then, I've not been able to get past your Dad. But he did say she wasn't well. That's probably an understatement. I don't know what to do. I'm sorry, that's not really helpful, is it?"

They agreed that they would both keep trying and Tabitha said she would go to see her sister if she hadn't heard from her by the end of the week, whether by invite or otherwise.

"I know you've got your hands full, dear. It's just dreadful. Martin's been through a really rough time so God knows how you've coped. At least you have the lovely George! The sweet voice of calm and reason."

After the arrests, the Coroner's office was in touch, informing her they needed to wait to see if the Defendants accepted the Pathologist's report or whether they'd be seeking their own. Kim's body could not be released until that issue had been resolved.

Sara had decided to return to work. Her days were long and aimless. Structure and routine might help her sleep. Gloria and the team welcomed her back, some better than others at acknowledging her loss. Her mug was still on her desk where she had left it, specs of mould on the surface of the tea she had abandoned when the police turned up to tell her about Kim. Gloria and Sara sat in a room set aside for case conferences and discussed what had happened in Sara's absence. Sandy's partner, the boys' father, had relapsed and there was no prospect of the children returning home whilst he remained living there. Sandy knew this but seemed unable to act on it. Sara needed to set up an urgent meeting with her. Seven children, from three separate families, had been taken into care whilst Sara was away. The department was struggling under the work load. Things had been complicated because local foster placements could not be found for 3 of the children and siblings had been separated. The children's Guardian demanded that they find a local placement, particularly for the two-year old who was traumatised at not only being removed from her parents but also losing her older brother and sister. And the parents are angry too, *understandably*, said Gloria, pushing her escaping hair back behind her ears.

"The father was in here yesterday, battering the door down. We had to call the police."

Exhausted by this litany of disaster, she paused to draw breath.

"So, it's good to have you back, Sara. How are you? Or is that a stupid question?"

Sara smiled, indicating her answer and Gloria, a woman of experience in understanding non-verbal behaviour, nodded.

"I'll leave you to catch up."

Much of the irritation which began percolating through her system, Sara ascribed to tiredness but, a few days down the line, there was something more than mere irritation present in her attack on her colleague, Patsy. They were close, having worked with each other for many years. Patsy was getting married in six months' time. The wedding was being planned with the meticulous attention once reserved for Generals in battle. At desks facing one another, they were both eating chicken pasta out of plastic trays. Already that morning Patsy had made two telephone calls in which she discussed some aspect of the forthcoming nuptials. One was connected to the number and price of the chairs at the venue and the second with her mother about whether she should buy or rent a hat and, if so, what sort would suit a woman in her sixties. Patsy smiled contentedly to herself as she put her mobile down and carried on picking the chicken pieces out of her pasta - to keep the calories in check.

"It's tricky," she said.

Sara made a noise to indicate that she was listening.

"You know, what sort of hat to wear. My mother wants a proper hat – as she calls it – with a brim - not one of those little things, Alice bands with feathers in them! Fascinators they're called." She raised her perfectly arched eyebrows at Sara and laughed. Throwing the remains of her lunch into the bin, Patsy continued on the theme of wedding hats.

"What d'you think?"

Sara looked over at her. Patsy's mobile was placed on her wedding planner, a large colourful file which had assumed the status of an essential accessory, always in reach. Inside there was a calendar of the crucial dates leading up to the special day, swatches of fabric, the guest lists (for the ceremony *and* the evening event), the seating plan (forever under review), menus and mobile numbers for the soloist and celebrant. On the cover of the planner, which Sara had seen so often she could have sketched it from memory, was a drawing of three thin women: the bride in white flanked by two bridesmaids in matching pale green dresses. They were holding up a banner *How to Achieve Your Perfect Day* and, naturally, they all exhibited wide smiles. There was even a glorious sun shining down on them, suggesting there would be tips inside on how to organise the weather too. *Although always be prepared – it can still rain in June!*

Sara's response was to shrug and hope it would satisfy the Bride to Be.

But no, the subject of fascinators was just too fascinating to be dropped.

"You see, I *do* like them. Although choosing one to suit the shape of your face is quite an art!"

Patsy leant forward, scrutinising Sara's features.

"You'd look *really* good in one of those *Percher* hats, worn at an angle."

Sara had had enough.

"Have you heard yourself, Patsy?"

Patsy's smile dropped from her face. She picked up her mug and stood up. Before she could murmur her apologies and creep away, Sara spoke again.

"Believe it or not, wedding hats are not at the forefront of my mind at this moment. And neither is your fucking wedding. I'm about to plan a funeral - so you'll forgive me if I don't join your debate on mummy's headwear."

Sara's raised voice had been heard by the rest of the team and a brief, painful silence descended in the office.

Patsy did not say anything. She headed off in the direction of the staff toilets and one of the admin staff, relishing any respite from the tedium of her work, scurried after her.

Sara did not look around her, just put down her plastic fork and returned to her screen. She typed into Google the question which had been preoccupying her ever since she'd received the news about Flood and Timms.

"What's the difference between murder and manslaughter?"

It appeared to be something to do with the *intention* behind the assault. Someone in the CPS had decided that there had been no intention on the part of Gary Timms or Gail Flood to kill or seriously harm Kim. In the particular circumstances of Kim's eventual death, their vicious actions could not amount to murder: only manslaughter.

Paul Burley was not available on his mobile. Sara prevaricated over whether to leave a message but, after her second attempt following the bleep, she asked him to call her back. She was standing in one of the office stairwells, knowing she should return to her desk. Someone from the legal department had arranged to call her at 4pm concerning one of her cases and it was nearing that time. As she turned to walk back up to the office, the familiar image of herself standing at the door of the mortuary gazing at Kim's covered body resurrected itself in her mind. She tried to dispel it, closing her eyes tightly and digging her nails into the flesh of her forearm. After a few seconds it faded.

Patsy did not look up when she sat back down opposite her and she didn't ask her if Sara wanted any tea when she got up to make her own a few minutes later. When Sara dared to glance at her, she could see that her mascara was smudged under her eyes. The wedding planner appeared to have disappeared from her desk. It was not feasible to maintain their silence. They were dependent on one another. Sara decided she would apologise before they left for the evening but, in the event, Paul Burley returned her call and when she came back from speaking to him, Patsy had gone.

"I just wondered," said Sara to Paul Burley, "why the couple you have in custody haven't been charged with murder. Because that's what it is. In my eyes anyway."

"It's not straightforward, Sara."

He had intended to expand on this comment but was not given the opportunity.

"It seems pretty bloody straightforward to me."

She was breathing heavily. The dregs of her composure were trickling away.

"Sara. Listen. Just listen. I can come round tonight and we can talk it through. Will you be in? I was going to phone you today anyway as they're up in the Magistrates court on Thursday and it'll be reported."

"Can I go?"

"To court? Anyone can go. But nothing will happen. The matter will just get transferred to the Crown Court for pleas to be entered."

"I want to see them."

Paul didn't respond to this.

"I'll come over later. What time is good for you?"

George was trying hard not to show his dismay when Sara told him that Paul was coming over at 7.30 to talk about *recent developments*. Arsenal was playing. If they were in the living room, he would be forced to watch it on his laptop in the kitchen. He wondered if it would be grossly insensitive to leave them to it and go over to his mate Sam's for the match. Paul came to the rescue on this one.

"Not watching the game tonight?" he asked George when he opened the door to him. He knew about George and football. Last time they met, they had used the subject as shorthand to check out each other's male credentials. Missing the game was a bitter blow to Paul too.

"George, you watch the game in here," said Sara. "We can go into the kitchen. If that's ok, Paul?"

Paul refused the offer of refreshment. He wanted to get on and get out. This was difficult territory to those looking at the law from the outside.

"You asked me a question about the charges brought against the defendants. In short, why it's been decided to charge them with manslaughter rather than murder."

Sara nodded.

"For a charge of murder to succeed, we would need to convince a jury that when they launched their attack on Kim they did so with the intent of killing her or causing her serious bodily harm. There's no evidence of that, particularly as Kim started it by pushing Flood. Which is not only what they say happened but what witnesses have said also. Anyway, the Pathologist is clear about the cause of death. She died from a fall down a flight of concrete stairs not from a head injury."

"But Kim told me that she only pushed the woman because they were both shouting at her and waving a bottle in front of her face."

"Sure, but the witnesses will be asked about her. She doesn't come out of it well, Sara. She'd been drinking *and* smoking and – we think - she *fell* down the stairs. She wasn't pushed. We have more than one witness saying she left immediately after the assault. On her own. As far as we know Flood and Timms left later. The pathologist describes the contusions and bruising to her face but concludes that the cause of death was a ruptured chest cavity, not a head injury from the assault. For any manslaughter charge to stick, we need to establish that Sara left the party immediately in a state of fear of being attacked further – that she acted the way she did because of the threat from Timms. Not only will the defendants argue self-defence but they'll also say she fell because she was drunk or stoned. We won't do any better than manslaughter. But have no illusions, they won't plead. We're in for a trial – and with no guarantees at the end of it."

His eyes were fixed on her face, gauging every flicker of her response.

"To be honest, I think we're lucky the CPS are going for manslaughter," he added.

"Lucky?" queried Sara.

"Sorry. I didn't mean it that way. I meant that the CPS could have decided that since Kim fell down the stairs and that the medical evidence is clear about the cause of death, a contested trial for manslaughter isn't a runner. But they haven't decided that. They think the chain of causation is sufficient to mount a case against Flood and Timms – that it's worth putting before a jury. Although we've a long way to go before then."

Sara pushed her hair back from her face and stood up. No-one could accuse Paul Burley of avoiding difficult issues

"I think I will attend Court on Thursday," she said. "I feel the need to be there. For Kim's sake."

Paul did not attempt to dissuade her, saying he'd text her if anything changed. He mentioned his visit to her parents, remarking that he had felt some concern for her mother's mental state. She appeared traumatised to the point of being unable to speak. He hoped she was seeking some treatment.

"How would you describe Kim's relationship with your parents?"

"Difficult. I'm not sure you could say that Kim and Dad had much of one. Mum had a hard time of it, sandwiched between them. But she – well, she seemed to have given up on her in the last couple of years. Perhaps we all did – in one way or another - although it's hard to admit it. Particularly now. Kim wasn't easy to help."

"Did the Coroner contact you?"

"No."

"The toxicology report is out. Kim was three times over the legal limit for alcohol when she died. There's a suggestion it may have contributed to her death."

"I expect that will be something else which will be used against her."

Sara went over to the sink, running the water and then filling her glass. She may as well have given Kim a couple of phials of poison to inject when she and Martin went over to see her on the night of her death. *Don't give me any grief, Sara, not today.*

In the living room, George was cursing loudly. There'd been a goal and he wasn't happy.

~ ~ ~

Gail Flood was a small, wiry woman in her late twenties. Dressed in black jeans and a hoodie, her short dark hair was plastered to her head, accentuating the shape of her skull. She was standing next to a tall police officer and she appeared nervous, her eyes darting around the court room as if she anticipated a jeering crowd. Every now and again, she sniffed, wiping her nose with the heel of her free hand in an upward motion. Two of her fingers were stained a dirty nicotine yellow.

Timms, older than his co-defendant, did not assume Flood's anxious demeanour. He stared into the middle distance and did not fidget. He was almost bald and had a stocky frame. He probably owned a Staffordshire terrier, Sara decided, which he would pull along on a chain, enjoying the wide berth which members of the public gave him on the high street on a Saturday afternoon. Parents would pull their children from his path, thinking of Bill Sykes and poor Nancy as they did so. She felt a fleeting sense of shame as she made this assessment. Despite her protestations to the more sceptical of her friends, her liberalism was just a thin veneer after all.

The front bench of the court was taken up by the lawyers, files and textbooks - *Archbold: Criminal Pleading, Evidence and Practice* - scattered in front of them. When Sara entered the court room they had been chatting and laughing amongst themselves, lounging back in their seats with the confidence of those who know their worth. The entrance of Timms and Flood silenced them. Thereafter, whilst awaiting the Magistrates, they only whispered or scribbled in their notebooks, occasionally turning around to make some request of the clerks who sat behind them, pens poised.

Sara was sitting at the back of the court, hoping not to draw any attention to her presence in case the press who were there, assuming nonchalance but fooling no one, spotted her. It was probably obvious that she was not there to support the defendants. In fact, she couldn't immediately see anyone who might be connected to them. But just as the Magistrates entered the room and the assembled persons stood up as one, the door behind her opened and a woman in her late fifties, in baggy tracksuit bottoms and a red puffer jacket slipped into the back row, a few seats away from Sara. Sara saw her gesticulating at Flood - a thumbs up sign which she converted into a little wave of her fingers, perhaps deciding that it was inappropriate to extend congratulations to someone in the dock on trial for manslaughter.

As Paul had told her, nothing dramatic happened. Flood and Timms confirmed their full names and addresses. The indictments for manslaughter were read out. The lawyer for the CPS said that, since bail was not in issue, it only remained for the matter to be sent to the Crown Court for a pre-hearing. No pleas were entered.

Sara didn't tell Gloria that she was going to the Magistrates' court on the Friday morning, just sent her an email to say she'd be in late. Paul had a prior engagement and Sara reassured him that she didn't need support. Courts themselves were not a foreign territory to her. But on stepping back onto the pavement after leaving court, there was an alien quality to the outside world. It had shifted on its axis whilst she was inside and things looked different. Her perspective had altered. When Kim's name was read out in the indictment, *Kim Madeleine Turner*, whatever had seemed unreal in Sara's situation, difficult to grasp, was now harrowingly real. The legal process, brief as it was, had made it so.

They killed my sister. She said it over and over to herself as she made her way back to the office. She thought back to the grieving relatives she had seen in the media, hanging on to their bitterness, unable to let it go because as time had gone by, *they had come to define themselves by their loss* - as she would observe blithely to herself. Well, now she was standing where they had stood at the door of the courtroom. And she didn't want to *understand* Flood and Timms or to examine their intentions. She wanted to watch Flood go white with shock when she was sentenced to ten years inside where bullying and fear would stalk her. She wanted to imagine Timms, in his first week, lying on the floor of the prison shower, nursing his damaged ribs: in no doubt of his position in the pecking order of the wing. She wanted them to suffer.

She had a meeting scheduled with Sandy, the mother of the cherubic twins, that afternoon. Sandy was late. When she did turn up, her eyes were blood-shot and she had a bruise just under her left cheekbone.

Sara, seeing the bruise, did not comment on her lateness.

"What's been going on, Sandy? Where did you get that bruise?"

Sandy put her hand up to her cheek.

"I fell," she said.

Sara laughed.

"Oh yeah. I bet. Come on, tell me the truth. *He's* back with you, isn't he? Was he responsible for it?"

Sandy shook her head miserably.

"You realise, don't you, that there's no chance of the boys being returned to you whilst he's on the scene. You need to get rid of him. You need to see a solicitor and get an injunction."

Sandy said nothing.

Sara looked at her, feeling the irritation rising like acid within her.

"Well?"

Sandy started to cry, her face crumpling under Sara's unrelenting, unsmiling gaze.

"You've got a choice, Sandy. Him or your children."

Normally, she would have put her hand out when Sandy started to cry, squeezing her arm and offering her tea. She'd start tapping into her computer, naming a couple of local solicitors who would help her. She might have suggested she make the appointment for her and run her there in the car, should she be free. But she did none of those things. She sighed instead and told Sandy to think about it. *Hard.* They talked about the date for Sandy's next contact with her sons and then

Sara terminated the interview. Sandy put up her hood and left the room without a goodbye.

Later, Sara passed Gloria in the corridor.

"How did your meeting go?" asked Gloria, stopping to talk to her, surprising Sara by her interest.

"Predictably," said Sara. "She'll never get around to kicking Dad out. She's a lost cause."

"Only when I popped out to the shop, I saw her sitting on a bench outside the shopping mall, sobbing her little heart out."

"I spelt it out to her. I decided anything else would be a waste of time. If she hasn't got the message now, she'll never get it."

Sara didn't wait to see if Gloria had any further questions. She went back to her desk. Patsy was in and she gave Sara a half smile as she sat down. Despite her previous intention to make it up with her, Sara didn't return the gesture. She fixed her eyes on her screen and started typing, bashing the keys wildly, the words blurring and merging as she fought for control.

~ ~ ~

"Why did you go?" asked Martin, who had already finished his glass of coke and was now bending his straw into different shapes.

"I wanted to see them."

He knew she wanted to talk about it. He wasn't sure he did.

"And?" he said eventually.

"She looked small and pathetic in the dock. He was the sort of man your mother would say you wouldn't want to meet in a dark alley late at night."

"I would have come with you, you know. If you'd wanted me to."

Martin wasn't entirely sure this was true. He was glad she hadn't asked. There would be other, more important, times ahead he decided, on this unexpected expedition, when he would be *expected* to show up

Sara nodded.

"I know. I felt I should be there for Kim. Bearing witness and all that stuff. I thought I'd be able to keep some distance from them. I've shocked myself with the depth of hatred I feel. You hear that phrase *mindless violence* bandied about in the press and think, it's not mindless – that's just a lazy way of describing something you can't be bothered to analyse. Yet that's precisely what I felt having seen them. They attacked her so *casually*. Mindless bastards. I wished them harm, Martin. I *wish* them harm."

At times, it had been difficult to hear her above the noise which surrounded them. This was a conversation at odds with the prevailing mood of a Friday night in a busy pub.

"They'll get their just desserts, I'm sure. Anyway, what happens now?" he asked, rocking back in his chair.

"We wait," she said. "They'll be up in the Crown Court for pleas in the next few weeks."

Martin was keen to move on to another subject and asked her about her return to work. He heard about the Patsy incident, surprised that she didn't appear to regret how critical she had been. He thought of reminding her that she and Patsy had shared some very difficult times in the past - how often she'd said "Christ knows what I'd have done without Patsy" or "Patsy bailed me out." He had spent the odd evening with them both. They were quite different. Sara was political and saw injustice in the current system which she wanted to change. Patsy adopted a practical approach and saw her job as encouraging *people* to change, so as to fit in with what was wanted, or demanded, by society. But they shared a passion for the work they did and appeared to complement one another.

Sara then recounted her meeting with the hapless mother, Sandy, even laughing when she got to the bit about Gloria seeing Sandy on the bench crying.

"Whoops!" she chuckled, pulling her mouth down, "perhaps I could have handled it better. Gloria didn't seem impressed. Still, better to be honest with her."

Martin was silent when she had finished. He wanted to leave and go back to his room and his boxes. But Sara was in for a session, not caring whether he wanted to drink or not.

"Where's George?" he said at last, resuming his rocking.

"He's going to Brighton tomorrow to see his Dad so he wanted to finish some work tonight, instead of leaving it until Sunday."

She drained her glass and held it out to him. Martin righted his chair and got up, moving his way through the throng to the bar. Whilst waiting to be served, he looked back at Sara. She was biting her nails and looked deep in thought. He was used to Sara's quixotic nature. No mood endured. As such, he didn't fear the heat of rage in her that she had described. But this was not a mood. Her words implied a lasting change, as if her belief system had been undermined by the manner of Kim's death and she was on the cusp of becoming somebody different.

When he escaped back into the night, running Sara home on his bike, he sat down at his desk and picked up the box he was working on. He had painted a green-blue sea with a whale making its way through the waves, its blowhole cascading water. He had not enjoyed the evening. Whilst Sara had not asked anything of him, she spoke as if he shared her perspective. She presumed his loyalty, wherever it may take them.

Deciding he had no appetite for his craft after all, he went to lie on his bed. He wished he'd found the strength to tell Sara he had made other plans for the evening. He thought of his mates, riding their bikes along the M4, the noise and speed consuming them and leaving no space for useless rumination. He couldn't recall a time when his longing to be with them had felt so intense.

CHAPTER 8

Gone

George was on the train going down to Brighton to see his father. He had asked Sara to go with him but she had said, with some ferocity, that she couldn't cope with his father *at this precise moment* in her life. A few minutes later, she apologised, blaming the events of the day and seeing *those bastards in court*. Whilst he changed out of his work shirt and trousers into his jeans she had sat on the bed and talked. She even followed him into the bathroom when he went for a slash, still talking, her voice rising in volume and pitch as she laid bare her feelings.

George had listened and nodded, not even attempting a response in case it prolonged her tirade. It wasn't even confined to the court hearing. There were frustrations in the office and she was sick to death of how slow *Legal* were at responding to everything. They'd sent a statement back, due to be filed that day, just before 5.30 saying *the checklist* needed some amendments.

There was a game on television he wanted to watch so he had to tread with some delicacy.

"I thought we could go for a drink," she said. They had moved on to the kitchen where George was eating a Danish pastry which had been left over from a colleague's birthday. He had spent some time with his head in the fridge, hoping that something for his evening meal might appear, miraculously, if he kept looking long enough. He hadn't planned to visit his Dad that weekend but during their telephone call the previous evening, in between the banter and listening to his father's new theories, he sensed his loneliness.

Pete Todd, widowed many years ago, now lived alone in a small terraced house in Brighton. Around once a month, George went down there for a Saturday night, occasionally with Sara but usually on his own. George's brother, Frank, three years older, also lived in London but was in investment banking and had a hectic social life – not that one inevitably led to the other. It was just in Frank's case he often presented his social commitments as mandatory. On the few occasions each year that he did manage to accompany George to the seaside, they drove down in Frank's silver Mercedes Sports to the sound of Chopin or John Mayer, depending on how the markets had performed that week. When Sara and George had got together, George worried much more about Sara meeting Frank than he did about introducing her to his father. He was sure that not only would she despise Frank for his lifestyle but also have no hesitation in telling him so. He was completely wrong. They got on famously from the beginning, sparring energetically with each other and then, to George's discomfort and, usually, everyone around them, moved on to some outrageous flirting. If Sara learned that Frank would be joining his brother on a trip to Brighton, she would *always* come, demanding to sit in the front passenger seat and seeming perfectly at ease in letting Frank pay for dinner in a restaurant she would, normally, lambast for its obscene prices.

"Your moral boundaries blur when it comes to my brother," George told her. "Not to mention your political principles."

"Jealous, are you?"

"Don't be pathetic." It was one of the rare times when George exhibited some annoyance towards her.

Where Frank had obtained his fierce ambition from was a question which various members of the family often pondered. To George, it was obvious. Their father was a wholly decent man, pleasant and kind but a bit of a wastrel, none the less. He had squandered his talents throughout the years, working only sporadically and then not at all since reaching his mid-fifties when his wife, the boys' mother, had died. Her life had been insured for a decent sum and Pete decided he wouldn't bother with the inconvenience of paid work any longer although, as Frank remarked – *not that any of us noticed the difference.* But Pete's example had horrified Frank – the cramped little house in one of the sleazier parts of Brighton, the prospect of an impoverished old age now that the lump sum had dwindled and the state pension was all he had to live on, the trips to Lidl and Morrisons with the vouchers he'd collected, getting rid of the car because he could no longer afford to run it but disguising the fact by saying he now had a Bus Pass and *it would be sheer madness to keep the old rust bucket*. Last year he could not afford to mend the boiler when it broke down and Frank had paid for the whole system to be replaced.

"After all," he'd commented to George. "Consider the alternative – Dad coming to live with one or other of us! What a fucking nightmarish prospect. Worth a few grand to keep him at arm's length in Brighton."

But for all his guff, Frank was a generous son and enjoyed treating his father whenever he could find an excuse – and the time, naturally. On Pete's last birthday, Frank had taken him to a hotel in Bristol and then for a ride in a hot air balloon. On his teacher's salary, George had not even tried to compete, deciding that the time he gave his father would always trump Frank's lavish gifts.

Pete had immediately launched into his latest theory when he'd called George the previous night.

"People just don't realise how much British values have changed over the last four decades. The newspaper headlines can tell us a lot. I've been researching them."

"Right," said George, wondering how long this particular discourse was going to last.

"I've started with The Guardian – The *Manchester* Guardian as it used to be, starting up in the industrial North, solid Labour then - anyway – the headlines were not about money the way they are now. In fact, if you compare the headlines of quite a few of the papers forty years ago with today's, you'll note a number of significant things. Firstly, the unions were big then and what they said mattered. Of course, they represented a lot more people than they do today."

"Did they?"

"Oh yes, I'll email you the graph I found in an article I've been reading about this very subject. Trade Union membership has fallen from a high of around 13 million in 1979 to under 6 million today. Cuts to the public sector and of course the rise of the gig economy have played their part but there are other, in a sense, more worrying reasons behind it."

"Like what?"

"Well, people don't align themselves with others in the same way as they did. Unions were about sticking together, a united workforce against the bosses. Nowadays, young folk particularly, align themselves in very different ways – through social media for instance."

After another ten minutes, George managed his escape by telling his father he'd come down to see him the next day. He'd skilfully organised his evening at home watching the football too.

"Actually, I wanted to get some work done tonight before I head off tomorrow. Instead of leaving it until Sunday evening," he said, in response to Sara's obvious need for self-medication in the form of alcohol.

"Why, for God's sake? You usually do!"

"I'm turning over a new leaf." George smiled. He hoped her remark, her little stab at humour, might signal that her rage had dissipated.

"I suppose I could ask Martin."

"What about Patsy? You're usually out with her at this time on a Friday."

"She's full of her bloody wedding. She's only got one topic of conversation these days. I'll see if Martin's up for a drink."

George put his arms around Sara and kissed her.

"I know you need to get out. I'll come if cuz can't."

She was only out for a couple of hours. He knew she was back when he heard the familiar purr of Martin's bike around ten. He hadn't done any work. A few minutes after she'd gone to meet Martin, he decided that, despite the expense, he'd take the train to Brighton and work during the journey. There was a lot of marking so he'd need to take his larger rucksack but, still, the decision enabled him to watch the game live and to order a pepperoni pizza which, obligingly, arrived during half time. He'd kept up a text conversation with his mate, Sam, throughout and they were still debating the ref's decision about a sending off when Sara came into room. It was clear that she had managed more than a glass.

"Did you eat?" he asked, as she eyed the pizza box on the coffee table.

She shook her head.

"Couldn't summon up any appetite," she said.

"How was Martin?"

"Same as ever. He drank Coke all evening. Pub was rammed."

"There's not much in the fridge," he said.

"Did you get your work done?"

He looked at her sheepishly.

"I knew you wouldn't!"

She pulled off her boots and lay down with her head on his lap.

"I just want to sleep," she said, closing her eyes. "Sleep and wake up in the morning, rather than toss and turn all night, thinking about things. But then, when I *do* sleep, I have that terrible moment as I resurface when I remember her. She comes back to me, sometimes quite clearly. Things we've done together."

George watched her face beneath him as the tears slid from the corners of her eyes. He had thought that her sadness was easier to experience than her fury. Feeling the little shudders of grief pass through her into him, he wasn't so certain of that now. He smoothed her thick dark hair away from her face.

"Come with me tomorrow. It will be good for you to have a change of scene, even if it involves my Dad. I'd like you to come. What are you going to do here if you stay?"

"I've lots to catch up on. Anyway, I think it's best if I'm alone at the moment. I'm not sure I'm the best company."

George was thinking about what she said as he unpacked some of Year 9's exercise books on to the table in front of him. The train had just left Victoria. He was sitting opposite a middle-aged woman and, he presumed, her elderly mother. The old lady had hearing problems and much of their conversation was repeated. It had been a relief when they went to the toilet together. George hoped he hadn't looked too eager to be of assistance when the daughter asked if he would keep an eye on their bags whilst they were gone.

He knew Sara was right about being better alone. He had failed to encourage her to talk about anything other than Kim's death and the charges against Flood and Timms. Although pleased when she returned to work, believing that it would bring some normality back into their lives, he was yet to see any. Bizarrely, he was looking forward to Kim's funeral – or, perhaps, the day afterwards when Sara might regain her balance. He heard his Dad's voice in his head. *All things must pass*.

Pete was waiting for George on the concourse of Brighton station. As he moved though the ticket barrier, George could see him chatting to a young woman who was playing the piano, the instrument serving the purpose for which it was installed: connecting travellers on their way through.

Pete beamed at him as he approached.

"Now here's a man who plays the classical stuff!" he boasted. The woman, early twenties, clear skinned and pretty, looked up at him.

"Come on, then," she said, getting up from the chair. "All yours!"

She smiled encouragingly at him.

"Oh, I don't know......" began George. It had been a while since he'd played although Pete still retained the family upright in his cramped little house.

"Just a few minutes, come on."

Sara had talked about him playing something at Kim's funeral and he hadn't dismissed the idea. He wanted to play his part in remembering Kim but, probably more than that, he wanted to make the occasion easier for Sara. She was worried about speaking, saying that someone needed to give the eulogy. Her mother was incapacitated with grief, such that Sara was not even sure she would attend on the day, and the thought of her father donning the mantle of the grieving parent made her *livid*.

George had gently reminded her that, however stormy Kim and her father's relationship had been, he must have still loved her.

"Albeit in his own way," he said, somewhat lamely, already regretting his intervention on the subject. He had intended to add – "after all, she was his daughter, his flesh and blood." But given the look of derision on Sara's face at hearing the word *love* in the context of her father and his first born, he left it at that. Only the foolhardy meddle in other people's families.

George sat down at the old piano and played the first chords to a Scott Joplin piece, immediately wondering how many times previously it had been played to the waiting crowds. His father nodded his head and looked around, hoping for silence in the wake of such obvious talent. But then George stopped and looking at the pianist he had usurped so abruptly, said,

"That was just too predictable, wasn't it?"

She laughed.

He turned back to the piano and played the opening to the Moonlight Sonata, which attracted more attention than the Joplin.

George and his Dad walked back to his house, picking up some baguettes on their way. They had an easy relationship, both sticking to subjects they had in common, seeking to please and entertain rather than otherwise.

After lunch, Pete got out one of the free newspapers from the stack of them piled up on his kitchen table. They searched through the listings, their heads bent together, looking for a film to see that afternoon. When nothing appealed, they ended up walking by the sea front and then going to a pub before dinner at a Chinese restaurant.

Over their meal, the subject of Kim, previously avoided, arose.

"I didn't mention her earlier. I thought I'd leave it to you to talk if you wanted to. When I saw you at the station, you looked, well, worn out really. It's why I asked you to play. Wanted to see a flash of the old George. My cheerful son."

George looked up from his sweet and sour chicken. His father hadn't made much progress with his meal. The concern in his father's eyes moved him. He doubted he'd shown him the same depth of compassion on the death of his wife of twenty-five years. All the focus then had been on him and

Frank, the motherless boys, because they were young and at *vulnerable* ages – as if all ages aren't vulnerable when it comes to coping with irreparable loss. George picked up his glass, swallowing down his emotion along with a mouthful of beer. But it was too late.

"I'm sorry," he said, putting his hand across his forehead, embarrassed by his tears. He felt his father patting his hand. "It's just been so dreadful, watching Sara going through it all. To begin with, I was amazed at how well she was doing, holding it all together. Now I don't know that she is."

"Only talk if you want to, George. If it helps. Don't worry about me."

He explained about the previous day's court case and Sara's mood on his return from work.

"She veers between grief and anger. I don't know what she wants from me."

"Nothing, I expect. Just to be there. Listening. You're good at that. She's lucky – in that respect."

George smiled, blowing his nose on the paper serviette.

His father continued.

"I've never been where you are now but I know one thing. Nothing's wrong or right. You're just going to have to see it through and hope you both emerge at the other end. Think of it as a journey across a land where the winds blow strong and fierce. Every now and again, you'll get blown off course or, even, blown over, but keep positive and keep going."

It sounded like something he'd picked up from an old copy of the Readers Digest.

"You're very wise, Dad," he said, kindly.

"I'm very old, George!"

They both laughed, marking an end to the melancholy, and then Pete passed his plate over to George and asked him to help him out.

~ ~ ~

Sara was still in bed when George left for the station. They'd agreed he wouldn't wake her if she was asleep, sleep having assumed such an elusive role in her life since the death of Kim. She was grateful to him for not making a fuss about leaving her alone. Lots of partners would have perceived it as a slight that she could cope without him for 36 hours during such a critical period in her life. George was different. He had no interest in infantilising her.

She had thought of her mother again during a long wakeful period in the night and resolved to call her. They had now not spoken for nearly three weeks. Sara thought back to when they had been quite close. Her moving away had changed their relationship. Once they had stopped seeing each other regularly, it had become more difficult to return to being relaxed in each other's company. In London, it had been easy to meet up, away from her father, and spend time together. Her father had been in work then. Now he was always around, making demands. Lots of their telephone conversations concerned Kim. She was in rent arrears, she was drinking heavily again, she had fallen and broken two bones in her hand. Her mother would defer to her husband as to how the latest crisis should be dealt with and the person *dealing* with it was, inevitably, Sara. She had come to resent the role which was forced upon her but, on learning from Tabitha that her mother was depressed and taking medication for it, she was, effectively, silenced. Instead the resentment bubbled away underneath her skin, being revealed to George or Martin or, in happier times, to Patsy, when her will weakened after a few glasses of wine.

Coincidentally, Tabitha contacted her mid-morning to say she had spoken to Martin and wondered how much Emily and Steve knew about the appearance of Timms and Flood in the Magistrates Court. She wanted to know *so that I don't put my foot in it when I speak to her, assuming I'm allowed, of course.* Sara explained that she believed that the FLO had visited them during the previous week, following the arrest of the defendants.

"So they'll be up to speed, I think. I was going to call myself this morning, actually."

"Look," said Tabitha, "You do that. And then let me know, would you?"

Sara assured her that she would.

She didn't ring immediately. She found other things to do such as going to the supermarket. She had felt lousy in the morning, waking up with a start when she heard the flat door bang on George's departure. She had a headache from the wine, probably still trickling through her bloodstream like a toxic drip. She wanted breakfast before tackling her father.

There was no answer from either her mother's mobile or the house phone. She left messages on both at around midday. She tried again in the early afternoon and then accepted, reluctantly, that she would have to speak to her father. He didn't answer his mobile either.

"Something's wrong," she said to Tabitha. It was three o'clock on a Saturday afternoon. Even if they'd gone out for the day, surely one of them would have taken their mobile phone.

"Christ, it's so damn difficult when they live so far away. I can't say to Martin, run me down there, will you, darling?! I'm tempted to just turn up at their door and risk your Dad's fury."

Sara said she would keep trying.

She got through to her father around 9 that evening. He spoke quietly and in monosyllables. *Yes. Sara. Sorry.* There was enough background noise to suggest he was in a public place.

"Where are you, Dad? And is Mum with you? For God's sake, I've been trying to contact you all bloody day."

"Hold on," he said, eventually, after she'd repeated her question to him with increasing annoyance.

She waited, hearing him saying something to someone about *going outside for a moment to speak to my daughter.*

She knew then. He was in a hospital somewhere with her mother.

"It's your mother," he said. His voice started to break. A tiny, and unfamiliar, wave of compassion for her father lapped over Sara as she imagined him - a stocky man with a flushed face, in an ill-fitting pair of Marks and Spencers trousers, slightly too short of his good black brogues, speaking of private things in a public place.

"She cut one of her wrists. I found her, on her bathroom floor, early this morning when I brought in her tea."

"Oh my God. Is she...conscious? How is she? Please, tell me, Dad."

"Yes. It wasn't a serious cut. Physically she's fine but the doctor wants a psychiatric assessment first, before she can be discharged."

"Have you spoken to her?"

"She refuses to speak to anyone. She won't even open her eyes to look at me. She's been bad for some time. I…I meant to contact you but I thought it was just temporary. That she'd come round after the shock of Kim had diminished a bit. She just needed time."

He started weeping into the phone.

"It's ok, Dad. I'll come down," she said, gently. "I'll come tomorrow."

"Thank you, Sara."

"Get back to her now, Dad. Let me know if there's any change."

After checking which hospital he was in, they rang off. Sara sat for a long time where she was, on her bed, her back against the wall. It was uncomfortably cold and hard. A headboard had been often talked about but never deemed a priority. *I just wanted an ordinary day,* she told herself, instantly appalled at her own selfishness. Now there were decisions again - whether to drive, when to go, who to call.

She rang Tabitha first, who received the news of her sister as if she'd been expecting it.

"Oh God, poor Em! But let's face it, Sara. It's been on its way for some time. Held at bay until Kim died. Why don't I come down with you? Some moral support. Unless you'd prefer to go on your own. I'll understand if you do."

Sara's gratitude towards her aunt expressed itself in the form of a sob. The sob did not escape Tabitha who waited, patiently, for Sara's answer.

"That would be great. I'd really appreciate it. George is in Brighton visiting his father."

"I'm sorry, dear," Tabitha said, "I've upset you with my big mouth."

"No, don't apologise, Tabitha. You're right about Mum. If you can get here around 9ish tomorrow morning, I'll drive us."

A wet Sunday morning was not an ideal time in which to navigate the motorways of the West Country.

"If we didn't know each other well before this journey, we will by the end of it," Tabitha joked.

Whatever her faults, Tabitha was not boring. Forthright without being judgmental, she believed in saying how she saw it and allowing others to do the same. Nothing was off limits like it was with her own parents. Sara was able to ask her about her relationship with Emily. Tabitha was the younger sister, less accountable to their parents. She admitted she had taken her freedom for granted. Emily, academic and serious, had been the receptacle for her parents' dreams. She had been a successful lecturer in early medieval history until she married.

"Even then, whilst her marriage to your Dad was not ideal, in my eyes, it was the birth of Kim that changed her life."

"You mean, Kim's cleft lip? It was only a minor disability surely? Easily rectified."

"Yes, but disability can affect attachment. For whatever reason – it's difficult to pinpoint these things and probably not helpful anyway – the relationship between Kim and your father was not right from the very beginning. I think he struggled to accept the child she was. He wanted her to be different."

"You mean he rejected her?"

"It seems harsh when you put it like that. But you know more about it than I do, after all, you lived it. Anyway, first there was a series of operations for Kim. Something went wrong. I can't remember what. Your mother went on extended maternity leave. She did go back to the university eventually, but only for a couple of terms. Kim wouldn't settle at the nursery and Steve persuaded her that she should stay at home with her. Then she became pregnant with you and I don't think she considered going back after that. Kim's behaviour became progressively more challenging. There were changes of school, as you'll recall, and Emily was in and out of meetings where Kim was threatened with exclusion. She and Steve differed on how best to cope with her. I'm not sure how they've survived it all, frankly. You've probably got something to do with that."

Sara looked at the motorway ahead of her, the endless lanes of traffic. They had been travelling for two hours and had still to reach the half way stage of their journey. Yet part of her was content to be on the move, talking to her aunt, postponing the moment when she would see her mother, lying silently in her self-imposed coma, her bandaged wrist an outward sign of her suffering.

"I never felt I could discuss Kim's problems openly with Mum and Dad. It was taboo. We focused on the *consequences* – all the things that went wrong for her - but we never tackled the cause, as if they couldn't bear to acknowledge she had a mental health problem. She may have got help had we done so. You know, the person I've spoken to most..."

Before she could say his name, Tabitha interrupted her.

"Is Martin. Yes, I know. It's one of the reasons I never really feared for you, Sara. You and Martin had a such a strong bond as children. Partners in crime, I used to say!"

"I think we still are."

There was a pause in their conversation. Tabitha, conscious of how difficult it must be for Sara to be reminded that her sister had not been happy in her short life, decided she had said too much and suggested she put the radio on. She cast a sideways glance at Sara. She always had an air of composure about her. Only the dark circles under her eyes signalled her unhappiness. She could only guess at the reserves of strength which Sara had been forced to draw upon. It seemed especially cruel that she was now plunged into another crisis.

Martin had been traumatised by his experience in finding Kim's body. He had stayed with her for a few days in the immediate aftermath. She would watch him in her garden, pruning and clipping, raking the stones on the footpaths, cleaning out the little pond, reassuring her that her precious waterlilies would survive the upset. He would surprise her by suddenly appearing in his leathers, announcing he was going off on his bike. Men of his age went jogging, played five a side football or went to the pub with their mates. Martin crafted boxes, loved plants and did a lot of solitary riding on his Harley. Whilst other mothers, in similar circumstances, may have fretted about their son's future, Tabitha revelled in his ability to stand aside whilst the herds galloped past.

The pure, sweet strains of Vaughan Williams *"The Lark Ascending"* erupted from the radio. Tabitha commented that despite living for over sixty years, she had never seen a lark but understood them to be *sweet but otherwise unremarkable looking* birds. Sara did not know the piece and was momentarily nonplussed as to why Tabitha had suddenly started talking about birds. When it was over, Tabitha turned the volume down.

"You know, Sara, we can support people but we can't *fix* them – not permanently anyway. I will sit by your mother's bedside today and wonder if I could have done more, like you feel about Kim now. But guilt achieves nothing. Believe me, I've learned that. Now, how about a break at one of those lovely service stations! I'm in need of a chocolate fix."

Sara didn't say that her aunt appeared to have forgotten the essential, glaring difference between their two situations. Her mother remained alive and could be supported. She may recover. To hope was reasonable. But Kim? Kim had gone.

CHAPTER 9

Abandoned

Tabitha and Sara reached Truro hospital mid-afternoon. Sara's father said he would be waiting for them in the café. He cut a forlorn figure, sitting alone at a table for four, stirring his mug of tea with the handle of a knife. An empty sandwich carton lay on a plate in front of him. He looked up with rheumy eyes when they came over to him and staggered to his feet.

"Steve," said Tabitha, hugging him to her. Sara nodded at him over Tabitha's shoulder.

"Hi, Dad. How are you? You look exhausted."

"I'm still standing. Just."

"Look," said Tabitha, already brisk, taking advantage of Steve's weakened condition. "Why don't you go home and get some rest - if you can. We'll take over from here, won't we, Sara?"

Sara nodded again.

"Sure, Dad. A good idea. We'll contact you if anything changes."

"It's a Sunday, Steve. Little happens outside emergencies in hospitals on a Sunday. Emily probably won't get looked at until tomorrow at the earliest."

"I assume you've got the car," said Sara. "Do you feel ok to drive?"

Steve didn't need much convincing that his stint at his wife's bedside was over for the time being. Before he left, he described again how Emily was just not communicating with anyone, except in relation to the basics such as asking for water or going to the toilet. He couldn't get anything out of her, no matter how he tried.

"I hope you have better luck," he said, as he picked up his overcoat from the back of the chair and started rummaging around for his car keys in one of the pockets.

Tabitha and Sara made their way to the lifts and up to one of the general wards where Emily lay, on her back, one arm, thin but woundless, lying outside the covers, the other safely hidden from the ward's afternoon visitors.

"Good Lord," breathed Tabitha as they stood together at the door of the ward, looking over at her. "Poor Em."

Sara's eyes welled up with pity at the sight of her mother. *I can't lose her too*, she thought. And then she corrected herself, stowing the pity away with such conviction as she could muster, *I mustn't lose her. She is still saveable.*

She moved toward her mother's bedside where a chair, no doubt previously occupied by her father, was awaiting her. Tabitha hung back, in two minds whether to stay or leave them alone. When she saw her sister open her eyes, as Sara placed her hand over her mother's, she turned and went back into the corridor.

"Hi, Mum," Sara said, gently. Emily looked at her and smiled.

"I'm sorry, my darling. So sorry that you should see me like this."

Sara put her finger to her mother's lips.

"I'm here, now. With you. And I'll stay, as long as you want me to. I promise."

Tears slipped down Emily's pale face and Sara cast around for a tissue. Emily's hand came out from under the covers to take it, her neatly bandaged wrist now visible.

The tears released something from within Emily and seconds later, she was pulling herself into a sitting position, cupping Sara's chin with her good hand - *so that I can see your lovely face.*

"What happened, Mum? Can you talk about it?"

As her mother looked away from her, she spotted Tabitha standing in the corridor.

"Is that my sister, coming to sort me out – as ever?"

Sara smiled.

"Yes, we came together. We've been worried about you."

She didn't refer to Emily's refusal to answer their calls. It was irrelevant now.

Emily returned her gaze to Sara, squeezing her hand, her eyes full of unshed tears.

"I can't live with myself, Sara. It's not complicated. I'm not sick. I just can't forgive myself for not ……..not caring for her better. I was her mother. She was my responsibility. Since Kim died, I've thought a lot about what happened to her in the last few years and I know I wasn't around for her. I abandoned her. You didn't. But I did."

"Mum," started Sara, anxious to prevent her mother from inflicting yet more pain on herself. But it was not a thoughtful interruption. This hurt needed to emerge: like her bandaged hand it had needed the presence of her daughter, one whose eyes held no judgment, to be revealed.

At that point, Tabitha came over, pecking Emily on the cheek - *Hi sis* - as if she were just visiting for the weekend, rather than showing up at her sister's bedside following a failed suicide attempt. She said she was off to the café for a little while and would they like her to return with some tea.

"That would be lovely," said Emily. As Tabitha turned to exit the ward, she added "Thanks for coming, Tabby." Tabitha shot her a warm smile over her shoulder and blew her a kiss.

Sara looked at her mother, recalling her father's words about her refusing to open her eyes, let alone talk to him. She was perfectly lucid. It was as she had anticipated, her parents couldn't talk about Kim. Her mother knew that her guilt would only irritate or enrage her husband. *You've nothing to reproach yourself for, Emily. She was a damned difficult girl.* If they embarked on this conversation, they would be lost to each other, possibly forever. In crude terms, thought Sara, Kim's death marked a tipping point for them. She couldn't help but wonder what Kim would have made of that.

"I can't give you any consolation, Mum," she said, "except to say that you've been a good mother to me and I'd like you to stay around."

A few fresh tears escaped on to Emily's sunken cheeks. "That's a wonderful thing to say. Thank you."

"You need to have this conversation with Dad, Mum. He needs to understand how you feel."

Emily shook her head, allowing one of the tears to slide into her mouth. She licked it away.

"I can't, darling," she whispered, suddenly conscious that they were having this conversation in the hubbub of visiting time on a Sunday afternoon. "He doesn't want to hear it. He doesn't feel the same way. He's just angry with her. He always has been angry with her. Her death hasn't changed things."

"What are you going to do, then? How can you recover if you can't talk to the person you live with?"

"There's no recovering from this, Sara."

"There has to be. For both of us."

Her mother closed her eyes. The significance of the conversation had exhausted her.

"Let's talk more about this when you're discharged, Mum. After the psychiatric assessment."

"I don't need that. I know what's wrong with me. I won't do it again. I promise. I'll get an appointment with my GP and a referral through her, if necessary. Hopefully, on that basis, they'll discharge me tomorrow."

They sat on in silence for a while, still holding hands, until Tabitha returned with the tea and a similar conversation ensued about Emily's wish to leave hospital the following day. But neither Sara nor Tabitha, for all her forthrightness, felt able to ask the most pertinent question which hovered, unanswered, over the hospital bed. Did Emily intend to return to Steve and, if not, where was she going to go?

In the car, after leaving hospital, on their way back to Polperro for the night, Tabitha had arrived at a decision.

"Forgive my interference, Sara, but your mother cannot go back to Steve for the moment. She needs – *they* need a break from one another. She needs some safe space – as I think those in the know call it – to talk about her feelings and process her grief."

"And guilt," added Sara.

"Whatever, it's both, probably. I'm going to suggest she comes back to stay with me for as long as she likes. Are you on board with that? I need you to be."

Sara wondered if she was asking her or telling her. Fortunately, for them both, she was more than happy to agree. She was immensely relieved that someone else was going to be responsible for her mother's welfare. She nodded.

"Yes, it's a good plan. God knows what Dad will make of it, leaving him on his own. That may concern her."

"Steve needs to contemplate his own behaviour in what's just happened. It was the clearest cry for help imaginable. He's just not able to help her. He must see that. I'm sorry if that sounds brutal but I can't see any point in hiding my true opinion."

Sara laughed.

"I can see that!"

Tabitha smiled ruefully.

"Sorry," she said again.

"Don't be," said Sara. "Actually, I admire you. And you know, she seemed ok with us. Happy that we'd come."

"Happy we came to rescue her?"

"Perhaps."

The remainder of their journey was spent on discussing whether Sara's father would have anything in for dinner and, if not, what options they had.

"Let's take him out, whether he wants to go or not," said Tabitha. "The alcohol may give me the courage I need to suggest we take your Mum home with us."

"Shouldn't we clear it with Mum first?"

"I think this way round is better. Let's see if he sees the sense in it first and then put it to her."

"And what if he's horrified by the prospect?"

"We'll cross that bridge when we come to it, hey?"

~ ~ ~

Strangely, having experienced the hell of insomnia, Emily had managed to sleep quite soundly in her hospital bed following her admission. She was contemplating the reason for this as she watched Sara and Tabitha leave the ward when visiting time ended. Occasionally, exhaustion defeats the mind, like an engine which has overheated and needs to be switched off before the flames of insanity destroy it. The silence at night in the house in Polperro was sometimes so suffocatingly dense, her aloneness was accentuated. Here, on Ward F 10, the clatter of trays and the sound of footsteps and voices allowed her to believe that, maybe, there was a route back to her previous life: the one she'd had before Kim died. It was not a life she had imagined she'd have, but it was a tolerably quiet one. It can't be unusual, she thought, to seek an *uneventful* life, predictable events on predictable days, having driven the bargain with some unknown God that in place of strife, she agreed to sacrifice passion.

But now, now that she was forced to examine Kim's life in detail, now that it was over, *her* role was the most significant. A mother's always is. She had never stopped loving Kim. Kim had stopped loving her. That was the conclusion she had reached so many times when Kim rejected help, refused her phone calls, slammed doors, whether metaphoric or real, in her face. She hadn't given up either. She had withdrawn to gather her breath, so that she could make the plunge again and, just perhaps, this time, save them both.

Steve did not see it like this. His reality was that Kim was a lost cause and that it was only she who could save herself. They had many arguments over *lost causes*, Emily baffled at how a father could determine his daughter should be placed in such a category. It seemed the greatest dereliction of parental duty to her: to give up on one's child. Phrases like *the triumph of hope over experience* were thrown at Emily time and time again. Steve's anger dominated all such exchanges. He was *a realist*, he maintained, not a fool. *Kim holds her fate in her own hands, like we all do. We can't live life for her, Emily.*

Since that first evening, she had resolutely avoided seeing any photographs of Kim, or anything else which held the essence of her daughter. She doubted such time would ever come again, when she might derive solace from seeing or sensing her, rather than sadness. She and Steve did not have many family photos displayed in the home but the one she had on her desk in the spare room, of Sara, Kim and Martin, their arms around each other's shoulders, in the garden of their old house, she had placed in a drawer. Kim was in the middle of the trio, included - for that moment. Sara and Martin's close relationship had not helped Kim although, to Emily's knowledge, Kim never voiced any jealousy. The *cool* she thought she had and which, she believed, they admired was not the reality. Sara would always choose Martin over her sister. Not only was he clever and thoughtful, he was equable. He loved Sara with a wholesome, brotherly love which Kim could not replicate, even had she wished to.

Emily was now engaged in picking over Kim's life, looking for reasons why it ended as it did. The memories flooded over her, each extracting pain: a walk barefoot over a coral reef. The attack on Kim was random, she knew, but the path that had taken her there that night was not. The 34 year old Kim should have been at home on a Sunday evening, with kids or a partner, or both, or out with friends - not wandering the street, chatting to strangers, vulnerable and lonely in a life without purpose.

Instead of starting at her birth, putting to one side, conveniently, Kim's relationship with Steve, she tried to reconstruct the trajectory of Kim's journey from hopeful expectation to disillusion - her trust in the world diminishing with each new loss, the drink killing off feeling so that disappointment was more easily endured.

The incident in the park held significance. At the time, she and Steve were both convinced that Kim would be shocked into taking stock of her life and behaviour; that she would mature and think more carefully about the choices she was making. *Surely*, Emily had remarked, *things will be different from now on.*

It was early in June, a hot spell producing floral abundance in the parks and gardens of suburban London. Kim was 17, no longer in school, disaffected with the idea of education. She'd taken up that spring with a gang of similar minded girls she'd met in a shopping mall one afternoon, the recruitment process involving a trip to a dingy studio somewhere in White City where her left eyebrow and the top of her right ear lobe were pierced. Her new friends cheered her on as, smiling bravely, she waited for the gun to puncture her tender skin. Her faint anxiety about the horror it would cause her parents was mixed with the elation of realising her own autonomy: the little metal studs a physical reminder that she no longer belonged to them.

The thirteen-year old boy they taunted in the park on that sultry June afternoon, was privately educated. Despite the heat, he wore a purple blazer, slightly too big for him, with a gold crest on one of its pockets – *hey, posh kid, you must be fucking hot in that thing*. His shoes were black leather and his glasses were wire-framed, quite trendy but looking odd on a pubescent boy. They separated him from his group of friends, like wolves isolating their prey before moving in en masse for the kill. Except he was just pushed around, humiliated rather than hurt. They took his money and his mobile and one of them, the girl with the Mohican, Megan, snatched his glasses from his face. He flailed around with his arms, the tears spurting from his eyes in frustration, provoking more laughter from his attackers, trying to grab them back. But Megan won, throwing them onto the ground, screaming with excitement at her success. Kim, hanging back at first, had moved forward then, anxious for approval. She had stamped on them using the heels of her ugly black boots to break and twist the metal rims so that when, after they'd scarpered, the boy had bent down with shaking hands to retrieve them, they were beyond repair.

Martin and Sara were coming up for fourteen at the time. Any admiration they'd had for Kim's wilfulness, her courage, began to evaporate when they learned about the smashed glasses: *the taunted turned taunter*, Tabitha had said to her, quoting Martin. He appeared genuinely mystified, she told Emily, how Kim – whose own scar had drawn the occasional callous and thoughtless remark – could have collaborated in such cruelty. She didn't add that she thought Martin saw himself there, where the poor hapless lad had been, saved only through circumstance. And nor did she say that Martin must have wondered why Kim herself had not made that same connection: it could have been him.

Ashamed Steve had shouted at Kim, over and over again, his face blotchy with rage. Emily had emerged from her desk upstairs to meet Sara on the landing. They stood at the bannisters together looking down into the hall below where the confrontation was taking place. Kim was by the front door, adopting that familiar stance of adolescent boredom, her pink hair, flat and unwashed, highlighted in the beam of light which shone through the stained glass in the panel above her. Emily had looked at Sara, catching her arm when she thought she was about to intervene in the argument, knowing that despite everything, even the smashed glasses, Sara felt the same overwhelming sadness for Kim. She too had wanted to run down the stairs and tell Steve – *she knows, for God's sake, you don't have to destroy her because she's shamed you* – but Steve did. He put the flat of his hand on the front door to prevent her from leaving and yelled until he'd exhausted every adjective in his vocabulary in telling her who she *really* was. And those loathsome boots, thought Emily, why did she continue to wear them when they all knew how she'd used them?

The Magistrates were told that poor Tim Ayers hadn't returned to school for some weeks, so traumatised had he been by the attack. The five girls had been identified quickly and charged with robbery but by pleading guilty and showing remorse, they avoided a custodial sentence. Apparently, the *opportunistic* nature of the crime also assisted them. They were placed on probation and ordered to pay the full costs of the mobile and the broken glasses. It came to several hundred pounds which was divided between them. Megan had been angry with Kim about this, declaring that she should foot the bill for the glasses as she had been responsible for their ultimate destruction. Ironically, it was this bitter exchange that marked the end of Kim's involvement with the group. Steve and Emily were adamant that Kim should write to young Tim and apologise for her behaviour and they also made it clear that she should repay every penny of the compensation awarded from her own funds – not that she had any.

In the following few months, Kim had stayed in her room, clearly contrite but unable to express it. Emily offered her support, when Steve was safely out of the way, but Kim appeared too proud to accept it. Occasionally, Emily would be bold and beg her to accept some help from elsewhere. There were grandparents still alive then, she could go and stay with them. It would get her away from the neighbourhood for a while. Nothing she said permeated Kim's stoicism, as if Kim was afraid that accepting her mother's love would destroy the only self she knew.

Kim left home when she was eighteen, getting a job in a pub in Acton and renting a room on the premises. This was her introduction to drink, hooking up with one of the landlady's sons, a regular at the *lock-ins* which occurred most weekends, when the spirits came out and payment wasn't sought.

Emily thought back to that time. What was she doing that was so important that she ignored what was happening to Kim? She wasn't engaged in anything very significant. It was just an enormous relief when Kim moved out and she gained some respite from the role of mediator which she had adopted during most of Kim's teenage years. She'd wanted to save Sara too from all the conflict, the tension between Kim and Steve hanging over the house like a pall of smoke. In this way there was something sacrificial in what had happened to Kim.

Strangely, Emily had *not* been in that place, totting up the cost of her choices, when she decided she wanted to hurt herself and took the nail scissors to her wrist, digging the points in and trying to drag the blades across her skin. She had yet to make the connections, the ones she was making now as she stared up at the hospital ceiling, the lights blurring as tears gathered in her eyes. There was only one image in her mind when she'd crouched down on her bathroom floor in the dawn of that Sunday morning. It was of Kim, in her chair, alone. And dying.

CHAPTER 10

Lowlife

In the town, down by the harbour, the Tavern was busy. They'd had to wait twenty minutes at the bar, drinks in hand, for a table to become free. By then, Sara had lost what little appetite she had, dreading the conversation with her father, seeing his awkwardness as he tried to retain his pride in the face of his wife's clear message that, when it mattered, he had failed her.

Tabitha outlined her proposal for Emily, describing its purpose in terms of a holiday rather than a separation from him. At some point in the ensuing conversation they all employed the phrase *a change of scene*, passing it on to each other like a verbal baton. Steve, recognising that this was a battle already lost, readily conceded that Emily should go back with Tabitha. Sara noticed that he didn't ask if Emily herself had agreed to the plan. It made her uneasy, colluding in the assumption that, by her actions, her mother had forfeited her right to a say in her own future.

"You'll cope without her, won't you?" Tabitha enquired of Steve, watching with some distaste as he tucked into his roast dinner like a man who'd been deprived of home cooked food for a long, long time. Sara was picking her way through some vegetarian concoction, more intent on the wine than the dish. When she asked if anyone wanted another drink – the third – she returned her father's stare without flinching.

"Well, Dad, one for the road?"

He shook his head as he speared another roast potato. Tabitha requested a sparkling water, looking from one to the other of them, sensing some tension. Alcohol occupies its own special place in this family, she decided. She thought of Martin, virtually tee total out of love for his Harley, ordering his coke and shouting after her *–remember to ask for a straw, please, Mum*. He liked to be able to take off whenever the desire for speed and movement swept over him, day or night. Witnessing other families in operation he was gloriously uncomplicated, she concluded.

Having bought the drinks, Sara stayed at the bar for a few minutes, sipping her wine. She wanted to be on her own, to walk out into the night and stand at the water's edge. Back at the table, she gave Tabitha her water and said she needed some air.

As a family, we were never without conflict, she thought, as she gazed out beyond the harbour's lights over a treacly black sea, but now we're truly fractured. In the murder of Kim, Flood and Timms had also taken great bites out of all those attached to her. Within the ripples of their crime, her mother had lost what little balance she'd had, equilibrium had been stolen from them all in one way or another: a continuum of loss. The label of *bereaved sister* would attach to her forever. Anger swelled within her as she recalled the sight of them in the dock that day: still living and feeling and having a life, however spent, ahead of them. They may yet become parents, walk by the sea, eat dinner with friends or family, laugh. All those things which, by their hands, had been stolen from Kim.

Paul had told her that a date had now been set for pleas to be taken in the Crown Court. But she hadn't made a note of it. She'd focused on what he'd added when supplying the date – *I doubt they'll plead guilty but I may be proved wrong*. She'd asked him what sentences were likely if they did enter guilty pleas. He was vague, purposefully she decided as clarity was his hallmark. He said the Judge would request reports before sentencing and, thus, it depended on what was in them - *like whether they have any previous*. Sara knew that sentences were usually reduced for those pleading guilty: an incentive so that the victims were spared the stress of a contested trial and, of course, because the State saved money.

"Even if it results in shorter sentences, I hope they plead guilty," said George when she referred to her conversation with Paul.

She wasn't sure. Part of her wanted to hear their voices, wanted to know how they would justify their brutality, the punching. It would be known then, by everyone who cared to know, the extent of their savagery, what *lowlifes* they were.

George baulked at her use of the description *lowlife*, when she'd spat out the word, her large, dark eyes glittering with fury in a manner which frightened him. Even Frank didn't demean himself with such crude terminology. Sara appeared to have forgotten her previous condemnation of categorising humankind so thoughtlessly. But, he decided against making any comment, acknowledging that this was *her* loss, *her* experience.

As she breathed in the clean Cornish air, she remembered that Paul had also said that they should be able to have Kim's funeral in the next few weeks. The Coroner's office was likely to be in contact shortly. The news about her mother had dominated her thoughts in the last 48 hours so she had yet to contemplate telling her parents, discussing *the arrangements* with them. Now it loomed like a giant obstacle in front of her, another test of endurance. She imagined herself in the middle of her parents walking into the crematorium, propping them up, her mother's anguished gasps in one ear, her father's heavy breathing in the other. There was the eulogy too. How did she make positive a life so full of disappointment? Martin and George, both good with words, would help her. Between the three of them, they might just arrive at something acceptable. *Just get through it*, she told herself, *just get through it* - repeating the phrase so many times as to render it meaningless.

Emily managed to get herself discharged by mid-afternoon on the following day. Tabitha, with terrier like determination to get things moving, had spoken with one of the senior nurses about wanting to take Emily back with her where she would be looked after and nurtured. Tabitha would ensure that her sister saw a GP to discuss a treatment programme. It was crystal clear, she maintained, that Emily needed the support of her family after such a traumatic loss. Her advocacy won through, assisted by Sara referring to her own occupation, trusting it would underline the safe hands into which Emily would be placed. A doctor came by just as they were wondering if another overnight stay with Steve was on the horizon. Steve did not return to the hospital to see Emily. When her discharge had been confirmed, Tabitha called him and said they were leaving immediately in view of the long drive and because Sara could not miss any more work. He answered her in monosyllables, seemingly keen to dispel any illusion she might have that he was grateful for her intervention.

"Ok."

"So, I'll make sure Emily calls you after she's settled in this evening – or, more likely, tomorrow."

"Ok."

"She'll be exhausted after the journey home."

"Yes."

"We all will!" she added, when she realised that no more words from her brother-in-law would be forthcoming. She hoped she sounded positive and friendly, whilst also admitting to herself that there had never been any *like*, let alone love, lost between them. It was certainly not going to manifest itself now.

"Right, I'll say goodbye, then."

"Goodbye." Her name was not added to the word, as is the custom.

"Oh, Steve, do you want a last word with Sara?"

"No."

He rang off before Tabitha could embark on any more unnecessary conversation, going into his shed to start the second coat of oil on a wooden bench which had been bleached of all colour by its exposure to the sun over the course of the summer. He switched his little radio on to distract him from thinking about Emily and how determined she had been not to engage with him in the hours that followed his discovery of her slumped body in the corner of the bathroom, the nail scissors, smeared with blood, by her side. Even before he'd attended to her, he'd picked them up and dropped them hastily into the sink, as if they were a living thing carrying disease.

Sara had not asked to speak to her father. Relations between them had been relatively harmonious during her visit. He seemed touched that she had come so swiftly to his aid, to see Emily, recognising how difficult it must be for her to take yet more time off work. But when she and Tabitha had left for the hospital that morning, he'd not lingered, as if reluctant to spend time alone with her in case he revealed a level of emotion he would subsequently regret.

The long drive home came almost as a revelation to all three of them. Emily accepted her sister's invitation to sit in the front with Sara and they all chatted, easily and happily, on their way back to the capital. Each mile put distance between Emily and Steve; he who had wrapped her in self-doubt, disguised as concern, pulling the knots tightly around her so that escape was impossible – until then. Each county they passed through seemed to allow Emily to regain a little more of her sense of self. Kim's funeral wasn't mentioned. That subject could wait a couple of days, Sara decided.

They drove straight to Sara's flat, her mother and Tabitha insisting that they would take an Uber to Tabitha's house given the lateness of the hour.

After she and George had seen them off and suddenly feeling cheered that some of her mother's balance had been restored, Sara called her father. She wanted to let him know that they had reached London safely and that, although it was early days, Emily appeared to be on the road to recovery. By then it was after 10pm and Steve was facing the first night on his own for over a decade. Exhaustion from the events of the weekend were provoking questions he'd never really expected to ask himself prior to that evening. How had he, a grieving father, ended up alone, deserted by his wife and daughter - neither of whom had attempted to hide how keen they were to be rid of him? The blame for Emily's little escapade with the nail scissors had been laid squarely at his door, of this he was certain. No doubt Tabitha had had plenty of time to work on Sara, had she needed any encouragement, on their cosy car journey down together. He was not in any doubt that his name had cropped up – and not in any gratifying way – any number of times in the plan they were busy hatching to kidnap his wife *before he can inflict any more damage on her*. He could almost hear the words spoken by Tabitha - meddling, self-opinionated Tabitha - who had, by Emily's own admission, begged her sister to think again before marrying him.

He thought back to his conversation with Emily on the night before her botched attempt at self-destruction. He'd gone up to her room just as the pips had sounded at 6pm, to enquire as to whether she wanted any dinner or should he just cater for himself.

She was lying on her bed, her head turned towards the window, her eyes wide open. She did not look at him when he came into the room, just shook her head in answer to his question. He'd looked around trying to establish what she'd been doing all day as she had not emerged from her room at any time, as far as he knew. There was a glass of water on her bedside table. Her long greying hair, wild and untamed, fanned out across the pillow. There were streaks of dirt on her bare feet, as if she had been roaming the hills, searching for something – or somebody. In her stillness, Steve glimpsed despair and had he believed in his own intuition, respected it, he might not have spoken as he did.

"Emily, you can't just lie here all day, not eating or drinking. You need to get up." The words came out more harshly, perhaps, than he had intended.

"Please, Steve, just leave me be," she said.

"You're not helping yourself, locked away up here. Are you *trying* to make yourself ill?"

He could have taken her hand in his, or gathered her to him in his arms, silently. If she needed him at all, she needed him to join her in the place where her sadness lay, not stand to one side, looking on, admonishing her.

When she did not respond, he left the room with an audible sigh.

"Suit yourself," he muttered as he closed the door. He banged and clattered around the kitchen for the next half hour, hoping the noise would raise her from her bed but it didn't. The next time he ventured into her room was when he'd found her.

Reflecting now, he could see quite clearly that she had been heading for her collapse for some time. She had ceased communicating with him in the days following their return from London. Her appetite had disappeared gradually. He wasn't even sure she was showering regularly, her self-neglect indicating she was depressed. He just couldn't quite admit it in case such admission released his own demons now gathered at the gate of his mind, demanding not only to be let in but to be heard also.

~ ~ ~

In Tabitha's care, some change came over Emily. She wasn't cossetted. Tabitha was bossy and determined most of their daily activities, seeing her role as relieving her sister of responsibility so that she could focus on her recovery.

"We'll go to the Portrait Gallery today, shall we? I love the place, so intimate. We can go over to the Crypt for lunch if you fancy it. I can't remember if you've been there before. I forget you used to live in London!"

They ate out occasionally, Tabitha taking pleasure when Emily began to take some interest in what she was eating. Whilst it had taken a measure of self-restraint, she resolved to allow Emily to navigate her marital difficulties without further interference. She was content in the knowledge that she had facilitated Emily's escape from the strait jacket of her marriage.

For Sara, also, there was some brief delight in hearing her mother's voice when she answered her calls. She had become so accustomed to her mother's voicemail message declaring her unavailability that, when she did answer, she was taken by surprise.

"Oh, hi Mum, just ringing to find out how you are?"

"I'm fine, love. There's no need to sound so anxious."

But there was. On that occasion, Sara was ringing to talk to her mother about Kim's funeral. She had put off making the call, wanting to give her mother as much time as possible before introducing some new cause for stress into her life. She had news about the trial, too.

Sara hadn't been able to attend the first hearing at the Crown Court. She'd been in court herself that day, standing in for Patsy who was on annual leave. Paul had called her almost immediately she'd arrived back in the office that afternoon.

He came straight to the point.

"They've both pleaded not guilty, I'm afraid. The matter has been listed for a mention and further directions in late November and for trial at the end of March on a 9 day time estimate."

"Christ, that's months away!" said Sara.

"Yep. But at least you have a fixed date. That's something. They'll be on remand until the trial obviously."

The following day, the Coroner's office called her to say that they were releasing "the body". The funeral could go ahead.

"Mum, the Coroner has been in touch and said we can now arrange Kim's funeral. Do you want to discuss things with Dad tonight? Decide what you want..... and things."

"I don't know," Emily said, eventually.

Sara imagined her mother's face, drained of colour, as she absorbed this news and instantly regretted not arranging to meet and tell her in person.

"Look," she said, after a few seconds of silence. "Have a think. Talk with Tabitha about it and call me back tomorrow. There's absolutely no rush. We've waited this long after all. A few more days won't matter."

Her mother murmured her agreement and they rang off.

It was much later, when she was telling George that she had managed to make the call to her mother about the funeral arrangements, that Sara remembered she hadn't told her mother about the not guilty pleas and the trial date. George said he thought that it was probably for the best, given her mother's *fragility*.

It hadn't occurred to either of them that the matter would be reported in the local press. Tabitha saw it, purely by chance, when she was having a coffee in Starbucks and someone had left a copy of *Metro* on the table near her.

Greenford couple plead not guilty to manslaughter of local woman after fight at party.

She picked it up and scanned the short paragraph which referred to the death of *34-year-old Kim Turner*. The starkness of the words shocked her as did the realisation that the trial would almost certainly be covered both in the press and on social media. She took her mug of coffee back to the counter and asked for a cardboard cup.

Outside, in the fading light of an afternoon in November, she called Sara to check whether she knew as neither she nor Emily had been aware there had been a hearing, let alone that Flood and Timms had pleaded not guilty.

"I'll have to go back and tell your mother immediately. It would be awful if she found out another way."

Half-heartedly, Sara offered to come over that evening to talk to her mother instead but, as was her talent, Tabitha knew that Sara was dealing with as much as she could manage. Brushing the suggestion aside, she said she'd speak to Emily and she'd probably give Steve a call too.

"Mum and Dad need to come to some decisions regarding the funeral as well," admitted Sara. "But I'll call her tomorrow evening after work about that."

"It's truly terrible, Sara," said Tabitha, feeling the emotion well up in her as she contemplated the impact of the news on her sister's already damaged spirit.

Sara did not reply. For some inexplicable reason, Kim's face had come into her head with startling clarity. She was happy too: a mischievous grin. Her image popped up every now and again, without invitation. Sara would be engaged in something mundane like unloading the washing machine or brushing her teeth when Kim appeared. Whatever triggered those images – a smell, a colour, the feel of the air around her – Sara could not decide. They were fleeting and not always welcome, emphasising her loss like a blow to the head. *She's not coming back.*

"Sara?" queried Tabitha, thinking they'd lost signal.

"Yes, I'm still here," said Sara, although it wasn't true. She was somewhere else. Still loving and feeling and reeling, yet again, at the finality of it all.

CHAPTER 11

Saved

Martin was sitting directly behind Sara. She'd asked him to or that's what he thought she meant when she said, "You'll stay close by, won't you? You know, just in case. I need you right behind me."

It occurred to him now that she was using a figure of speech and that he hadn't needed to push in between his mother and her cousin, June, making overweight June scrape one of her fat knees against the pew in front as she leapt up to let him past. Tabitha had cast him an anxious look. She knew her son. Whatever he was doing would be for good reason. She realised his purpose when she saw him lean forward and put his hand on Sara's shoulder. She'd managed to suppress her tears up until that moment. But when Sara, sandwiched between her parents, had turned around, after putting her hand on Martin's acknowledging his gesture, Tabitha had no control over the sob which hiccoughed from her. They had once been children, she thought, remembering them together - roller skating, swimming, giggling, reading out loud to one another at bedtime in the twin beds – pushed together – in Martin's room, Sara's arm flung around Martin's shoulder. Now they were here, adult mourners at Kim's funeral, Sara about to give the eulogy for her murdered sister. Whatever challenges she had expected they might face in later life, this had not been even at the margins of her imagination. She dabbed her eyes with the old-fashioned cotton handkerchief which June passed to her and, as Martin squeezed her hand, she interpreted the look he cast her as an exhortation to be brave.

George and his father were sitting on the front row on the other side of the small chapel. He'd said he thought it more appropriate that Martin take over if Sara faltered when speaking, rather than he. Martin agreed, partly because he had faith in Sara and whilst believing she might have the occasional stumble, was certain she would see it as her duty to her sister to remain in control and speak without breaking down. He did not think there was any real chance he would be called upon.

The three of them, Sara, Martin and George, had got together the week before to draft Kim's eulogy. The occasion had not been without some jocularity, none of it planned for, not least because Martin had walked over instead of coming by bike and declared – as he produced a bottle of wine – that *this is one of those rare occasions when alcohol is a necessity.* This declaration had set the tone and, by the time Martin left around 1 am, they were on their third bottle and Martin was slurring his words.

They had begun seriously enough, nodding at each other's contribution politely, Sara taking notes, George swallowing a lot – which he did when nervous, Martin restless because they were in the sitting room and there was no chair on which he could rock back and forth.

"I want somehow," Sara said, glass in one hand, biro in the other, "for people to know that there was another side to Kim - the things she was good at, the fun she could be. Everyone thinks she was just a difficult person with a drink problem. She wasn't always like that."

George decided he'd be hard pressed to remember her any other way and hoped this inconvenient truth was not reflected in his expression. When he glanced up, after pouring more wine into his glass, Martin was looking at him. There was no evading his scrutiny.

"The best of her, you mean," said Martin, switching off his penetrating gaze and smiling at Sara.

Sara nodded. "Yep," she said.

"Well, I can remember a few things. You know, way back. Before things got... well, bad."

"Go on, then," said Sara.

"Like that time our mothers, our mad mothers, agreed she could take us to Colwyn bay camping for a couple of nights. I think we were twelve and she was 16. I know I'd just finished my first year in secondary school."

"Christ, yes! Yes! We went in the sea. We had no tent poles. She left them on the train in an old duffel bag."

Sara bounced up and down excitedly, some of her wine sloshing over the side of her glass as she did so. George looked on, baffled at the sudden change in not only Sara's mood but in Martin's too. They were beaming at one another as if they'd cracked a code and the evening would be plain sailing from thence onwards.

"So what happened, if you couldn't put the tent up?" asked George.

"We slept on the beach in our sleeping bags," they said, almost in unison, laughing when they heard themselves.

"Yes, it rained as well," added Sara.

"Like it always does in bloody Wales," said Martin. "We only lasted one night. She took us for breakfast in a greasy cafe."

"Yeah and you, surprise, surprise, told her you didn't eat fried stuff."

"And she said, *well, Marty, let's see if they've heard of poached eggs* and that's what I got."

"We went in the sea, didn't we? And it was quite rough with big waves."

"Yes. As soon as we got there. We said we'd have a paddle and Kim said we were a couple of wimps so we got properly in, practising our front crawl, and she sat with the stuff on our only towel…"

"Smoking!"

"So, it was a good memory?" ventured George. "Despite the lack of a tent."

"Definitely," said Sara. "Kim could be wild at times. Unpredictable."

"Never boring," Martin added. "She had a savage tongue as well. If she had used that more constructively, things may have turned out differently for her."

Sara nodded.

"You know, I sometimes thought that was the real problem between her and Dad. She could outwit him easily. He didn't like being challenged all the time."

"She wasn't afraid, was she?" said George. "That's a good way to start your speech. Something along the lines of - *My sister Kim was a bit wild. She wasn't afraid and..*"

George stopped. This wasn't an English lesson. He swallowed.

"That's great," said Sara. "Getting started is always the most difficult, getting the right angle."

She jotted a few lines down, taking a sip of her wine as she did so.

"The party," said Martin. "Her twenty first."

"Christ, yes!" said Sara and started bouncing again.

"She started to take her clothes off, didn't she?"

"What?!" exclaimed George. "You can't put that in!"

Martin laughed.

"She got one of her mates to put that striptease music on…"

Sara let out a loud snort of laughter.

"And then a group of them started to strip until…"

Sara and Martin looked at one another.

"Your Dad came into the room and saw them," explained Martin. "Christ almighty! What a shitstorm."

"Actually, Marty, *you* tried to stop them," said Sara. "Little you suggested to this gaggle of raucous, drunk women, that it wasn't a good idea. I distinctly recall you handing Kim her top and telling her to put it back on. Then when Dad came in, it looked as though you were involved somehow. Standing right in front of Kim as she was struggling with her bra straps."

"Don't remind me. It's the sort of memory you generally suppress out of embarrassment. It doesn't quite fit with what we want to achieve, does it?"

Sara gave another yelp of laughter, looking at George, pleased to note he seemed intrigued rather than appalled.

"Didn't you once tell me a story of how Kim came across someone standing on the side of a railway platform and befriended them?" asked George.

"That's right," said Sara. "She did. She was still quite young herself at the time. She brought this really weird girl home with her one afternoon after school and told Mum that she needed help. I have this vague picture in my mind of a thin, sad girl sitting at the kitchen table not speaking."

"What happened to her?"

"I can't remember the details. I think Mum took her back to her home in the car. That evening at dinner my Dad gave Kim a lecture about not bringing *waifs and strays* into the house because we weren't equipped to help them. Kim asked him whether she should have just looked on and watched the girl throw herself under a train. It led to one of their familiar arguments. Nothing constructive came out of it, just the usual clash of opinions."

"Values," said Martin, as if correcting her. "It was a clash of values."

"Perhaps that's something you could emphasise," said George. "Her values. She had them. She acted on them."

"And what about the incident in the park? How do I get around that if I'm making her out to be such a paragon?"

"We're all a mixture, aren't we? Kim made some mistakes like people do when they're young but, fundamentally she was a good person. And she could be good company. You've always said that."

George looked over at Martin, inviting his response.

"Yes. It's true. We shouldn't be defined, or remembered, by just the negative things we've done in life, our mistakes."

George gave a snort of derision. Drink had pushed open the gate and allowed cynicism to worm its way onto the premises.

"But we are. Even just one mistake is enough. One mistake in a career spanning a few decades and no-one will remember all the minds we've educated and influenced, the lives we've improved. Look at your profession," George said to Sara.

"Damn right. You can rescue dozens of children from lives of squalor and abuse but you'll not only be remembered for the one that couldn't be saved, you'll be crucified for it too. By the tabloids *and* the wonderful public who will see no distinction between you and the person who was responsible for hurting the child. Lock 'em both up! Anyway, getting back to Kim, we'll have to come up with a bit more," said Sara, rounding off her little tirade, a familiar one, with a few gulps of wine. *I'm turning into my sister*, she thought.

In different circumstances, Martin may have taken issue with the simplicity of their analysis. Social workers *were* hounded, sometimes unfairly, but there was something to be said for holding people in authority to account in a manner almost unheard of forty years ago.

"We're doing fine," said Martin. "It's early. Time for another bottle, George."

Some skill is required in refining anecdotes so that they fit the profile being built: just the right mixture of embellishment and hyperbole. After all, most would choose a eulogy designed to bring comfort to those looking *at* the coffin, rather than one questioning whether the defunct being inside it had *really* accomplished anything worthwhile in their years on earth. By the end of the process, Sara was content that Kim's essence was captured in the stories she would tell. In years to come, whenever another wave of grief came rolling towards her, Sara would use that night as a rock to cling to. The happy memories were all there: you just had to allow yourself to *be* happy when you found them.

Since there was only access to an organ in the crematorium, George had to abandon his idea of playing a piece on the piano for Kim. Choosing the music to be played during the service, deciding what was appropriate, was more challenging than they had expected. After listening to Barber's Adagio for Strings and a section from Brahms' cello concerto, Sara became tearful and Martin disappeared into the kitchen, ostensibly for a glass of water but staying there for a lot longer than it took to drink one. Meanwhile, George having scrolled through a selection of poetry on his mobile, joined the group descent into melancholy. He'd kept his own mother at bay for the last three hours but reading Charles Causley's *Eden Rock – My mother shades her eyes and looks my way* – he was reminded of her funeral, his father lingering after the service, asking his sons to leave him be *just for a moment.*

Then, as speedily as they had retreated from each other, they were together again. Sara had recovered and was looking for more wine, Martin was back from the kitchen and George had switched his mobile off.

"You know, I think it would be a better idea to let Mum and Dad pick the music and any readings or poetry they want. I'll stick to the speech. They need to feel a part of Kim's farewell and that way they will," said Sara.

"Yes. You're right," said Martin. "My Mum will be able to read if they don't feel able to. I'll mention it to her before Friday."

"Christ, I'm starving! Sandwich, anybody?" said George, making Sara roll her eyes and Martin smile.

~ ~ ~

"Will you be coming home with me, afterwards, Emily?" Steve had asked of his wife, only moments after she, Tabitha and Martin had arrived at Sara and George's flat on the morning of Kim's funeral. They were standing, surveying each other in their funereal garb, waiting for the limousine and wondering what topic of conversation was the least inappropriate for the occasion. Martin was wearing a grey suit and an open-necked white shirt. He didn't own a tie and had decided against borrowing one. Kim had not been one to conform to the conventions of dress. His tie-less state was hardly an act of rebellion: Tabitha had not even remarked on it. But when he'd shaken Steve's hand on arrival, he was certain that Steve had looked pointedly at Martin's neck before shuffling away to stand beside Emily. No one could fail to hear his question – nor her response.

"Later, Steve," she said, before turning to Sara to ask where George was.

"Meeting his Dad at the station. They're going directly there."

Emily looked less gaunt than she had done when rescued by Tabitha and Sara. She felt like she had been practising for this day since she'd arrived at Tabitha's some three weeks ago, building up reserves of strength so that she could survive the few hours ahead of her without crumbling. She was dressed simply in a black suit and cream top which Tabitha had dug out for her from one of her overstuffed wardrobes. The night before, Tabitha had been thrown into a mild panic when she realised her sister did not have any matching shoes. Emily remarked that she and Sara were the same size and rather than rushing out to buy some, they should wait until they got to Sara's. She was now wearing a scuffed pair of black, knee length boots, seemingly oblivious as to how shabby they made her look.

Sara, dressed in the one suit she had for court purposes, could not help but notice the difference in her father since she had last seen him. He appeared strangely vulnerable now that he was responsible only for himself. He had been quiet when they had all eaten the night before. She was certain that he'd been expecting, hoping, that her mother would be at the flat to greet him when he arrived in the cab from Paddington, glancing around the living room looking for signs that she was there. *Surely, she would want us to be together on the eve of our daughter's funeral?*

Now, overhearing her parents' exchange, Sara and Martin had locked eyes for a few seconds. She felt the pressure of tears begin to build behind her eyes until his steady gaze steadied her: a pinpoint of light in the pitch-dark.

Tabitha was standing at the window looking out for the arrival of the cars. Kim's body was being taken directly to the crematorium. They would follow her coffin into the Chapel once they were all gathered. Sara had made several calls to her parents in the days previously, repeating information to them patiently. Around fifty people would be present; the service would be a short one; she'd contacted her father's relatives, a brother and a sister, in Gibraltar and told them of the arrangements; she would start with the eulogy - which she'd emailed in preparation, her mother saying it was *beautiful,* her father merely acknowledging its receipt. Her mother had chosen two poems which Tabitha and Steve's brother had agreed to read.

On that drunken night with Martin and George, Sara had suggested that they arrange a few of Kim's *things* on a table: a tangible memorial. Martin wasn't sure and wanted the details. *What things?* He thought of Kim's voice at that moment. *The voice which should have saved her.* But there was no recording of Kim singing. Privately, he thought a collection of her modest belongings would only serve to underline the sadness of her final years. It wasn't necessary. When Sara was forced to consider exactly what she would put in the collection, a similar thought had occurred to her and she abandoned the idea.

When it came to it, Sara did not find it hard to stand up, leave her parents and walk to the lectern to speak. When she looked up from her notes, ready to begin, she noticed that her parents had moved together and were holding hands. Their eyes, fearful and tired, were fixed on her face, awaiting the words which would wound as well as comfort.

*Kim, my sister, my complicated sister, was a bit wild. She wasn't afraid to speak out when she thought it important. And there were times when I valued that. Other people might say that, tragically, Kim "lost her way" in the years before her death but I refuse to use such euphemisms. She became an alcoholic and the ramifications of that illness were such to rob her of much of her vitality and spark. But, even then – even in those last years – **if** you heard her sing, **when** you heard her laugh and – at times – before the drink took hold and she spoke of things other than her troubles – she could dazzle you. And that's what I ask you all to remember today. The Kim who dazzled, who was herself, however flawed, in a world which can be cruel and unforgiving.*

Before Sara continued to the anecdotes which had been collected at the eulogy soiree, she looked up again. There had been some audible gasps when she had used the word *alcoholic*. No-one was expecting that. She hadn't even run the amendment past George or Martin. She'd just decided on it when, the previous evening, she mulled over the contents of her speech. The version she had emailed to her parents was not the version she delivered.

But neither of her parents looked particularly shocked. If anything, they looked relieved of a burden, a lie, which they'd had to carry around for many years. Perhaps too, in describing Kim's alcoholism as an illness, they were unbuckled from some of the guilt which attaches to all parents whose children fall far from the path of convention.

CHAPTER 12

Sounding Board

There were three months between Kim's funeral and the trial, a hiatus in which Sara and her parents might regain some balance before the next phase of their ordeal.

At work, relations between Sara and Patsy remained strained. They still sat opposite each other, their conversations, once diverse, now limited to the necessary for getting through the workload. Patsy never referred to her wedding again, taking any such calls away from her desk. On occasion, Sara was aware of the silence which descended as she entered the kitchen where Patsy might be holding forth to a posse of interested listeners. If she missed the friendship she had once valued, Sara would not admit it, telling George that she now saw Patsy as being *a bit vacuous*.

"I just don't get why anyone would invest so much time and money into one day of their lives."

"It's the romance, I suppose."

"Well, not that she's asked me, I won't be going on any hen night with her. When we talked about it, you know, way back, she said she was keen on a weekend in New York. How are people supposed to afford that? Why can't she be satisfied with a night in the pub?"

George had teased her a bit, saying he'd always looked forward to seeing her in the sacrificial white of a wedding dress.

"Lifting your veil and kissing those full red lips," he moaned, nibbling at her ear.

She'd pushed him away, unamused.

Patsy had not attended Kim's funeral. She hadn't been *officially invited*, she explained to one of their colleagues, making the unilateral decision that she would be better employed in covering Sara's work that day instead. Gloria Bostock had turned up, despite never having met Kim. It touched Sara enormously when, looking towards the back wall of the Chapel when giving her eulogy, she glimpsed a smiling Gloria: her face bobbing up like a sunflower in a sea of grey faced mourners. Paul Burley was there too, on the other side, but also on the back row. Neither of them stayed behind afterwards. They melted into the crowd as they all filed out and Sara lost sight of them.

Gloria was concerned about Sara. Mildred from the Contact centre had telephoned her the week before to voice her disquiet at Sara's attitude towards Sandy during her contact with the boys.

"It wouldn't have been so bad if she'd spoken to Sandy after the contact session but she was very sarcastic and, well, *horribly* rude to her in front of them. It wasn't fair to Sandy and it was certainly not in the best interests of the boys to see their mum so upset and tearful whilst she with them. I was really quite shaken when I overheard her."

Gloria could not recall any previous occasion when Mildred had considered it incumbent on her to comment on the professionalism of one of her social workers. She knew that Sara was wildly exasperated with Sandy following a recent visit. She had allowed the boys' father back into the family home contrary to her agreement with Social Services. Sara had discovered him in a downstairs cupboard when she'd made an unannounced visit to Sandy at her home. She'd noticed there were two smoking cigarette butts in the ashtray and asked where he was hiding. When Sandy had clammed up, she'd gone looking for him, *like a sniffer dog* – as she joked to Gloria – and found him sitting on a bucket next to the vacuum cleaner. The aftermath had not been pleasant. He'd threatened Sara and she'd called the police even though he'd retracted his threat immediately and apologised. Asked by the police if she wanted to take matters further, she'd said she did and he was arrested for *threatening behaviour*, handcuffed and taken to the station. Sandy became hysterical, fearing the consequences for her sons' future. Sara had not stayed around to comfort her, telling Sandy that she didn't want to waste time listening to her explanations. Sandy *knew the score* and a formal letter would be coming out to her shortly confirming the action she intended to recommend.

Gloria told Mildred that Sara was under some family strain, although she hadn't provided any details. She did not choose to confront Sara. Instead, she suggested that Sandy's contact be supervised by someone else. She juggled a few schedules, freeing up a family support worker for the session and telling Sara she needed her elsewhere. To her relief, Sara did not argue with her. Gloria was convinced that Sara's old compassionate self would return once Kim's funeral was over. She had been one of her most steadfast and reliable workers and she intended to retain faith in her. Who wouldn't be going through hell in her situation? This was a blip.

Emily and Steve had returned to Cornwall together after the funeral. To Sara, there appeared little affection between them. She would not have described them as *reunited* and this feeling was underlined when she and George visited for New Year. Her mother appeared to spend much of her time outside walking in the hills around the town or reading in her room. She admitted the same to Sara, saying that she and Steve only came together in the evenings for dinner. They are *sharing a house*, she remarked to George, *not sharing a life*.

It was Tabitha's belief that Emily was not strong enough to resist the pity she felt for her husband.

"I'd like to think she has not all but given up on life," she said to Martin, who felt ill-equipped to comment on the subject but was prepared to listen. It was a Saturday evening, an odd time for him to visit her. "But I think she has. I think she went back because it was the easier option and, anyway, she likes the solitude of that little house by the sea. I could tell that she felt confined in the flat with me." Immediately she had given voice to her theory, she felt sorry. Kim had been dead for a mere three months. It wasn't fair of her to comment on any aspect of Emily's behaviour when her wounds were still so fresh.

She gave Martin a wry smile.

"Take no notice of me. I'm too quick to judge – as always. Imagine if I'd lost you."

"No, Mum, let's not *imagine* anything of the sort."

Tabitha laughed and said she would need to leave in a few minutes, to meet a friend. They were going to the theatre. She picked up their cups and began carrying them to the kitchen. Martin followed her.

"Have you no plans, darling?"

Martin shook his head.

"I'm off on my bike for an hour or so."

"I've not seen or spoken to Sara since the funeral. How is she?"

"She seems ok. Counting down the days to the trial."

"Is she going?"

"I don't think she can attend the whole thing. But she feels she should be there as often as she can. She thinks it's the least she can do for Kim."

"Are you going with her?"

Martin stood up, zipping his jacket and fiddling with his helmet.

"I don't know, yet. I don't want to. But if Sara asks me to go with her, I suppose I'll have to."

"I expect there will be some form of closure for her once the trial is over, depending on the result – of course."

"She's not mentioned that word – closure. She talks about justice for Kim. She bangs on and on about it, raging against her attackers. Raging against those who didn't help her - the onlookers - with just as much hatred."

Tabitha sat down again.

"What d'you mean?"

He shrugged, wishing he hadn't invited her curiosity.

"Just that. She seems, sort of, blinded by anger at times. As if there's nothing else in the world."

Tabitha would never describe her son as happy-go-lucky. He just wasn't given to outbursts of emotion, whether joyous or angry. He was much the same - almost all the time. That evening he seemed adrift in a territory he was being forced to occupy.

"I suppose she has every right to be angry. Just like my sister has every right to surrender to her grief. We have to give them time."

"Yep. I know. Look, I'm off. The bike awaits its master! See you next week sometime."

He was gone, abruptly, before she could say anything else. Within the minute, she heard the familiar start-up riff he played on his bike, making her wonder why she hadn't suggested he gave her a lift.

Martin came very close that night to confessing that he had begun to avoid Sara's calls. He'd extricated himself before he revealed it, already feeling some disloyalty to her. But, whether he shared what he felt with his mother or not, it was the reality. Sara's obsession with the assault on Kim, the fury she felt towards Flood and Timms, was alienating him. He wanted to say to her – *I'm not just your sounding board, you know* – but he'd occupied that role for too long. She took it for granted that he would always be by her side, listening to whatever invective spewed from her mouth. He had gained the impression too that, because of his tolerance, George was spared these outbursts from Sara. She didn't inflict them on him because she knew George would turn away or change the subject, indicating that he would not collude in fanning the flames of her rage: enabling her.

Sara had called Martin earlier, leaving a message when he didn't pick up, asking if he fancied coming over. George was out at a football match. *We can catch up*, she said. He'd texted her to say he was going over to his mother's, even though he'd had no intention of doing so prior to her call. To assuage his conscience, he'd then got on his bike and made the visit. The last time they'd met up on their own, when she'd called in at the garden centre after an appointment she'd been on her way to was cancelled, he'd spent so much time listening to her that he had to work through some of his lunch hour.

Following her text announcing her surprise visit, Martin had tracked her down at a table under one of the fake palms in the tea room. She was looking at her phone when he came over in his overalls with his mug of coffee. She looked up at him but didn't greet him.

"Guess what I'm doing?" she asked.

"Oh, hello, Martin. How nice to see you," he said, sitting down opposite her.

She smiled sweetly at him.

"Sorry, darling," she said, leaning over and pecking him on the cheek.

He raised an eyebrow, signifying that he might forgive her.

"What madness are you engaged in now?" he asked. If he kept it light, perhaps she would follow his lead.

"I've been searching for any files on them."

"Who?"

"Timms and Flood, of course. You know, any history of social services involvement. Any dirt on them."

"Do you keep files that long?"

"Flood's not that old. She's only in her late twenties. Anyway…"

"Are you allowed to do this?"

"As long as I don't get found out," she said, with a fake beam on her face. Martin remained expressionless.

"Anyway, I'm reading her file now! I traced it and took a few screenshots."

"Right."

"Oh, come on! Don't look so disapproving," she implored. "They've forfeited any right they may have had to decency. I want to know."

"And what will you do with this…. this information?"

She shrugged.

"Don't know."

She looked back at her phone and started reading from it aloud.

Martin looked around at the other tables where people, of all ages, had gathered to share their morning coffee. Nearby, there was a woman with a new born baby. The couple with her, the grandparents he assumed, were gazing at the child in adoration. The tiny bundle had three pairs of eyes watching its every twitch, squirm and grimace.

"Best not announce it to the whole world," he said, interrupting her.

Sara put her phone down and looked at him. He could see the irritation in the set of her jaw, the way she ground her teeth together when she was annoyed.

"You're not interested, are you?"

Martin sighed.

"Perhaps, not quite at this moment, no."

"Right then."

Sara returned to drinking her coffee and stared over his head, pointedly.

"Stop it," he laughed. "Here, give it to me. I'll read it myself."

She handed her phone to him and waited whilst he skimmed through the contents of the Flood family file. It made him uncomfortable: peering through a keyhole, spying on a family, unguarded and vulnerable. He was shocked too at the detail in the reports, the judgments:

I asked Bev Flood how often she bathed Gail as she seemed to have some nappy rash. I also said that Gail should have been potty trained by now and what was she doing about this. She gave me very vague answers which concerned me. She seemed tired, as if she was on something. I asked her if she was taking any medication and could I make some enquiries of her GP. I also reminded her that she needed to take Gail to the baby clinic to be weighed and generally checked out. Said I'd be back (<u>On an unscheduled basis?</u>).

"She was on the Child Protection Register, as it then was," said Sara. "For years. I'm surprised she wasn't removed. Her Dad was in prison too on and off. For assault and petty theft. She also suffered from nocturnal enuresis throughout her childhood, which means -"

"Yes, I know what it means," said Martin.

"That bed-wetter caused the death of my sister."

"Sara!" Martin said. A look of distaste swept over his face.

"What?" she snapped back. "Aren't I allowed to hate her and vent in private to the person who knows me best. You."

Martin looked away from her. He needed to get back on shift.

"I hate her," she repeated, her eyes welling up with tears. "I'm sorry if that offends you."

"I know," said Martin quietly. "But condemn her for the right reason. Not because she had a shitty childhood and her parents lacked the capacity to care for her. As you've commented, numerous times, her parents probably had shitty childhoods too. The cycle of deprivation – or whatever."

They were silent for a moment whilst Sara pressed a tissue into the corner of each eye. She had never been able to bear any criticism from Martin. It was so rare that when it came, she knew it was deserved.

"Anyway," Martin went on. "How on earth does any of this help?"

He could have expanded on this train of thought. He could have gone on to say that Sara had devoted her professional life to trying to help the Gail Floods of this world, arguing for second chances, asking that people criticised a little less and enquired a little more, looked to understand first before they raced to judgment. Instead, when she didn't answer, he said he had to get back to work but they could meet up later and go for a drink, if she wanted to.

"I'm sorry," she said, suddenly. "It just consumes me at times. I'm really sorry."

"It's ok, I understand," said Martin, although he didn't *really* think it was ok and neither did Sara *really* believe he understood. They were standing on opposite banks of a stream. Perhaps, until that moment, they had been able to stretch out their hands and touch or jump the water to join the other. But now, after that day, the stream had transformed into a raging torrent of a river and was, or *felt,* unbridgeable.

It was almost midnight when, speed and concentration having failed to relieve his restlessness, Martin rode back over to Kim's flat, looking for Marie Chambon. He repeated her words - *vous survivrez a cette* - into the biting wind of a winter's night. He was searching for consolation: consolation which never came.

CHAPTER 13

Causation

The prosecuting barrister, Miss Emilia Swinburne, reminded Sara of an actress whose name she couldn't remember. It was Miriam *something*, she was sure, but she couldn't retrieve her surname. A rotund woman in her fifties, the plumpness of her jolly face was accentuated by a horsehair wig which slipped a little when she became over excited in her examinations in chief. She was the *mistress of the exhibit bundle* – as christened by her colleagues – from Day 1 referring them to the right document in the right lever arch file in a matter of seconds and then watching with some irritation as her opponent barristers scrabbled through theirs. Such was her commanding presence in the court that she was rarely interrupted by the Judge on matters *other* than when he wanted her opinion on something. By way of contrast, the male defence barristers, both younger, were subject to much sighing and even some tutting on his part. Flood was represented by a young, smart Asian lawyer and Timms by a scruffy, if handsome, man with an attractive Liverpudlian accent. The three lawyers together with their acolytes and hangers-on, not to mention their clients, made for perfect theatre.

 Miss Swinburne spoke in clipped, clear tones, matching the precision of her language. She employed only a small range of expressions, as if conserving her facial muscles for some important event in the future. Her most popular was to roll her lips together tightly. This usually indicated that she was pleased with the answer she had managed to extract from the witness. If she was frustrated with the hapless individual on the stand, her nostrils would flare ever so slightly. A particularly significant response from the witness would result in a few seconds silence and then a stern look at the jury. *You'd better be concentrating*, it said.

Timms' barrister, the one from the North, smiled a lot when he was on his feet and managed to charm whoever he was questioning. A couple of the older female jurors seemed unable to stop ogling him, even when, tabs askew, he was slumped in his seat tapping away on his laptop. He and Flood's advocate would occasionally whisper together, which usually meant some point of law or procedure had arisen on which they needed the Judge's direction. When this happened, the jury got sent out and the trial came to a halt. The advocates appeared to relish these little intervals, as if they could be themselves now they weren't having to perform to the members of the jury. Robes were adjusted and there was much stretching and yawning.

The twelve good men and true were split seven to five in favour of the male sex. There was an elderly man who shuffled in and out with the aid of a walking stick. A tall middle-aged woman with her hair in a bun had assigned herself the role of his minder, hauling him to his feet when they had to stand up and taking charge of his stick so that he could extricate himself from the bench with two hands. He didn't look entirely appreciative of her attention but, since the jurors were expected to sit in the same places throughout the trial, he was stuck with Mrs Good Intentions. One of the young women studiously took notes as if at a university tutorial whereas at least half of the jurors did not appear to take any notes at all. Presumably, they were not looking to put themselves forward as the foreman in due course.

Sara had missed the prosecution's opening and arrived on the second day of the trial, as Miss Swinburne trudged her way through the disparate bunch of party goers who witnessed the attack on Kim on a night the previous September. Mr Finch was her second victim.

"Mr Finch," she said, once he had taken the oath and given his full name to the court.

Robert Finch was a thin, pasty faced man in his late thirties. He was wearing a rather grubby shirt, once white, now grey, and denim jeans. His eyes flicked around the court room until they alighted on the defendant Timms, whereupon a look of surprise came over his face - as if he had suddenly realised why he was there, facing this bossy woman with the posh voice.

"You've given a statement to the police confirming that you were at a party at Flat No 38 on the night of September 17th 2017. Do you recall providing that statement?"

"Sort of."

"Does that mean you do or you don't recall giving a statement?"

"Yeah, yeah, I do but it was a long time ago."

"I'm going to ask you some questions about what happened on that night."

Mr Finch nodded.

"The defendants Mr Timms and Miss Flood do not dispute that they attended the party on the 17th September last year. Nor do they dispute that they were both involved in an incident concerning the deceased, Miss Turner. Did you witness any incident between Mr Timms, Miss Flood and Miss Turner?"

"Yeah. I was in the room when it happened."

"Which room?"

"The kitchen."

"Where were you in the kitchen?"

"I was standing by the cooker. You know, sort of leaning against it."

"Was the room crowded?"

"People were coming in and out all the time. It was quite crowded."

"How far away would you say Miss Flood and Mr Timms were from you?"

"A couple of feet, I suppose. Near, like."

"And what happened, Mr Finch? Can you tell the court exactly what you saw?"

Mr Finch swallowed.

"There was a fight."

"There was a fight," repeated Miss Swinburne in a teacherish tone of voice, indicating that this was yet another witness from whom evidence would have to be dragged bit by torturous bit.

She continued.

"What did you see, Mr Finch?"

Everyone looked at Mr Finch expectantly, save the Judge who was indicating to one of the ushers that his water pitcher was empty.

"Er… I remember seeing the other lady.."

"Who?"

"The lady who was, like, hurt…"

"The deceased, Miss Turner?"

"Yeah. I saw her push her," Mr Finch jerked his head over in the direction of Gail Flood where she sat with Timms behind a glass screen at the back of the court.

"Go on."

"And she fell backwards onto the floor."

"Just hold it there, Mr Finch. Who did you see push whom and who fell backwards onto the floor?"

"Miss Turner pushed Gail onto the floor."

"How?" Mr Finch mimed an outwards pushing motion with the flattened palm of one hand.

"Where did she push her?"

"Onto the floor, like I said."

"No, I'm sorry, Mr Finch. I didn't make myself clear. Where on Gail Flood's body did Miss Turner push her."

"I don't remember. Somewhere in her chest region, I think."

"Is there anything else you remember about the actual push?"

Mr Finch's brow wrinkled indicating his confusion.
"Like what?"

"Was it a soft or hard push?"

"I wouldn't describe it as hard. Gail slipped."

"How? On what?"

"The floor was wet. Y'know, like there was water or beer or something like that spilled on the floor. She fell backwards."

"Right. Let's pause again there, Mr Finch. I want you to tell the court now if there were any words exchanged between Gail Flood and Miss Turner and, if so, can you recall them?"

"Gail was shouting at Miss Turner, saying she'd drunk her vodka."

"Was Mr Timms involved at this moment?"

"I don't remember. I just remember that Gail was saying that Miss Turner had drunk her vodka."

"Can you recall any of the exchange between them?"

"As I said, Gail was saying she'd drunk her bottle of vodka and what was she going to do about it and Miss Turner told her to, you know, fuck off out of my face."

Mr Finch glanced at the Judge when he uttered this profanity in case His Lordship hadn't heard such language before and might be shocked. The reality was that Mr Justice Barrington-Smythe was immune to such language. His days were peppered with much worse: in particular, the 'c word' was now so acceptable as to have lost some of its impact. No longer could one ascribe any specific characteristics to the user of such language. It was ubiquitous amongst all classes, albeit in private in the upper echelons of the professions.

"Out of my face," repeated Miss Swinburne. "Those were her words, were they? *Out of my face?"*

Mr Finch nodded.

"Is that a yes, Mr Finch?"

"Yeah."

"Thank you. That suggests that Gail was very close to Miss Turner at this point. Was she?"

"Yeah, she was sort of right up against her face and she had the bottle in her hand."

"I see. What was she doing with the bottle?"

"She was showing it to her, you know, showing her it was, like, empty. And then Miss Turner grabs the bottle from Gail and pushes her."

"And what happened then, when Gail went down onto the floor?"

Mr Finch swallowed again. He knew that Timms was staring at him, his wide blue eyes boring their way into his skin, his fists balled. Timms had a load of mates. He might run in to them when he returned to the estate. He'd not checked to see if one of them was sitting in the public gallery, committing his words to memory so that he, Finch, could be reminded of them when cornered in one of the stairwells.

Miss Swinburne raised her eyebrows at Mr Finch as she waited for his reply. His Lordship looked up expectantly and Timms' barrister glanced away from his laptop.

An uncomfortable silence settled over the court room.

"I.., I don't remember much after that."

"That's not what you said to the police in your statement," said Miss Swinburne, crisply.

"I don't remember what I said to the police."

"Are you sure about that, Mr Finch?"

After another swallow, Mr Finch started talking.

"Yeah, well, I remember Gail's fella moving in then and hitting Miss Turner."

"I assume you are describing Mr Timms as Gail's 'fella'?"
"Yeah."
"Where was Miss Turner when Mr Timms was hitting her?"
"She was standing with her back to the sink."
"Where was he hitting her?"
"In the face."
"With his fists?"
"Yeah."
"How many times did Mr Timms hit Miss Turner in the face?"
"Two, I think, or three. I can't be sure."
"Were they hard hits?"
"Yeah. I suppose so."
"Did Mr Timms say anything to her?"
"I can't remember exactly but I think he called her a bitch."
"Did he say anything else?"

There was now a sheen of sweat covering Mr Finch's face. His tongue flicked out to lick his lips. He knew – they all knew – that the *anything else* words were crucial ones.

"He told her to, like, scarper."
"Is that all he said?"

Mr Finch nodded again. The judge looked up from his laptop. Ms Swinburne persevered: a climber inching her way up the rock face towards the summit.

"Mr Finch," she repeated. There was a sharp edge to her tone. "Is that all Mr Timms said to Kim Turner after punching her?"

"He said she'd better leave before he did her some more damage."

"Did he use the word "more"?"

Mr Finch looked confused.

"Are you sure he said *more* damage? Because you said something a little different in your statement?"

Ms Swinburne asked the Judge for permission to read from Mr Finch's statement. Neither defence counsel voiced an objection.

"In your statement, you said *real* damage – you said Mr Timms said to Kim Turner "I suggest you leave before I do you some *real* damage."

"Yeah. He may have said that."

"Said what?"

"That she'd better leave before he did her some real damage."

"And what did Miss Turner do then?"

"She left the room."

"How did she seem?"

"How d'you mean?"

Miss Swinburne stifled a sigh.

"Did she appear unwell? Was she bleeding? How would you describe her?"

Mr Finch looked around the room as if planning an escape. There was none. He was cornered.

"Yeah. I think her face was bleeding and she looked, you know, a bit unsteady on her feet. Shocked, sort of."

Miss Swinburne was visibly pleased with this response. It fitted her case. Kim was dazed, bleeding and unsteady on her feet when she fled from the flat in genuine fear of further attack.

"Did anyone help her?"

"I don't think so."

Ms Swinburne could feel that a hush had settled over the court room as most of its occupants asked themselves if *they* would have helped Kim Turner as she fled from her attackers. Accordingly, she allowed for a moment's pause in her examination of Mr Finch. Any sympathy for the victim was welcome.

"Did you see Miss Turner leave the party?"

"No. I stayed on. I didn't know anything about what had happened until later when someone told me an ambulance had been called."

"Please wait there, Mr Finch. There will be some more questions for you."

Miss Swinburne sat down.

Sara got up from her seat in the public gallery at that moment and made for the door, tripping over someone's feet as she did so. Instead of an apology, which she had intended to offer, she released the sob which had been crouching inside her throughout the course of Mr Finch's evidence. The official on guard in the gallery leapt up to open the door for her and then joined her outside on the landing. She muttered her apologies and was surprised when he did not admonish her. She didn't linger, just ran down the stairs, back out through the security scanners and into the tunnel which led out onto the street. In the half light of a still, grey March afternoon, she rifled through her bag looking for her mobile before remembering that she had left it at home. Mobiles were not allowed in the Old Bailey. There was a nearby shop which would look after them for you for a small fee but she'd decided she could cope without it. But not now. Now, she was regretting that she was standing alone, her tears spilling from her, an unstoppable flood of heartbreak and fury.

"Oh, Kim," she moaned softly to herself, pressing a rapidly disintegrating tissue, the only one she could locate, into her eyes. "Oh, Kim."

Paul had warned her. He'd said she would find it immensely difficult and she should be very sure before attending the trial. But he'd warned many families before and very few heeded him because, ultimately, there was no other way of honouring their dead than by being present when that final story was being told.

"Sara."

She looked up, her vision blurred, and there he was, like a Guardian Angel, Paul Burley.

He fixed her with a steady gaze but, since he knew that any words he uttered would be more for his own comfort than for hers, he said nothing. He stood by her side, on the busy street, and waited. He waited whilst she cried, at one point handing her his handkerchief when he came to the realisation that she might not be choosing to wipe her eyes and her nose with her fingers. He waited a full one minute.

"I didn't see you in there," she said eventually.

"I was sitting in the well of the court at the back with the police officers. I guessed it was you when I heard someone leaving the gallery."

"I'm sorry," she said. "It's just very hard to listen to. I knew it would be but perhaps I'd underestimated the impact it would have on me."

"You loved her," he said: a stark and simple statement which brought fresh tears to Sara's eyes.

She nodded.

"Can I buy you a cup of tea or coffee?" he asked.

"Thank you."

In the café, after their coffees were brought to them by a waitress with pink hair.

"Kim went through a stage of having pink hair," Sara said.

Paul told Sara that he'd heard Miss Swinburne's opening speech to the jury the day before.

"The basic facts aren't disputed, as you heard today. Timms and Flood don't deny that they were involved in an altercation, although they say she started it and they were defending themselves. The prosecution must show a causal link between the attack on Kim and her eventual death. The jury will be asked to determine whether they accept that link, answering the question *"but for"* the assault would Kim have fallen down the stairs and sustained the injuries which eventually led to her death. Timms threatened Kim as we just heard. She left in an injured state, fearing she was going to be further assaulted if she remained at the party."

Paul stopped talking briefly to take a sip of his tea and to look round the café, as if he feared he was being indiscreet in releasing such details into a public place.

"The party was on the eighth floor of the tower block so Kim using the stairs might support the theory that she was trying to escape quickly, didn't want to risk hanging around waiting for a lift. The lifts – there were two – were both in working order although we haven't been able to trace the two men she came to the party with and who might have been able to say that she happily used the lift on the way up. Anyway, not only are the defence raising self-defence in relation to the assault, just as crucially they're saying it can't be conclusively proved that the assault led to Kim's death. There were, or may have been, intervening events."

"You said it wasn't straightforward."

"We're calling someone who opened the door for her when she left, saw her injured and unsteady on her feet. That's important evidence too in what's called the chain of causation."

"You mentioned earlier that there'd be medical evidence."

"I've only seen the hospital's report which describe her facial injuries as being consistent with being hit or punched hard. The Pathologist's evidence is very clear as to the cause of death, as you know. It was the fall. But no doubt, the prosecution's medical expert will also be asked to comment on whether her injuries would mean she'd be dazed and her balance might be affected. We'll have to wait to see how that evidence comes out. It's impossible to speculate. However…"

At that point, Paul Burley put his hand on Sara's arm. He'd never touched her before: a stringent adherence to professional distance had prevented him. It was her first real intimation that it was perfectly possible they might lose the case. Until then, she'd believed that any jury would make Flood and Timms pay for their vicious assault on Kim by returning a verdict of manslaughter. Now she realised that even a bit of uncertainty as to the chain of events on that night would be enough to make the jury wobble.

Paul removed his hand and carried on speaking.

"Essentially, the jury could accept the possibility of self defence and also conclude that Kim fell down the stairs, not because she was anxious to get away, but because she was drunk and stoned."

"But what about the head injuries affecting her balance?"

"The defence will also produce their own medical evidence with a view to muddying the waters. But, you know, I'm a police officer, not a lawyer or a doctor. I just wanted you to be aware of the possibilities. What we're up against."

Sara looked away and out towards the street. After what he'd said, all his misgivings, she wasn't sure she wanted to sit through an afternoon of cross examination where Kim's demeanour on the night in question would be scrutinised and dissected. Sara knew that Kim could be aggressive when drunk. She'd rarely been the subject of it but she'd witnessed it often enough when she'd not had the opportunity, or foresight, to escape before Kim got going. She remembered how uncomfortable it had made George when he first encountered a ranting, red-eyed Kim, angry because the barman had decided she'd had enough and he was within his rights not to serve her. Even George, with his ability to defuse tension, had failed in persuading her to accept the situation and move on. On that particular night, it was only when the police arrived that Kim gave in and allowed two women police officers to escort her off the premises. Even afterwards, Kim hadn't apologised, just looked offended when Sara and George said they were calling it a night and going home.

"Where's she going on to?" George enquired of Sara as they waited at a bus stop, watching Kim lighting up a cigarette before moving on to where she might find some other establishment with lower standards.

"I don't know and at this precise moment, I don't care either. I never thought I'd say this, but I just don't want to be with her sometimes. I'm sorry she ruined the evening."

If George agreed, he didn't say so but thereafter, Sara noted, if a meeting with Kim were suggested, he would ask who else was going along. Kim's alcohol problem was less evident when she was absorbed into a group.

After Sara admitted to Paul that she'd had enough and was not going back to court, they parted and she headed off in the direction of the tube, going over in her mind all the information he'd passed over to her that afternoon. He'd not said he'd call her to let her know how the afternoon's proceedings progressed, simply reminded her to call him if she needed to talk.

When she got home, she dozed in a hot bath, hoping she'd have half an hour to herself before her parents were on the phone enquiring as to the day's events at court. She'd tell them of her conversation with Paul in the café so that they'd be prepared for the worst. Her father would be angry – *are you telling me they're going to get away with it, Sara?* She might suggest he ring Paul himself. Her mother would be more sanguine, resigned. *What will be, will be, Steve.*

Sara thought back to the two defence barristers, imagining them on their feet running through a list of questions which would be adapted to suit each particular witness but, nevertheless, seek to support the same scenario.

She started the row. She hit Flood first. They were entitled to defend themselves. Who's to say the silly cow didn't fall down the stairs because she tripped? After all, she was out of her fucking head. Just like she was most days.

CHAPTER 14

Jubilant

Sara did go back to court. She'd taken two weeks' leave for the purpose of attending the trial. She would see it through. Martin had called her around nine that first evening, asking how things had gone. He'd proffered the view that the first day was bound to be the most difficult as she adjusted to the experience although, when she recapped on her meeting with Paul, he conceded that the day of the verdict might be equally challenging.

"I'll definitely be with you on that day. I promise. And I'll try to make it this Friday too. I'll let you know."

There were two more days of prosecution witnesses. The witness after Mr Finch, Paula Lowe, largely corroborated his evidence, seemed less unwilling to describe what she'd seen and was adamant that Mr Timms had hit Kim at least three times, *hard like*, and with his right fist. *She didn't stand a chance against him* she maintained. Miss Lowe was in her thirties and sported an array of tattoos so dark they appeared like bruises along her muscular arms. She so relished her dishing of the dirt on Gary Timms that his defence counsel would have been derelict in his duty had he not probed a little deeper to establish a motive.

Mr Grant, Timms' barrister, rose to his feet and bestowed a fleeting smile on Miss Lowe, introducing himself as he did so.

"Do you know Gary Timms, Miss Lowe?"

Miss Swinburne looked up from her notes. Her nostrils flared.

"Yeah, I know him." *So what?* was implicit in the shrug of her shoulders as she conceded the fact.

"In what capacity do you know him?"

"We live on the same estate."

"Is that all?"

"We were friends once, if that's what yer mean. A long time ago. He's been with Gail for the last couple of years."

"You were romantically involved with him, weren't you?"

For the first time since she'd been in the witness box, Miss Lowe showed some discomfort. She wiped her hand across her upper lip.

Mr Grant took a sip of water whilst he waited for an answer and then shot a look at the jury.

"Yes. We were. But I know what I ..."

Mr Grant cut her off, raising his hand at the same time.

"We'll come to that in a minute. For the moment, let's stick to your *past relationship* with Mr Timms."

He flashed her another disingenuous smile.

"How did the relationship end?"

"I don't remember."

"Well, put it like this. Did you remain friends?"

At this point Miss Swinburne got to her feet, questioning the relevance of Mr Grant's cross examination.

"I think we've got the point, Mr Grant," said His Lordship. "Let's move on, shall we?"

Mr Grant seemed as if he had been expecting this interruption. He murmured something obsequious and switched tack.

"How long had you been at the party when you witnessed the assault?"

"A couple of hours, perhaps."

"Did you drink anything whilst you were there?"

"Yeah. I had some vodka I think."

"How much?"

Mr Grant didn't make much ground in this line of questioning. Miss Lowe accepted she had drunk *quite a bit* but was unmoveable on what she had seen happen. He made more headway with his questions about Kim.

"Did you know Kim Turner?"

"I'd seen her around but not, like, to speak to. We weren't mates."

"Where had you seen her?"

"In The Arms, you know the pub opposite the estate. I saw her in there quite a few times."

"How was she when you saw her?"

"What d'you mean?"

"Well, how did she seem on those occasions? Is there anything you'd remember about her?"

Miss Lowe smiled then, providing a glimpse of her tobacco stained teeth.

"She was usually pissed."

"How could you tell?"

"She was very loud. You couldn't miss her."

"And what about at the party? How did she appear then?"

"She looked like she'd had too much."

"How?"

"Just the way she was leaning against the sink. And then when she was shouting at Gail, she just sounded, you know, pissed."

Of the two witnesses produced by the prosecution in relation to their seeing Kim leave the party, one was very clear that he had opened the door of the flat for her. She was *in a bad way*, he said, seemed anxious to get out. He'd wondered whether he should go after her as she appeared dazed and was bleeding. But she'd ignored him when he'd asked her if she was alright so he hadn't. On cross examination, he accepted that she might just have been *very drunk*, accepted that he did not have the medical knowledge to distinguish between the effects of a possible head injury and extreme inebriation.

The second witness was nervous and unsure. *Neither* had witnessed the assault and nor could they be sure as to the exact time when Kim left the flat. Whilst Miss Swinburne's re-examination was skilful enough to retrieve some of the ground lost, enough holes were left to cast doubt on whether Kim, as the prosecution alleged, fled from the party *immediately* after the attack or at some later point – for example, after another couple of cans.

Miss Heather Baker, consultant neurologist, was being called by the prosecution to provide her expert opinion on the nature of Kim's head trauma. That opinion was a paper exercise: she had not seen or examined Kim. Her comments were based solely on four reports provided to her – the paramedics', the hospital's following Kim's admission and the two Pathologists'. Miss Baker maintained that it was easy to distinguish between the injuries to Kim's face and head inflicted at close range and the bruising which may have resulted in the fall. The pattern of injuries usually sustained in a fall down a flight of stairs was well documented, although the stairs in question were uncarpeted, stone ones. She identified four 'punch' contusions to Kim's face and gave evidence to the effect that they were likely to have caused her pain, confusion and dizziness which may have led to some unsteadiness on her feet. Miss Swinburne knew exactly the angle of attack lying in wait for Miss Baker once Mr Grant and his learned friend were unleashed on her and pre-empted their questions in so far as it was safe to do so.

Kim's intoxication was referred to in the hospital notes. Her belligerence and non-cooperation were also made mention of, confirmed and highlighted by the fact of her discharging herself against medical advice.

The medical expert for the defence emphasised that any opinion on the effect on the victim of being punched in the head was speculative. It was not possible to be certain about the consequences for any individual. All he would concede was that the blows were sufficiently hard to have caused the bruising noted although he also made two observations: firstly, the blows had not been so hard that Kim fell over and secondly, she was not knocked unconscious and there was nothing in either pathologist's report to suggest she'd had a bleed on the brain. The cause of death was due to fractured ribs, sustained in the fall, which had ruptured her chest cavity. She would not have died had she remained in hospital.

At lunchtime, Martin and Sara sat in a nearby café and mulled over the evidence they'd heard that morning.

"Surely, Kim's failure to seek proper medical treatment will be fatal to the case?" said Martin, peering into his ham and cheese sandwich as if he suspected someone was trying to poison him.

Sara nodded at him. She was eating a berry yoghurt with granola.

"You should have had what I'm eating. It's delicious. And, no, Kim refusing treatment is not – apparently – relevant. You take your victim as you find them. But I'm not clear about her drunkenness and the relevance of that. As far as I can make out from the line of questioning by the lawyers for Flood and Timms, their main contention is that there is no cogent evidence to support the prosecution's case that Kim's fall was as a consequence of the attack. It may have been, it may not have been."

"And that's not really enough is it?"

Sara scraped around the rest of her yoghurt pot.

"Probably not," she said. "Paul obviously doesn't think so."

"So, what happens this afternoon?"

"The defence start their case and I understand that both Flood and Timms intend to give evidence. Although I doubt that will be today."

Mr Grant opened his case that afternoon by calling a witness who had seen the assault on Kim and who was adamant that she had not left the room *immediately* afterwards. He said Kim had leant over the sink and spat into it. Someone had given her a paper towel to stem the blood from the cut on her eyebrow.

As Miss Swinburne was getting her teeth into this witness who, perhaps, was one of the more articulate of the lay witnesses to have appeared on the stand, Martin glanced at Sara. She looked back at him, knowing what his eyes signified. Like sand running through their fingers, the case against Timms and Flood was trickling away as their lawyers exploited every single factual discrepancy with terrier like tenacity.

Flood and Timms gave evidence during the following week. They both described Kim as being aggressive and unpredictable because she was *out of her head on booze and weed*. Timms maintained with vehemence that he was defending Flood.

"Yeah, I, like, hit her. I was angry. She'd pushed Gail on to the floor. I was defending us."

"Didn't Gail slip?"

"No. Kim Turner was pissed out of her mind and pushed her. She was acting aggressive. Wasn't sure what she might do next. She had the bottle in her hand, too. Waving it around. How was I to know that she wasn't going to smash me in the face with it?"

"Are you suggesting, Mr Timms, that a man of your height and size was scared of a woman less than half your weight and six inches smaller?"

"She was drunk, like, you know, unpredictable. And she had a weapon, like I just said. But I didn't threaten her with any more violence. I just sort of made my point, like, and then she left."

"You punched Kim Turner hard, didn't you?"

"Not that hard."

"The medical evidence shows that you punched her hard three times, not once. Three times. As I've suggested already, Mr Timms, you are a big strong man. Surely, you would have been able to restrain Ms Turner had she attempted to attack you or Gail? It wasn't necessary for you to punch her so excessively."

Mr Timms did not respond, merely fixed Ms Swinburne with an angry glare.

"Well, Mr Timms? Do you accept that you punched Kim Turner hard in the face three times?"

"I accept I punched her a couple of times. Definitely not three. I don't know how hard it was. I was worried she might come at me with the bottle, like I said."

Ms Swinburne looked down at her notes for a few moments before resuming her cross examination.

"A few minutes ago you said – *I just sort of made my point and then she left* - what was your point, then, Mr Timms? What did you say?"

Mr Timms smoothed his hands down over his jeans, wiping away the sweat that had accumulated on his palms in the face of Ms Swinburne's probing.

"I don't remember much, you know, in the heat of the moment-"

Ms Swinburne took advantage of his hesitation: in like a falcon swooping down on a bit of carrion before other, lesser creatures, could even blink.

"But sufficient memory to recall how often you punched Miss Turner?"

She fixed him with a contemptuous stare *I've been here much more often than you, Mr Timms, you're on my patch now.*

"Well, what did you say to Miss Turner after you punched her?"

As she posed the question, she cast a meaningful look at the jury.

"I called her bitch and said she'd better leave."

"And?"

Mr Timms returned her look but said nothing.

The court waited.

"Do you deny, Mr Timms, that you said as stated by Mr Finch in his evidence to this court *I suggest you leave before I do you some real damage*?"

"I don't remember."

"I put it to you, Mr Timms, that you *do* remember and that you're lying about the exact words you used to threaten Miss Turner on the night in question.

"I'm not lying. No way. I didn't threaten her."

"I suggest to you that your words were so threatening that having already demonstrated that you were capable of causing her some real harm, Kim Turner fled the party immediately. That was your intention exactly, wasn't it, Mr Timms?"

"Wasn't it, Mr Timms?" she repeated when he refused to answer.

As the Defence case progressed, the scenario that Kim had left the party, bleeding, in pain and in fear, was just one of many. There was no certainty around times, let alone Kim's movements.

In his summing up, the Judge said that the jury needed to decide whether Kim's actions – in leaving the party and falling down the stairs – were within the range of *foreseeable* responses following the assault. Had the prosecution proved the causal connection between the attack and Kim's death? Did the jury consider – as put forward by both defence teams - that Kim's fall was *an intervening act* which broke the chain of causation? If so, they should find the Defendants not guilty of unlawful act manslaughter. They were directed to ignore the fact that Kim had been her own worst enemy in discharging herself from hospital the following morning.

The jury went into their deliberations after the luncheon adjournment on the Friday afternoon. Sara watched them file out. She felt she discerned some excitement on their faces. It was a Friday. The trial was over. Their lives could return to normal. They just had to get on with things that afternoon and they might even be able to beat the worst of the rush-hour. Their return was swift, taking even counsel by surprise. There seemed to be some confusion as to where Mr Grant's team had disappeared in the interim. He scurried in eventually, fiddling with his wig but looking pleased. He had clearly concluded that the swift return of the jury indicated a not guilty verdict.

He was correct. The jury found both defendants not guilty. Behind Sara and Martin in the public gallery, a group of individuals started whooping and pumping the air with their fists. Martin felt the rush of air as they rose to their feet, screeching in his ear. Sara knew that the woman she had seen at the Magistrates' court and whom she assumed to be Flood's mother was also in the gallery. She had vowed to herself that, whatever the verdict, she would not look at her. She would not participate in any spectacle of triumph. But, when the noise erupted, she could not help herself searching her out. And there she was, her face a jubilant blotchy red, as she gesticulated at her daughter with a raised closed fist. As Martin hauled her to her feet, saying *for God's sake let's get out of here*, she looked down at Timms and Flood jumping around behind the glass screen. They were waving to their audience, like a couple of celebrities, and laughing.

The judge called for order and then thanked the jury for their service. He went on to inform Timms and Flood that they were free to go.

CHAPTER 15

Threshold

Expecting something, anticipating it, rarely equates with the reality when it eventually occurs.

Sara knew it would have been polite to wait to see Paul Burley outside court following the verdict but she didn't suggest it to Martin. They went directly home, in virtual silence, Martin sensing an aura of despair surrounding Sara. He'd expected anger from her and was relieved when none emerged. When her conscience pricked her later that evening, she decided that Paul was probably the person she least needed to be concerned about on that day of reckoning. He'd forecast it, tried to prepare her. He didn't need to speak to her to know her anguish.

As she was lying, in familiar position, with her head in George's lap on the sofa, a text had come through from him.

I'm sorry, Sara. Take care. Paul.

Although she felt a rush of tears on seeing his words, she fought against them. That evening marked an end to the whole wretched affair. It was over. There was nothing left to endure, save the absence of her sister which would last for the rest of her life. And grieving was a private process, very different from the public space she had been forced to occupy with the police, at the funeral and during the trial. Those had all demanded such energy from her.

She'd phoned her parents before George had arrived home, wanting to get it out of the way immediately. After their previous conversation, it wasn't that difficult. She gave her father little opportunity to vent his frustration.

"There's nothing left to be said, Dad. It's finished. There's no point railing against it."

"But I can't understand how they could…"

"That's our criminal justice system, Dad. Take it up with the Attorney General or someone. Not me."

It wasn't the most compassionate of responses.

"Sorry, Dad. I'm tired. I just want to spend a normal weekend with George before I go back to work on Monday. I'll speak to you both next week. Give Mum my love."

She rang off and went to pour herself a glass of wine.

Later, after they'd finished a rather unsatisfactory dinner, George asked her what she wanted to do with the rest of their weekend together.

Sara looked drawn and pale after her incarceration in the court. She'd remarked that court number 13 in the Old Bailey had no natural light in it at all. Winter never suited her olive skin, anyway. She needed sunshine and whilst they were unlikely to get much, if any, in March, some fresh air would be equally beneficial.

"Maybe we could go away for a night somewhere quiet and rural where we could walk and you could recuperate. Have dinner out, perhaps go to a market on the Sunday morning."

George pushed her off his lap and reached over to grab his phone from the table.

"What are you doing?"

"I'm looking to see what's available," he said. "The Cotswolds, I think. One of the Slaughters. You like all those little twee and overpriced shops in Broadway, don't you?"

"I don't know what I want," she said. "Perhaps just to sleep and not go anywhere at all until the horror of Monday morning arrives."

George was disappointed but did not press her. When he thought beyond his immediate enthusiasm, he remembered the planning work he'd promised his head of year he'd complete by the end of the following week.

"Sorry," she said.

George gave her one of his puppy dog looks, making her smile.

"We don't really have the money, anyway," he said. "Poor us."

The following morning, Saturday, Frank called him, saying he was taking Pete out for a meal to a steak house in central London.

"The old man could do with a change of scene," he said. "Can you come?"

George explained about the trial and its outcome.

"Christ, I'm really sorry, George, I forgot all about it. What a bummer! How's Sara taken it?"

"She half expected it. It's over, anyway."

"Well, Sara can come too. Dad's always pleased to see her."

"I don't know, Frank. Perhaps we'll just stay in. I'm not sure she's up to socialising at the moment."

"Ok, ok. Just a thought. Not a problem."

But it was, because no sooner were they off the phone then Pete was ringing George on the landline. Sara answered it, assuming it would be her parents. When she heard what Frank had planned, she was insistent that George should go too.

"Absolutely. It's not that often the three of you get together. Your Dad will be so disappointed if you don't go. I'll be fine just chilling here. I'll watch a film or something. I don't mind. Honestly, George. Please go."

George went in the end, without too many misgivings about leaving her alone. At 4am that morning, he'd awoken to find her missing from their bed. Assuming she'd gone to the bathroom, he'd not immediately worried. When she hadn't returned after ten minutes, despite his body's insistence he turn over and go back to sleep, he got up and went to find her.

She was standing by the window, looking out, one of the blinds half-raised to enable her to do so. There wasn't a view, as such, but it was a clear night and there was a three quarters moon. She almost glowed in its light.

"Sara?"

She turned.

"Are you ok?" he asked.

"I had a really vivid dream about Kim. I was happy in it because she wasn't really dead, after all. She was still here."

George went over to her and pulled her to him, without saying anything. She leant into his naked chest and then kissed his neck. Pressing herself hard against him, her lips moved up to his mouth. He reached for her hand to lead her back to the bedroom but she said, *no, here, now* and knelt down, taking him with her. When he bumped his elbow on the edge of the window sill, she started giggling, asking him if she should *kiss it better* and was there anything else she should kiss whilst she was *in the mood?* His face was such a picture to her, a mixture of surprise and childish glee, that she laughed out loud. And whilst the sex was welcome and fulfilling, when George lay in bed afterwards, it was the sound of Sara's laughter that he thought back to. *She's going to be ok, thank Christ, she's going to be ok.*

~ ~ ~

Whilst George, Pete and Frank were perusing the menu at the Argentinian Steakhouse in Piccadilly, Sara was looking up which bus she would take should she decide to undertake a trip to The Arms, in Greenford, the pub that was referred to in the trial as being opposite the estate on which Timms and Flood lived.

She'd logged into her Facebook account that afternoon and saw that there had been some significant activity on it regarding the outcome of the trial. There were posts from a number of Kim's old school friends, the ones who had attended her funeral, commenting on the injustice of the outcome and *how hard it is to watch those bastards walk free.* One of them, Julie, also said that she'd heard from a friend of a friend that there was to be a party for Flood and Timms in their old watering hole, The Arms, that night, Saturday, to celebrate their *so-called victory. I cannot believe,* wrote Julie*, that anyone considers a celebration to be appropriate in these circumstances where a person lost her life in such tragic manner. I almost feel like turning up and telling them what I think of them face to face, disrupting their fucking stupid get together with the rest of the scum they knock about with. RIP Kim. We were good mates in the day.*

The fury which Sara had been so successful in locking away during the previous 24 hours was unleashed. Like petrol being poured onto the dying embers of a bonfire, the flickers of fury had turned into red hot flames shooting out at unpredictable angles. *Don't get in my way.*

Meanwhile.

"We could start with a cocktail," suggested Frank. He looked smart in an open necked dark blue shirt and black jeans, his hair short, dark and neat. He was wearing light leather Italian shoes which looked uncomfortable to George who had texted him before he left the flat to ask whether it was *ok to wear trainers.*

George and his father looked at one another when Frank sprang the suggestion on them. *What in God's name would they look like*, it said, *three grown men sipping cocktails though coloured straws?* Frank stopped studying the side orders and looked up.

"What?" he said to his father. "I bet you've never had a cocktail, Dad. Try one. Try a Highland Fling."

Pete laughed.

"A beer will do me. But it sounds intriguing. What's in it?"

"Grouse whisky and pineapple juice."

"What an insult to decent whisky! Mixing it with fruit juice."

"Bro?" Frank turned his attention to George. "Are you going to stick with Dad in his strait jacket?"

"No. I'm happy to join you. I'll have a Negroni, thank you."

"The steak is excellent by the way. We come here quite a lot. Never had a bad one yet."

"Whose the we?" asked Pete.

"The guys from work. And I've been here recently with Tammy." He looked over his shoulder and beckoned one of the waiters.

"Tammy? Your new lady?"

Before Frank could tell them that she was actually more than that, they were engaged now - and an announcement to that effect was the principal reason for his arranging the evening - the waiter appeared at his shoulder.

As George was debating whether to have the fillet or the sirloin, Sara was searching through her wardrobe to find something suitably nondescript to wear on her expedition to gate-crash a party. She knew she had a black leather jacket somewhere. She'd stopped wearing it when it developed a rip in one of the side seams. Before she left, she downed what remained in the wine bottle from the night before, disappointed that there wasn't much more than a glass left.

She didn't have a plan, as such, just liked the idea of walking in, introducing herself – *my sister died alone and in agony, anything you'd like to say to me –*. Perhaps she'd explain to them that not being held criminally responsible did not absolve them *one fucking jot* from the moral responsibility they bore for their actions. *Remember I saw her face afterwards. She'd been battered. By you.* An embarrassed silence would descend when she confronted them. The revellers would put down their glasses and some might smile or laugh nervously as they listened to her. The landlord would come over and ask her to leave and she would go, gracefully, thinking of Kim: *the least I can do for you.*

"Why didn't you bring her tonight?" Pete asked his son, having learned of the impending nuptials. He slapped him on the back, manfully.

Frank shrugged, stirring his cocktail.

"I wanted to tell you in private, I suppose."

"That's great, bro, look forward to meeting her. What does she do? Where did you meet her?"

"She's the sister of a colleague. We were introduced at a dinner party. In fact, I'm damn sure we were set up although it was denied. She works in finance too. She's Head of Risk at one of the smaller banks. She's smart and lovely and…"

He stopped, smiling at them both.

"Spit it out, man," guffawed Pete. "She's got one leg. And a beard."

George frowned at this father.

"It's not ok to say things like that anymore, Dad. Assuming it ever was."

Frank was not bothered by his father's remarks.

"She's older than me."

"So?" said Pete.

"She's 44."

"Lord," said Pete. "Have you thought this through?"

Frank had reddened. It was an unusual sight. He rarely lost his composure.

"Of course."

George was doing rapid calculations in his head. There was a twelve-year age gap. When she was 70, Frank would be 58. He was also thinking, *they may never have children.*

As if reading his mind, Frank went on.

"Tammy has never wanted children and she still doesn't. We've had that conversation, don't worry. I'm happy about it. I'm passing the entire burden of producing grandchildren on to you, George, and Sara of course, from here onwards. Sorry, Dad."

Pete started shaking his head in a typical old man style he adopted from time to time.

"You might change your mind, you know."

"And also, we're not intending to have a big wedding. We've decided to get married in a Registry Office with a couple of witnesses and then go off on honeymoon somewhere exotic."

"Sounds sensible," said George. "Anywhere in mind?"

"Tammy has her eye on a Wellness spa in the Himalayan mountains."

"A what spa?" asked Pete.

Sara, in the crowded upstairs of a double decker, realised that she was probably on the wrong bus but decided that provided she alighted somewhere recognizable in Greenford, she'd be able to find her way to the pub without too much difficulty. It was getting on for 9pm. The sky was heavy with dark grey clouds: rain threatened but had yet to fall. She had her earphones in and was listening to a playlist full of melancholic ballads. It drowned out the noise from a group of young people sitting at the back of the bus. Already hammered, their ability to find every comment uproariously amusing met with stony stares from the other passengers around them.

Looking to the left of her, the tower blocks from the Grenadier estate loomed into view and she hastily rang the bell and made her way down the steps. Stepping out of the bus onto the pavement, Sara was suddenly struck by the futility of her mission. She didn't look for the pub. She walked a few hundred yards along the A40 until she came to where Kim used to live. The house appeared unoccupied. The same net curtain, half on its rail, was still hanging in the window *in the room where she died,* she thought. If there was something subconscious in her making a pilgrimage to Kim's last resting place, there was also an element of masochism in it. It made her *hurt,* physically. But there was method in that. It emphasised her appalling loss, reminded her of Kim's suffering and, thus, enabled her to justify whatever act of vengeance she was in the process of formulating.

As she thrust her hands into her pockets, her fingers touched something metallic and cold: a lighter. The last time she wore this jacket she had been a smoker. Taking it out to test it, a flame shot up in the darkness. Briefly, she wondered if she should make her way to the nearby shop and buy some cigarettes: any prop was better than none. But she turned away, looked for a convenient place to cross over the road and walked back towards The Arms.

After an odd discussion about the derivation of the word *wellness,* Pete, George and Frank were now gazing at their steaks, straight from the grill and glistening with succulence in front of them. The side orders were accumulating around the table, large chunky chips and onion rings, salad and sweet potato fries.

"Lord, we'll never get through all this!" exclaimed Pete. He sat back, admiring his boys, his face full of pleasure. "This is wonderful!"

Frank was back to looking for a waiter.

"Where's the bloody wine?" he said. "You know, it's not a lot to ask, is it? We've come in here for a steak meal and some drinks. We're not asking them to remember anything complicated - just the food and the wine. It's pretty standard in a restaurant."

"Chill, Frank," said George, who was musing over his lot in life: preventing those he loved getting things entirely out of proportion.

Within a few seconds of catching Frank's eye, their waiter realised the omission and sped off to seek out the St Emilion which Frank had ordered. He presented the bottle to Frank, muttering his apologies. Frank refused to meet his eye and merely nodded. George smiled at him encouragingly and Pete, unaware, continued to look around him as if he was eating his last meal on earth and needed to saviour each moment.

"Would you like to taste, Sir?"

Frank put down his knife and fork with a sigh. George already knew that his brother would be asking for the service charge to be removed from the bill. Frank gave no quarter once riled.

"No, just pour it - please."

"Of course, Sir."

There was a lot of noise coming from The Arms as Sara approached it. A crowd of smokers had congregated around the door. Clouds of smoke swept into her face as she squeezed past them and into the lounge bar. There was no pretence about the place. It was functional. The clientele preferred cheaper beer to money being wasted on soft furnishings. But it was packed solid. A few men turned around to look at this lone woman as she wended her way through the throng to the bar, trying to look purposeful. It took her a while to be served, the various locals appearing to take precedence with the bar staff over any stranger - especially a female one. Ordering a large glass of white wine, she glimpsed a space at the end of the bar where the, largely redundant, coffee machine was situated. She took her drink and moved over to it, standing with her back to the bar and looking around.

Over to her left, there was a corridor and a sign for the toilets. The number of people Sara observed disappearing into the passageway with drinks, and emerging from it with empty glasses, indicated that something else was going on in a back room or another bar. She downed her drink quickly and, already feeling the effect of one third of a bottle of wine on an empty stomach, headed down the dingy corridor before caution prevented her.

Her first stop was the Ladies. Any female knows that if you want the lowdown on any gathering, what's kicking off, who's making an arse of themselves, head for the powder room. A gaggle of girls were congregated by the sinks, applying mascara and lip gloss, combing hair and swapping information. Sara disappeared into a cubicle and sank down onto the toilet seat.

"She looked dreadful".

"Yeah. Lost a lot of weight inside."

"Hey, Tara, you seen 'em yet?"

"No, I just got here. Had to wait for Mum to come and sit with Bailey."

"Gail's had a fucking awful time. Can't believe they've been banged up for over seven months and then found not guilty."

"How did Gary get on?"

"Home from fucking home for him! He's been inside before. Probably met up with a few of his mates!"

At this point, neglecting to flush the toilet, Sara emerged from her cubicle and four pairs of kohl rimmed eyes looked at her. She washed her hands and then started rummaging in her bag, pretending to search for something. A minute later they all traipsed out in a line and she followed them, stopping dead as they entered a back room. Above the door there was a scruffy, makeshift banner – *Welcome Home, Gail and Gary!* Two red balloons hung either side of it, like a couple of afterthoughts.

Deeper into the room, so far as she could make out without being conspicuous, there were only around twenty people standing about, drinking. For a celebration, it seemed oddly low-key. A middle-aged woman was busily fussing around a side table, setting out plates of food. Sara recognized her as Gail's mother and retreated further into the shadows just as a shout emerged from her.

"Where the fuck are they? Tara, give Gail a fucking call, would you? It's gone half nine."

A male voice shouted back.

"They're still in the bar, Sharon. Talking to Frankie and that lot. I'll go and get them."

This piece of information seemed to motivate those assembled to depart the room for top ups or fag breaks. Sara stood well back as they careered past her like a herd of zebra, spooked by the scent of something nasty. She ventured a little closer to the door.

Having recovered from the trauma of the missing wine, Frank was now in full flow about some crisis at work. Pete and George were showing only scant attention as neither of them could quite work out why some false data in the Futures section was such a big deal. If they requested clarification, they knew they'd risk a tedious lecture so they both nodded politely and used the time to sample all the sides.

"What do you think of this glorious wine?" asked Frank, holding his deep bowled glass up to the light.

"It's just the ticket!" exclaimed Pete, whose face was now so flushed he looked feverish.

"Excellent," commented George, fervently hoping he hadn't misunderstood when Frank had suggested he *book a steak restaurant for the three of them in town*. Christ knows what the wine was costing. Frank drained the last of the bottle and began his now familiar scan of the room for their errant waiter.

"What are you doing?" asked George, leaving the word *now* off the end of his question.

"Surely, we can manage another bottle between us! *Come on*, guys!"

"But the cost, Frank."

"You leave all that to me, bro. No point earning the shekels if you can't spend them."

He picked up the empty wine bottle and started waggling it at head height. It all seemed faintly rude to George who treated everyone in service with gentlemanly respect, even when, as Sara would comment, they did not deserve it. Pete was ruminating along similar lines: how could two brothers have such utterly different value systems?

Another bottle of the excellent St. Emilion arrived within minutes. On this occasion, the waiter merely showed the bottle to Frank, opened it and asked if he wished him to pour. Frank granted him a cursory nod of his head and three large glasses were soon sitting in front of them. George was wondering whether he'd be fit enough to undertake *any* work the following day whilst Pete excused himself, weaving his way, a little unsteadily, across the restaurant in the general direction of the Gents.

"Better go easy on the wine for Dad," said George.

"Don't worry, he's staying the night with me," said Frank. "We'll cab it back. Anyway, we can get a couple of coffees down him and perhaps a pudding before we leave. Look, I haven't brought it up tonight but I have been thinking about Sara. How is she?"

George gave him a flavour of the issues which had determined the outcome of the proceedings.

"So, the trial has been very difficult for her and of course, the outcome. She was exhausted last night but, well, seemed ok."

He thought of her then, back to the night before when they lay together under the lounge window. He recalled her lips searching him out, her dark hair falling over her face under the light of a March moon. Now, she would be curled up on the sofa, catching up on some drama, perhaps in her dressing gown, perhaps finishing off the wine and thinking about an early night.

"I think the worst is over, actually," he said, taking up his glass and gazing thoughtfully into it.

Frank clinked his glass against his brother's.

"Let's hope so."

"What are we drinking to now?" asked Pete, sending the table rocking as he settled back down into his chair. Both his sons snatched up their wine glasses, fearful that some of the precious liquid might get wasted, eliciting a roar of laughter from their father.

"This *is* wonderful!" he repeated.

Frank and George looked at one another and smiled.

Meanwhile, Sara had moved forward to the threshold of the back room and was contemplating whether she had the nerve to enter. Her right hand was in her jacket pocket, clasping the lighter.

CHAPTER 16

Tempest

Martin was at his desk, working on a box which was much bigger than the ones he usually crafted. It was a commission. He'd recently started inviting commissions, not entirely sure if he was prepared for the pressure it might entail. It felt a more serious pursuit of his art than simply creating what he wanted and then seeing if it appealed to anyone. But he'd received the odd email asking him if he would make something to order so he'd decided to *test the market*, as it was termed. He'd received three requests that week already and was now feeling vaguely apprehensive about his ability to fulfil the orders.

The one he was currently working on was to be a wedding present. The client had specified the size and given a vague description of the shape of receptacle they wanted. It was to hold memorabilia from the big day and the interior had to be divided into compartments of varying sizes although Martin could not envisage what might actually be placed within them. He had been sent a colour photograph of the wedding venue: a rather forbidding detached Georgian house situated by a small lake. Martin was to reproduce this scene in oil or acrylic paint on the top of the box, with the bride and groom's names underneath together with the date of the marriage. And that wasn't all. A few lines from a poem were to be inscribed on the inside of the box lid, preferably employing the ancient art of calligraphy. They were from Shakespeare's sonnet 116, often quoted at weddings, the one about impediments and minds not altering and *love being an ever-fixed mark.* Its overwhelming popularity was lost on Martin. He was not sure he completely understood it. He got the gist but felt the message could have been delivered with more clarity.

He was now having to undertake a crash course in calligraphy, perfecting the up and down strokes, the paunch and the serif. It was a difficult, if fascinating, skill to acquire so he hoped that his perseverance would be rewarded in the new opportunities it opened to him.

The thought of creating a unique gift which would be cherished by the recipients for the rest of their married lives gave him a lot of satisfaction, which was just as well as it would, fittingly, amount to a labour of love. He had miscalculated on the cost of the materials – the pen, the nibs and the ink had been left out of his calculations entirely- and his labour worked out to less than a couple of quid an hour. He promised himself he'd try to be a bit more savvy in the future and at least look at making a profit.

The previous evening he'd gone out for the usual run along the M4 with his biking gang. After being cooped up in the bowels of the Old Bailey for a few days, it was the release he'd craved but that night, Saturday, he'd vowed to stay put and do some serious work. He'd been listening to a phone in on *the battle between the generations* but, irritated by the endless whinging, he'd eventually re-tuned to Classic FM. He knew he was expected to reproduce the photograph accurately but it was such a gloomy looking building, he was tempted to add some embellishments – perhaps a little copse to one side, a spatter of pink on the branches to give an illusion of blossom and life?

At 9.45 he put down his brushes and went over to fill the kettle and make some coffee. He intended to work through the night if necessary to get the box finished, although he wouldn't be able to apply the varnish until the paint was thoroughly dry.

But fate had other plans for Martin Mactaggart.

Before he could take a sip of his thick black coffee, his phone started buzzing. It was Sara.

"Hi…" he started to say.

"I need you to come and get me." Sara was out of breath.

"What?"

"Please, Marty, I need you now. I need to get away fast and I…"

"Where are you?"

"Greenford. Not far from Kim's."

"Why? What have you done, Sara? What's the matter?"

Martin sighed and went to sit on his bed, the coffee abandoned.

"I can't tell you. I just need you to come and get me. *Please* Marty."

"Where's George? Does he know where you are?"

"No."

"Where exactly are you?"

There was a silence.

"Sara! Where *exactly* are you?" he repeated.

"At the back of Kim's old place."

"Ok. I'll be there as soon as I can. Keep your phone handy in case I can't find you."

Martin rang off, grabbed his bike keys, jacket and two helmets and careered down the stairs, almost bumping into Mrs Twist who was by the foot of the stairs.

"Off out, love? It's awful out there. Be careful!"

"I will!" called Martin over his shoulder as he banged the front door shut. Mrs Twist was right. The rain was coming down in sheets and there was a gale force wind blowing, buffeting him as he wheeled his bike out from Mrs Twist's garage. Before he could even click the straps of his helmet into place, his curly mop of hair was plastered to his face by the force of the rain, almost obscuring his vision. Only a fool would take to the streets on a bike in weather like this, he thought, but she had given him no choice - just presumed, as ever, on his allegiance. He could not imagine what Sara's crisis was but the fact that she was in the vicinity of Kim's old flat – and alone - made him apprehensive.

The rain had come down so fast and so fiercely that the drains were unable to cope, water overflowing and spilling out onto the pavements and roads, creating deep, hidden, treacherous puddles. Martin wound his way at such speed as he could manage between the cars and buses, which had slowed to a crawl to accommodate the conditions. Eventually, he made it to the A40 and speeded up for the last stretch, turning left in to the nearest side road to Kim's. He saw her immediately, standing under a streetlight, her collar up against the rain. He slowed, then stopped. Keeping the engine running, he handed her a helmet.

"What is this about, Sara?" he shouted at her, aware that his voice was likely to be carried away by the wind which was gusting round them as if they were climbing at high altitude.

"Just get me out of here," she said. "Let's go."

He didn't challenge her. She climbed on and he did a quick u turn in the street, heading back on to the main road. Ahead of him, outside a pub, he could see that a crowd had congregated. It was evident they hadn't chosen to endure the tempest. They'd been evicted for some reason. That reason became clear as a fire engine, lights flashing, siren sounding, appeared behind him in his mirror. He pulled in a few yards from the pub, allowing it to pass. Immediately, he felt Sara pummelling him on his back. Before he could turn around, she bellowed in his ear.

"For God's sake, *go*. We need to go."

The pub's name had seemed familiar to him although he knew for a fact he had never been there. Then he remembered. He recalled Sara telling him that a couple of the witnesses at the trial had made reference to seeing an inebriated Kim in there, which made sense: it was Kim's local. No doubt it was Flood and Timms' local too. It flashed into his head that Sara's palpable anxiety to be gone from the scene they now surveyed suggested that she was, in some way, connected to it. He tried to dismiss any such notion. Even Sara, in all her madness and fury, would not suddenly have resorted to arson, he told himself.

He checked his mirror and moved off. As his speed increased, so did his discomfort. If she was involved in any way, then, now, so was he. And if he were then this was the consequence of his unfaltering obedience. Because that's what it is, he decided: obedience under the guise of loyalty.

Since he hadn't chosen to venture out that evening, the ensuing accident could be laid at Sara's door. But, in the aftermath, Martin never made this accusation, possibly because whatever the reason for his being on a flooded side street in Ealing at 10 45 on a Saturday evening, it was *he* who was in control of the bike and it was *he* who should have taken the corner with more care. A police siren had unnerved him. He didn't really believe they were chasing him, but he swerved off left down the side street just to make sure and hit one of those hidden puddles on the bend. They both came off. He tried to control the skid and the bike landed on his lower leg. Sara was bruised but fine: the leather jacket protecting her. Someone saw the accident from a neighbouring house and called an ambulance. Martin was carted off to hospital and admitted. An X-ray showed that his left tibia had been fractured. Sara stayed by his side until, about 6am in the morning, a bed on the men's ward became available. Martin was in a great deal of pain for which some morphine was prescribed. A junior doctor told him he'd need to await the consultant before any final decision could be made but the fracture appeared uncomplicated and it was likely that no surgery would be necessary, just a splint to hold the bone in place whilst it healed. But it would be a few weeks before he was able to resume his normal activities – like riding his bike.

Martin had been in too much shock and pain to say much to Sara before they got onto the ward. Later, following the words they exchanged, he would look back and be grateful that he *did* enquire after her welfare. He asked her if she was hurt when they were together in the ambulance. She just shook her head although he could see her hands were badly grazed and her jacket ripped along one shoulder. It mattered to him, on some moral plane, that he had kept true to himself throughout the whole sorry affair; that he'd behaved in a civilised manner.

At one point, she tried to hold his hand but the paramedic in charge wanted to monitor him, so she sat back to allow her access. This was probably fortuitous. Martin's fury with himself was increasing with every moment and he had no intention of letting Sara touch him. Whether she recognized his resentment at the time, read the portents of what was coming, is doubtful.

Once he was on the ward, Sara placed his jacket in the locker beside the bed and said she would return at visiting hour with a charger for his phone and whatever else he might want her to bring him. In the meantime, did he want her to get in touch with the neighbour who had said he'd look after his bike and given Sara his contact number?

"No," said Martin, propped up on the bed, pale faced, his swollen leg exposed ready for inspection. "I want you to go."

Sara looked at him quizzically, unable to understand what he meant.

"What d'you mean?"

"Just go and please, don't come back."

Tears started to Sara's eyes as she moved towards him.

"Please, just go. I don't want you here. Just let Mum know. That's all I ask."

"Martin, please, you *know* I'm sorry. Sorry about it all."

Martin looked away.

"It isn't enough, Sara. I don't know what you did last night but…"

Before he could finish, she interrupted.

"I was going to explain. Of course, I was. I didn't get the chance. I'm sorry about it."

"I don't want to know," he said, his voice choked with emotion. "You dragged me in without any thought as to what it might mean for me. Like you always have. You make me ashamed of myself. Well, it's at an end. You can go your own sweet way without me. I want no part in the vengeful, bitter world you've created since Kim died. You're not honouring her, if that's what you think. You've just got sucked into some warped idea of victimhood."

"I know," said Sara, softly, hoping that if she stayed, if she *listened*, Martin would relent. She wondered if she should just let the tears fall to prove how ashamed she was. "Please, Martin."

"You use me. You always have. Just go."

"Please, Martin, let me come back later."

"No. I don't want you to. I want you to leave me alone. Please."

He turned his head away again and she left the ward.

Martin closed his eyes, oblivious to the sad, broken figure he portrayed.

CHAPTER 17

Consequences

Tabitha had the good sense not to enquire what had occurred between Sara and Martin. When she turned up at the hospital at visiting time that Sunday afternoon, Martin gave her only a brief account of the circumstances surrounding the accident. Naturally, she asked what Sara was doing in Greenford on her own on a Saturday evening, but the vagueness of his reply suggested that he didn't wish to impart any further detail. Happy anyway that her son had called on her in his hour of need, Tabitha knew she might get the complete story in the fullness of time - if he felt it necessary.

Marjorie Twist had been worried when Martin did not return home that evening. Martin always told her if he was staying elsewhere so that she could lock the back door and put the chain on the front. He had never let her down previously so, after she couldn't reach him on his mobile, she'd called Tabitha around 11 am on the Sunday and been informed of the calamity. She recalled her words to him as he'd left the house on the night of the storm. She recalled too that Martin was carrying two helmets and had guessed he had been summoned - *probably by that attractive cousin of his who seems so reliant on him*. Mrs Twist didn't wait to be invited to visit him. She just turned up at his bedside half an hour after Tabitha arrived. She had a tupperware box of homemade flapjacks with her. Her eyes sparkled with tears at the sight of her precious lodger and confidante laid up with a broken leg. Like Tabitha, she knew exactly what it would mean to him to be unable to ride his beloved motor bike whilst the fracture healed.

"Oh, you poor darling," she cooed, engulfing him, so far as she could, in a bosomy embrace. Tabitha was amused, trying to catch Martin's eye and winking at him. Martin was used to Mrs Twist's demonstrative shows of affection and didn't recoil. His eyes lit up at the sight of the flapjacks.

"The day looks so much brighter now, Marjorie, thank you."

Marjorie looked at his mother, momentarily beaming at the compliment and then assumed a grave expression.

"Your wonderful son was on a mission of mercy, Tabitha. He would never have gone out in such conditions. That's one thing I know for definite. I trust the person he was rescuing realises the trouble they've caused."

Her many chins wobbled as she shook her head signifying her disapproval. Had Sara been there, Marjorie Twist would have tackled her.

Martin didn't need his mother to deal with his landlady.

"It's ok, Marjorie," he said, patting her hand. "It's ok."

Marjorie's eyes filled with tears again and she dabbed at them with an embroidered handkerchief.

Tabitha explained that Martin would return to stay with her for the foreseeable future and that she'd come over and get some clothes and his craft materials the following morning. Marjorie looked a little disappointed at not being entrusted to care for him but nodded and said she understood. They arranged a time and then left Martin to have his tea and flapjacks. A couple of the young nurses had taken a shine to him and almost rushed over when the two middle aged women left, teasing him about the flapjacks and telling him he should just call if his backrest required adjustment or he needed help to go to the toilet.

He was trying to adapt to the idea of being housebound for some weeks. His mother had already contacted the kindly Samaritan who'd taken his bike into his driveway. It was scratched but not badly damaged, so far as the man could ascertain. He even said he'd wheel it over to Martin's if she liked as it was less than a mile away. At least, Martin decided, he'd still be able to work on his boxes and getting through his backlog of orders would no longer be a problem.

There appeared to have been no consequences from the fire. No-one had been hurt. Sara had checked on the internet where she'd found a brief local report. The fire brigade had been called as a precaution. When she'd entered the back room, hesitantly, she had been surprised to see that no one was in there. She'd torn down the banner, leaping up like a teenage vandal, throwing it on top of the buffet and then setting fire to it with her lighter. She'd also destroyed the cake, by turning it upside down and squashing it, hard, the sponge and filling oozing out of its frilly bottom onto the tablecloth. She thumped it a couple of times to ensure that there would be no question as to its edibility. For good measure, she'd also set alight some of the paper doilies on which the sausage rolls and sandwiches lay. When she left, smoke was beginning to fill the room. It had taken only around 45 seconds. Her heart pounding against her ribs, she'd made her escape through a nearby fire exit which meant she could avoid going back through the lounge bar. Fearful that the sassy girls she'd encountered in the Ladies might connect her with the destruction, she'd run off in the direction of Kim's, and then called Martin.

On their way back through the rain-splashed byways of West London, the wind battering at her even though she was sheltered by Martin from the worst of it, she felt some elation. Flood, Timms et al would receive the clear message that not everyone saw the outcome of the trial as just. There were people around whom they should be wary of. If it made them just that little bit more cautious when they walked the streets, then the gesture had been worth it.

The re-evaluation came about when the accident occurred, when she saw Martin's body momentarily crushed by his motorbike and feared he might be seriously injured. As she picked herself up from the pavement where she had landed, stumbling over to him, wiping the rain from her eyes, whatever demons had possessed her earlier that evening retreated. They were sent, skulking, into the shadows. She sobbed when she saw that he was conscious. He could move everything, he said, apart from his lower leg which was twisted. The ambulance arrived ten minutes later. Watching him being rolled onto the stretcher, Sara began to calculate the cost of her selfish little venture even if, at that point, she had no real idea just how costly it would be.

Even before Martin's harsh words at the hospital, she'd decided that she would come clean to him about what she'd done and acknowledge her rank stupidity. She knew he would condemn her actions outright. She had not contemplated the extent of his condemnation – nor had she imagined losing him altogether.

Sara had kept in touch with George throughout the night at the hospital, glossing over the full facts at that stage. He'd said he'd come over in the car to collect her from the hospital until he remembered that he was probably still under the influence of the St. Emilion. She'd taken a bus back to the flat. Whilst she was exhausted by the lack of sleep, it was overridden by the bludgeoning which Martin's words had amounted to. When, eventually, she went to lie down, after George had fussed over her, making her toast and tea and inspecting anxiously her cuts and bruises, she couldn't relax. Each time she drifted into sleep, she would hear Martin's words echoing in her head.

You use me. You always have.

George knew there was something she wasn't telling him. When he asked her if she wanted to visit Martin later that afternoon – *maybe for just ten minutes at the end of visiting time* – she said no, *it's not a good idea*, he wondered if perhaps Martin blamed her for the accident. It didn't sound like Martin.

"Did you and Martin have words or something?" he asked, suddenly. They were sitting at the kitchen table, a take away pizza in front of them. It was the first thing George had eaten all day. Sara had taken a few bites out of her slice and then abandoned it.

She nodded. She knew then she would have to tell him, if only because Martin might do so himself at some point - when he came around, that is, once he was out of hospital, no longer under the spell of the morphine, able to think more clearly, when he'd forgiven her. *If* he forgave her.

Sara recounted the events of the previous evening whilst George listened, unable to prevent a look of appalled astonishment settling over his features.

"My God, Sara, you've been lucky. The fire could have been serious, people hurt. If you'd been caught, you'd have been done for arson. You still might. It's a crime, a terrible one. What the fuck were you thinking of? I know you're angry that they got away with it but how does it help anyone, least of all you. Where's all this coming from? Wherever it is, you need to get some control."

George got up and went to the sink, running himself a glass of water. When he came back to the table and sat down, he looked unwell. He wondered whether she'd already planned it when he'd said goodbye to her before meeting up with Frank and his father – whether she'd been glad to get rid of him. Martin was justified in his response. She had assumed consent to his being an accessory to her crime.

"Are you going to turn against me, now?" she said in a small voice.

"Don't be ridiculous. It's just, well, an unbelievably stupid thing to do. I'm finding it hard to get my head round it. No doubt Martin feels the same."

There was a silence.

"Perhaps you need professional help," said George, after he'd downed his water.

Sara nodded. Perhaps he was right.

"I know. And I'm ashamed."

She put her head down on her arms. George, unable to bear her misery, squeezed her arm. She pushed him away.

"Don't," she said. "I don't deserve it. Martin's right. You're right."

"Yes," agreed George, "we are. But, listen, you regret it now. You've been an idiot. Seized of a temporary madness! I'm sure Martin will forgive you. Come on, give him a few days. It'll be ok. Probably."

She looked up, like a child believing the words of an adult when all her instincts told her otherwise.

"Do you really think so?"

"Yes. He's a decent guy. One of the best. Just give him time. He'll get over it. But, Christ, Sara, promise me…promise me I can trust you." He didn't wait for her answer. He swallowed down any further words and left the table.

The next time she saw him, he had his coat on and said he was going for a walk. She didn't ask if she could accompany him. She watched him as he made for the door, his familiar walk and scruffy jacket pulling painfully at her heart. In a manner which George himself was utterly incapable of, she'd let him down: sullied their relationship.

Whatever was hers over those next few hours, vengeance was not.

~ ~ ~

George came back from his walk and went over to where Sara was lying on the sofa. He sensed the sadness, like an invisible blanket, lying over her. He bent down and kissed her on the cheek.

Opening her eyes, she looked up at him. A solitary tear ran down her face.

"I love you, George," she whispered.

"I love you too," he said. "Now budge up. Let me sit down. What are we watching?"

In the morning, despite everything, Sara got up and went in to work. The night before she'd felt so exhausted, she'd considered calling in sick but when she saw George heave himself out of bed at 6.45, she got up with him and they enjoyed a rare breakfast together. On arriving in the office, the first thing she did was to speak to Patsy, telling her about the trial and then apologising for *the stranger I've become over the last few months.*

Patsy was forgiving.

"It's ok, Sara. I can't imagine what you've been through since Kim died. It must have been hell. I just wish you'd allowed me to give you a bit more support. You seemed so….. so unreachable."

"I made myself that way," said Sara. "Building that wall of hate and bitterness around myself. I didn't want to be reached. I just wanted to wallow in it and punish anyone who wouldn't wallow in there with me."

"We've all been a bit worried about you, you know, where the old Sara had gone. But I don't suppose you would be the same after what had happened to you. It's a stupid thing to expect, isn't it?"

They arranged, events permitting, to go out for lunch together on one day during the week and, thus, harmony was restored between them.

Sara managed to get through the week without calling Martin. She checked her mobile numerous times a day, hoping for a message, a commutation of the sentence he had imposed upon her. Nothing came.

She rang her mother on the Thursday evening. First, she felt obliged to tell her about the recent accident, reassuring her that Martin was going to be fine. She didn't mention their estrangement. Instead she moved on to the trial which they spoke about briefly, if meaningfully, it being evident that to dwell on its outcome would serve no one's interests. Sara said she hoped to come down to see her mother in the Spring, when they could spend some proper time together *now that it's all over*. They chatted for the first time about things other than their shared loss, things other than Kim. Apart from Sara's promise to visit, they didn't quite stray into the future but it was glimpsed - like an island, once appearing impossibly distant, now emerging slowly into the sunlight after being obscured by layers of cloud.

With the weekend upon them, George encouraged her to call Martin to see if he wanted any visitors. Her call went straight to voicemail. The joy she felt at the sound of Martin's familiar message – *don't panic caller! I'll get right back to you* – was only momentary. It disappeared a few minutes after she'd left her message.

It's me, Martin. I just wondered how you are. Please call me. Please. –

But the weekend passed and her call was not returned.

"I'm going over there," she announced to George, one sunny morning in April. George didn't need to ask where *there* was.

"Are you sure, Sara? He'd call if he wanted to see you, wouldn't he?"

"We're at an impasse," she replied. "One of us needs to breach it, or whatever you do with an impasse."

George looked uncertain but said nothing further, just watched her from the lounge window. He felt pity for her at that moment – pity mixed with love. His instinct was to run after her, bundle her up tightly, protect her from any further pain. Instead, he went back to the sofa and turned on Five Live.

She walked over to Mrs Twist's, the sunshine inducing some optimism in her, even though there was no rationality to the feeling. Nothing had changed. She'd hoped Tabitha might call her and suggest she visit Martin. She imagined her telling her he was lonely and needed some company - *a break from those wondrous boxes of his*. But she heard nothing from Tabitha either. It had been three weeks since the accident. He'd still be in the splint so was unlikely to be back at work at the garden centre.

After some delay, Mrs Twist answered the doorbell.

"He's not here, dear. He's still at this mother's. You know, after the accident on his bike."

"Yes, I know about that."

Mrs Twist gave her a look which said *I bet you do*. She'd established, through asking Tabitha directly as they were leaving hospital that first morning, that Sara was indeed his pillion rider on the night of the storm.

"Do you know when he might be coming back?" she asked.

"No, dear. I suggest you contact him."

With that last remark, Mrs Twist made to close the door, leaving Sara in little doubt of her disapproval.

She made her way disconsolately back to the flat, stopping off at Boots to buy a pregnancy test kit. Her period was late. She'd never missed one before and it was George who suggested it as a possibility for her overwhelming tiredness. She'd managed to ignore the significance of the missed period during the last few days but it wasn't fair to George to keep putting it off. They had pinned it down to their lovemaking on the floor in the moonlight. George was excited. She was not. She hoped the test would be negative.

But it wasn't. It was as clear as could be. She was going to have a child.

George danced around the room, waving the stick and shouting out possible names. *Bert! Gertrude! Maureen!* He'd been wandering about the flat in a tee shirt and his underpants, revelling in not having to go anywhere because it was a Saturday.

Sara sat, mute, on the sofa.

"What's the matter?" he asked. "Oh, sorry, I forgot to ask. Did you see Martin?"

He'd have thought the joyful news about their being prospective parents might have eclipsed whatever disappointment she'd experienced. Ok, so they hadn't exactly planned it: they'd not exactly *not* planned it either. They were often careless. They knew they'd be living in rented property for a few more years. They'd never seen it as an impediment to their plans.

"He's living with his mother at the moment. Presumably whilst he's recuperating. She didn't say when he'd be back. I doubt she'd have said anyway. She was pretty abrupt with me."

"What?" said George. "Why would she be like that with you?"

"She blames me for his accident. As does Tabitha, probably. And, you know, I think they have a point. If it wasn't for me, it would never have happened. I can't dispute it - even if I wanted to."

"But, *this*, Sara. Us. Please tell me you're pleased about it."

He beamed at her, his black hair sticking out at odd angles as he hadn't yet taken a shower. He was still clutching the stick. Someone on Five Live was becoming over excited about a local derby somewhere.

She looked away from him.

"I'm not sure, George. I can't lie."

"But we've talked so often about having children, maybe moving out of London. Living a different life. All that romantic stuff. Come on, be excited about it!"

"I..." she stuttered, "I feel crap about myself at this precise moment. I try not to look back but I can't stop myself. I think about Kim and what I could have done to support her. I'm a social worker for God's sake. What's the point of helping others when I couldn't save my own sister? What's that about? Why do people like me do that?"

George stopped fooling about and threw the stick down on the coffee table. He went into the kitchen and switched off the radio. Sitting down next to her, a heartfelt sigh escaped from him. Occasionally, he'd imagined this day, all it would represent, binding them together in the most significant event of their shared lives.

"People like you?"

"You know, thinking I'm doing a socially worthwhile job and, yet, sidestepping the really difficult part of my own life – like actually caring for my own sister, who needed me. More than anyone else."

"You're over simplifying the whole thing. You did try with Kim. You did everything reasonably possible."

Sara shook her head.

"No. I didn't. I could have done more. I gave up on her."

George took her by the shoulders and shook her.

"Stop it! That's rubbish. It's not a matter of saving people, Sara. They need to want to *be* saved before you can do anything for them. Otherwise you're just encouraging them not to take responsibility for their own happiness."

"I didn't do enough. You know, on that night, the night of the attack, she could have been over here with us. Instead, she was wandering around on her own. But I didn't see her that much, did I? I always found something else to take priority, rather than spend time with her. It became a duty and she knew it. That's what I'm talking about. Love turning into a duty. And the consequences of it."

She thought about Martin then. This was a conversation more likely to have been had with him. Not any longer.

"There's a gap between who we are and who we say we are. I think I always knew that: I just didn't know how big it was."

"Sara…"

"And now I've lost Martin too. I despise myself."

George tried to tell himself that this emotional outpouring was connected to the hormones coursing through her body, the ones sustaining their offspring. But he wasn't sure. Kim had only been dead a matter of months. This was grief and guilt and exhaustion, borne of events which any person might buckle under. And now she was pregnant. And missing Martin whom she loved.

He didn't say anything else, just put his arms around her and hugged her whilst she cried.

Outside, an April sun shone with surprising fierceness.

CHAPTER 18

Gift

Sara didn't give up hoping that, at some point, Martin might forgive her but as the weeks went on, she managed to stop obsessing about it. She adapted. She became more cheerful about being pregnant particularly when she saw how overjoyed her parents were at the prospect of becoming grandparents. In the light of their loss, she could see it was, possibly, the greatest gift she could have given them.

When Sara agreed that her mother could start informing people of the forthcoming event, Tabitha had been the first on the phone, congratulating her and saying what wonderful parents she thought she and George would make. After the niceties had been exchanged, Sara asked the question which Tabitha had been expecting.

"How's Martin?"

Tabitha assumed a breezy tone.

"Oh, he's fine. He's back on his bike and none the worse for the accident. He's back at the garden centre too. Oh, and his boxes are going great guns. He takes commissions now and he's been *so* successful. I'd say he could possibly go full time with them but he loves the garden work too much. Being outdoors is good for him, he says - the perfect combination!"

"Good. I'm glad he's happy," Sara said. She was – sort of.

"Is he back living at Mrs Twist's?"

"Oh yes, a week or so ago. Although he's thinking of moving out. Renting a one bed over by the river in Brentford, I think. But I get the impression he can't bring himself to tell Marjorie. She'll be heartbroken!"

That sounded just like Martin. She could imagine him, sitting down with Mrs Twist at the little stone table at the back of her garden, clutching their mugs of tea. He would broach the subject sensitively, assuring her he'd visit regularly and still help her with the garden. He'd make a joke of it, then, saying he *had to grow up sometime* and become *a bit more independent*. And her eyes would mist up *I'll miss you, dear.* His smile, as he patted her arm, would show off his perfectly white straight teeth.

In June, Frank invited Sara and George to dinner in town so that they could meet his fiancé, Tammy. Kensington Town Hall had been booked for a date in September and they were then going off for an extended honeymoon to the Atlas Mountains in Morocco. The Wellness spa in the Himalayas had been ditched: something to do with the type of yoga it had to offer. Tammy had very specific ideas about yoga, apparently.

Fortunately, the nausea Sara had experienced was waning so they were able to accept the invitation. They had both rolled their eyes when they'd googled the restaurant which Frank had booked for the Friday night. It was a Michelin starred place in Mayfair with the most expensive wine list they had ever seen. The eye rolling had turned to gasps of amazement as they perused it.

"Oh my God," breathed Sara. "Look at that! A Chablis Grand Cru for £250. How can that ever be justified when you're walking past homeless people on the streets of London."

George was peering over her shoulder.

"Wow. A bottle of the best Bollinger – whatever *best* means – for £2000. That's just ridiculous. The meal's going to cost the same as a week's holiday in the Bahamas."

"Oh well, they'll save money on me. I expect the sparkling water's not cheap. I wonder if I dare to ask for tap? What do you think? Shall we have a bet?"

"Oh Christ, promise me you'll keep your mouth shut about politics. At least if you're not drinking you'll be better able to exercise some self-control."

"Frank's used to me."

"Yes, but Tammy isn't."

Anxious not to be late, they arrived early at the restaurant. George had his school brogues on and had taken an old jacket with him, just in case it was obligatory to wear one. Sara was wearing her court trouser suit, only just able to do up the waist band on the trousers. She'd grown at least two chest sizes so had bought a new blouse, a shocking pink one with a high neck and sheer sleeves. She'd pinned up her hair too and slapped on some makeup. George had kept staring at her on the tube over to Green Park.

"What is it?" she asked, eventually.

"You look stunning," he said. "I would hardly recognize you!"

"Well, thanks a bunch. Talk about a back handed compliment."

"We're going to Mayfair," he said to her in a stupidly posh accent. "Fancy that."

She laughed.

"What do you think of when you hear the word Mayfair?" he asked.

"Wealth. Not that I know the area."

"I think of Monopoly," he said. "I'll mention that to Frank. He was always furious if I got to buy Mayfair before he did – not that I could ever afford to put hotels on it."

The approach to the restaurant was along a decked walkway lined with exotic ferns and palms. A giant bronze human head, bald with a zen like presence, emitted a soft light over the garden whilst little fountains of sparkling water appeared from time to time: a metaphoric cleansing of the soul after the grime and stress of the city. Sara and George stood awkwardly at the reception desk, George providing Frank's name and looking around anxiously for him. Their hosts had not arrived and they were invited to sit at the bar whilst they waited for them.

Tammy and Frank turned up a few minutes later, much to George's relief. He had been far too anxious about the prices to order any drinks. Tammy was nothing like George had imagined. He'd expected her to be dauntingly sophisticated. Whilst Sara looked as if she belonged in the place, Tammy didn't, he thought - somewhat uncharitably. Slim with her blonde hair in a pony tail, Tammy's features were quite sharp. She was dressed rather drably in a beige suit. The voluminous orange scarf draped around her neck was unnecessary on such a sultry evening and highlighted her pasty complexion. But she was pleasant enough. He just couldn't quite see why Frank was with her. Frank, a good-looking guy, with amazing prospects – if that's what turned you on – could have his pick of women, surely?

Sara, having decided against taking up her own challenge of asking for tap water, was drinking sparkling water whilst the three others were enjoying a white burgundy with their starters before moving on to one of Frank's favourite reds. There was talk of Sara's pregnancy and when she would be going on maternity leave and whether they intended to remain in their *rented* accommodation. Tammy didn't appear to have been appraised of their situation. She voiced some concern at the thought of the two of them, plus baby, living such *a tenuous existence* at the mercy of a landlord. Looking back on the manner in which the conversation developed from there on in, George could see that his brother had realised they were heading off shore, towards the open sea where danger lay.

Frank threw in a non-sequitur saying how wonderful Sara looked.

"I think the description of *tenuous* is a little exaggerated," said Sara.

"My souflee is a tad over cooked," Frank said, the banality of his comment indicating how desperate he was to avoid the clash of ideologies appearing on the horizon.

Tammy looked over at Frank's starter, almost blanching in disgust. Her nose wrinkled up and she started to wave her hand at a passing waitress.

"Over here, over here, please!"

The waitress, carrying two bowls of steaming mussels to another table said she would be there in a moment.

Tammy's hysterical response to the fact that her betrothed was not eating something absolutely perfect was such to induce a fit of giggling in Sara. George commented afterwards that she did not even try to hide it.

"It's only a souflle, Tammy," she spluttered. "He's unlikely to be traumatised by the experience."

Frank nodded vigorously.

"I'm fine, darling."

But it was too late. The waitress had now scuttled over and was being instructed to bring a replacement dish *properly cooked*.

"Why should you accept sub-standard food?" Tammy lectured poor Frank, who'd eaten most of the original souflee and had no wish for another. And then she turned back to Sara, who was trying to avoid George's *shut the fuck up* glare by pouring more water into her already filled glass.

"About living in rented accommodation, I just meant it must be unsettling to not know when you might be moved on."

"We're not living in a refugee settlement. We're entitled to notice. Anyway, a baby doesn't care where they're living provided they're loved and cared for."

Tammy smiled.

"Oh well, hopefully you'll be able to afford somewhere to buy in the future."

It wasn't a condescending smile really: it was just that Sara decided to interpret it that way.

"We're public sector workers. We've seen a decrease in our wages year on year over the last decade since our 1% pay increases have not kept pace with inflation. We're being made to pay, along with most of the working class in this country, for the lack of regulation in the banking sector which brought about the financial crisis in 2008. We probably don't have a hope in hell of buying anywhere. Ever."

Frank flinched at the words *banking sector*.

Tammy looked embarrassed.

"Yes, I know. It's awful. And you do such valuable jobs too."

"Valuable jobs which aren't valued, hey?"

"I think we should all focus on what unites us rather than what divides us," intoned Tammy.

"Right. And what does that mean when you have to go to a food bank to feed your kids?" asked Sara.

"No-one mentioned food banks, Sara," George said, determined to shut down the line of conversation before it became toxic. *I bet they don't in here*, thought Sara.

But Sara and Tammy hadn't quite finished with each other yet.

"What motivated you to be a social worker?" Tammy asked.

"I'm interested in people – and finding solutions. It's not all altruistic. There's some satisfaction in helping others achieve something they may not have done without my help."

"It must be challenging – dealing with those who've had diffcrent experiences and lives to your own."

It was a reasonable comment but made at that moment, in a place of such exclusivity and glamour, she was not inclined to deem it such.

"I don't see myself as particularly different. I've just had better luck in life. I'm where I am as a matter of fortune, in the main. We all are."

"You don't think we make our own luck, then?"

"We have choices but those are based on our opportunities, aren't they? The fewer the opportunities, the fewer the choices."

"But that's so depressing! To have so little control over our lives!"

Tammy took another sip of her wine and then dabbed at her lips with her napkin before continuing.

"Anyway, surely, we want to motivate people to make the best of themselves, whatever their background, rather than provide them with excuses to remain dependent and poor."

"I haven't said otherwise," snapped Sara. "But do tell me, what control to you think children born into poverty have over their lives?"

George winced and shot Sara another of his glares. Sara shot one back – *she asked the question, she started it.*

From the corner of her eye, Sara caught a glimpse of Frank. He looked miserable. Not only was he now so stuffed with souflee that he would struggle to eat his lobster, the evening was disintegrating in front of him. Any plans he had that they would make a happy foursome in the years ahead, were pure fantasy.

"I'm sorry," said Sara. "I didn't mean to… you know, get all heated."

Frank perked up immediately, taking large gulps of wine. Tammy looked sceptical but said nothing. George merely sighed.

The rest of the evening was relatively uneventful. All possible contentious subjects were studiously avoided. Tammy was a fan of opera and there was an awkward moment when she asked George and Sara if they'd ever been to the Royal Opera House. George jumped in to say, no, they hadn't, but he realised he was probably *missing out* and would like to do so at some point in the future. Tammy said she would make sure she got four tickets next time and they would be her guests. George smiled and said he would look forward to it and what would she recommend to *newbies in the world of opera*?

Sara was scathing on the tube back to Ealing.

"Newbies in the world of opera! Where did that come from?"

George laughed.

"I was trying to make up for your condemnation of anyone who doesn't see the world exactly as you see it."

"The whole place reeked of privilege."

"Well, you – we – shouldn't have accepted the invitation, then. Frank wanted to treat us."

"I didn't realise it would be so up itself."

"Funnily enough I think they both got that message. I doubt we'll be invited again."

"Are you mad at me?" she asked, smiling flirtatiously at him.

"Desperately!" he said.

George had a talent: an unusual one. He didn't seek out the worst in people and complain. He took pleasure in getting the best out of people. Perhaps that attribute is the hallmark of all effective teachers. And whilst Sara could be a liability, with her forthright opinions and impulsive nature, she was, simultaneously – to George - beautiful, beguiling and good company – most days. He was just never sure when the less attractive parts of her character might surface.

~ ~ ~

It was Martin's birthday at the beginning of July. Sara could not remember a year when they had not been together to celebrate it. To add to its looming significance, Kim's birthday fell on the day *after* Martin's. The year before, she, Martin and George had gone round to her flat to surprise her, carrying cake and balloons. They'd had an unnecessary discussion on the way there as to whether they should also bring booze; unnecessary because whether they brought it or not, she would drink anyway. A birthday was *hardly the occasion on which to tackle the issue of Kim's relationship with alcohol*, Martin said. The problem was that, unlike meeting in a pub or restaurant, there was no natural cut off to the evening. They knew that when they left, she would carry on drinking until she fell asleep – or passed out. But it had been a good evening. They'd played a couple of board games. One had involved guessing the moral choices made by the other players in difficult situations. Inevitably, this had led to much, largely good natured, disagreement between them. Kim had taken George to task over his decision not to inform a close friend of his partner's infidelity, dragging Martin into the argument by asking whether he would inform George if he knew Sara was cheating on him. When he said *probably not*, she had reversed the question and Martin's hesitation in answering, his transparent devotion to Sara, had made them all laugh. Sara had scrambled up from the floor where she was sprawled and gone over to Martin, kissing him on the cheek and pulling at his goatee beard. *My darling cuz* she whispered in his ear.

That Saturday, Martin's birthday, she had awoken early, remembering last year's party, remembering Kim's expression of triumph at Martin's hesitation, remembering Martin. Yes, she'd kissed him by way of thanks but she'd never doubted his answer. None of them had.

She'd not only that day to endure. Her agony of loss would be doubled as the weekend progressed. George knew the significance of the date. The most he'd achieve was to organise a day of distraction. Nothing would, or could, make up for Martin's absence. He'd considered calling him, imagining his voice, thick with emotion, begging Martin to call her. *Please, mate. She misses you.* But his instinct was against it. This was between the two of them. He knew too that the Sunday, Kim's birthday, would present an even greater challenge.

He insisted they spent Saturday out, wandering around Green Park and then on to the cinema, ending the evening with a Thai takeaway back at the flat. As their evening drew to a close, he watched Sara pushing her noodles from one side of her plate to the other. She sensed him looking at her and smiled.

"Thanks for today. Thanks for putting up with me being in the doldrums."

He smiled back, taking hold of the moment by the scruff of its neck.

"I was just wondering about tomorrow. If there's anything you'd like to do – anywhere you'd like to go. You know, to remember her."

Sara looked down at her plate, at the annoyingly present noodles, to hide the tears which ambushed her along with George's thoughtful words.

"I can't think of anything. There's no grave."

"Well. whatever you want is ok with me."

"Thanks," she murmured.

"And for God's sake, leave the noodles! I don't know why you ordered them."

Suddenly, she put down her fork and placed her hand on her lower abdomen.

"Christ, what's the matter?" George asked.

"The baby. I think the baby just moved. Our baby."

"Our baby," he repeated. He leant over to her and put his hand, gently, on her cheek.

Sara woke late on the Sunday. Images of Kim had been dancing at the edge of her mind all night but, somehow, she'd been able to banish her. *I'll be with you tomorrow, I promise.* But it wasn't true. The dazzling light of a summer's morning did not deliver the courage which Sara hoped it would. She still pushed Kim away.

George remained sleeping so she crept out of the bedroom and went to the kitchen to make herself a camomile tea. She rarely drank a whole cup, finding it mildly disgusting, but she'd gone off coffee and was trying to avoid too much tea. The sun blazed. The roads were quiet. A cacophony of birdsong sent her to the lounge window, where she stood, sipping the camomile, envying the frenzied energy of the tits and robins flitting in and out of the hedges and trees in the garden opposite. As she moved away, she heard the deep buzz of a motorbike engine. She stopped. Something stirred in her and, instinctively, she put her hand on her abdomen. But the baby was sleeping, like his father.

She stood where she was for a few moments, listening intently as the engine noise grew nearer. She knew then, knew without checking, who it was. She didn't bother with her keys, just ran from the flat, down the stairs and out on to the street. He was there, sitting astride his bike, in the process of removing his helmet when he saw her. She had her hand up to shade her eyes from the strong sunlight. Martin reached behind him to get her helmet and, as she approached, he handed it to her and replaced his own. He didn't speak and she found she couldn't.

She wondered only briefly about the baby before climbing on behind him.

CHAPTER 19

Damage

That no one was hurt in the smoke-filled back room in The Arms public house at the end of March that year was just fortuitous. That the fire was started intentionally, and thus there was a criminal act to be investigated, was without doubt. But the enquiries made by the police were desultory and, hampered by a lack of resources, the investigation – if such it could be called – was soon shelved.

Then, on a day in late September, Tara Bowling, a resident in one of the blocks of flats on the Grenadier estate, exited the lift on the ground floor on her way to collect her daughter, Bailey, from school. She passed two women outside, talking and laughing. One of them was dark and attractive and several months pregnant. Something about her made Tara look twice, feeling she'd seen her somewhere before but unable to place her. As she looked back at the pregnant lady, the woman smiled at her, warmly. Tara called out to her.

"I'm sure I know you! What's yer name?" She was probably a teacher from Bailey's school.

The lady with the dark hair stopped smiling and did not answer. When it was evident that Sara was not going to reply, Patsy obliged.

"We're social workers."

Tara nodded and went on her way. *Fucking social workers*, she thought, regretting her friendliness.

As Sara watched Tara break into a jog, she turned to Patsy.

"What made you tell her that?"

"Why not?" said Patsy, smiling. "Why should we be constantly apologetic about what we do? You're the one always saying that to me!"

It was true. It was wearing to feel a vague sense of dread every time she admitted to her occupation. And she thought no more about her encounter with Tara Bowling.

It came to Tara, around two hours later, when she was frying up some fish fingers for Bailey's tea. She remembered *exactly* where she'd seen that attractive woman with the warm smile and the dark hair: in the Ladies' cloakroom on the night of Gail's welcome home party before the fire had disrupted everything. The police had asked around when they were all huddled in the car park, getting soaked in the tempestuous conditions, but no one cared much at that stage. They just wanted to get back into the warmth of the bar and resume the festivities. They were yet to see the destruction on the food table. Gail's mother had yet to discover that the cake she'd spent so many hours planning and perfecting was now an unrecognizable mess.

Tara didn't think the woman looked like the type who'd be starting fires but, then, she didn't look like the type who frequented The Arms either. That's why she'd noticed her. She stood out. And she was damn sure that she'd been *lurking* in the cubicle that night, emerging as she did *without flushing the toilet* and looking *guilty* when they all turned to face her.

That night, after Bailey, who was being *a right little madam*, had gone down, Tara Facebooked the mates she'd been with on the night of the fire to tell them of her suspicions. All were outraged, naturally, but, moreover, hugely excited. Since Gail Flood wasn't on Facebook, someone kindly WhatsApped her to let her know that Tara would be going to the police station the following morning. Gary Timms became quite aggressive when he was roused from his slumbers on the couch by Gail that evening. He was sleeping off the seven pints of Pride and the curry he'd had earlier. But when he heard that some *toe rag of a social worker* might be getting her comeuppance, he recovered quickly from his little bout of ill-humour.

"You're fucking joking, my girl?" he barked, seizing the diminutive Flood by the shoulders. "You – are – fucking – joking!"

Gail was overjoyed that Gary had shown her some affection. Throughout the rest of the evening, she kept stroking the top of her arms where he had grasped her. Perhaps Gary's good mood would translate into some real passion later when they'd retired to the bedroom.

At the police station, the desk sergeant looked sceptically at Tara.

"I don't know her name," she explained. "But she's a social worker, local like, so it should be easy to find her."

"So, she was in the pub on the night of the fire, so what? Why would you leap to the conclusion that she was responsible for it? We can't just go marching into her office and drag her down for questioning. We have to have some reasonable cause for suspecting her – some basis for investigating her."

"I've told you. I definitely saw her in the Ladies. I've got a hunch she was up to something."

"If we went on peoples' hunches, we'd be in a right state!" the officer joked.

"So you're not going to follow it up?"

The officer shook his head.

"If you get anything more concrete, by all means come back."

It had never been reported that Sara Turner, the social worker, was Kim Turner's sister. But when Gail's mother, Bev, learned of Tara's suspicions from her daughter, she suggested they visited Social Services offices and found out the name of the woman in question. At least, that would be a start, she claimed.

In the event, neither she nor Tara had the courage to storm the offices.

"Brings back some fucking terrible memories to me," Bev said.

They hung around outside, debating whether they should make up some story about needing a crisis loan. They were having a fag when Sara came out of the building. It was just gone 1pm and she was in a hurry. She was due at the Magistrates Court for a hearing at 2pm and she'd been asked to be there early for a meeting with the local authority's barrister. She'd be lucky to get there in time for the hearing, let alone the conference with counsel.

As Sara dashed past, wishing her bag were not so heavy, Tara and Bev saw her. Bev recognized her from her days in the public gallery during her daughter's trial.

"That's her!" hissed Tara.

"Oh my God," breathed Bev. "She was at the trial. She must be related to Kim Turner. She was there every day that I was. I queued next to her one day. It's definitely her."

It was easy then to pop into reception and make enquiries to establish Sara's name. The description was easy – *dark, attractive, pregnant.* The receptionist was from an agency and not suspicious when some spurious excuse was given for wanting to know.

"That's Sara Turner," she said. "Why? Had you got an appointment with her? She won't be back today, I'm afraid."

They made some vague response, thanked her and shot out, managing to contain their exuberance until they were some distance from the building. There was some high fiving and Tara did a little dance around Bev, her hands pumping the air.

Fifteen minutes later they were at the police station. Bev was much less polite than Tara, insisting their account was taken seriously and that *Sara Turner* was questioned about her whereabouts on the night of the pub fire. Surely, Bev maintained, as the desk officer, tight lipped, was unable to mask his irritation at her hectoring tone of voice, there will be some CCTV footage that might pick her up in the vicinity? Eventually, he agreed that Tara should come back the following morning to provide a statement.

Sara was identified, interviewed and charged, ultimately, with the lesser charge of arson with intent to cause criminal damage. She'd been arrested in the office one evening. As she was putting on her coat to leave, she noticed two police officers, one male, one female, talking to Gloria in her room. Initially, she thought little of it as it wasn't unusual for the police to be in attendance. But then, something in Gloria's expression, a paling, the way she pushed her hair back behind her ears, made Sara wonder if there wasn't some *personal* element to the visit. As she started to walk out, she heard Gloria call her.

"Sara, can you come in here, please?"

As she entered, Gloria was closing the internal blinds. There was something symbolic in this action: *when you walk back out, your life will have changed.*

There were no introductions.

"Sara Turner?"

"Yes." What's happened, she thought. Not an accident, surely: not George?

"We need you to come to the station with us. We want to interview you about an incident at the end of March this year at The Arms public house in Greenford."

Gloria pulled out a chair and indicated to Sara to sit down. She asked her if she wanted a glass of water and then left the room. Thanks to Gloria and the fact that, due to the lateness of the hour, the office was largely devoid of staff, Sara's humiliation was limited. Her maternity leave was due to start the following week anyway. Her absence was already anticipated.

The officers performed that familiar action where they put their hand on Sara's head as she lowered herself, awkwardly, into the rear seat of the police vehicle. Staring at the back of the officers' heads on their journey to the station, Sara could not prevent herself recalling her previous ride in a police car. But this time, she was calm, resigned. She placed her hands on her abdomen and waited for the baby to kick.

At the station, she was asked if she felt well enough to be interviewed or should they call a doctor to assess her.

"No," she answered. "I know what this is about. I won't be any trouble. I had a momentary lapse..." She stopped, unexpected tears scalding her eyes.

The woman police officer leant forward, touching Sara's arm lightly before hastily withdrawing when she saw her partner's look of disapproval. *What are you doing, giving this arsonist sympathy just because she's been found out?*

Sara declined the offer of the lawyer she was entitled to. The tape recorder was switched on and the caution read out to her. Her confession was short and articulate. Bail was forthcoming but she needed to report to the police station once a week.

Citing the manner of Kim's death in mitigation, Sara was merely fined and ordered, much to the delight of Gail and Bev Flood, to compensate Bev for the destruction of the cake. Not only was Sara of previous good character but, when attending before the Magistrates for sentencing, it was taken into consideration that she was eight and half months pregnant. But given that you cannot sit in judgment on other peoples' lives when you've made some serious misjudgements yourself, the conviction ended her career.

Thereafter, Sara's life followed a very different trajectory from the one she had imagined for herself – as did George's, of course. Indeed, most people who had known Kim Turner, but especially those who had loved her, found that they were living in a different land from the one they had so casually, thoughtlessly, complacently, occupied before her death.

EPILOGUE

Kim

There was a band of light interfering with Kim's vision. It came on gradually, dim at first and then growing in brightness. Panic swept through her as the light intensified.

She stumbled her way out of the room amidst the stares. There were no familiar faces, just a blurry sea of people to wade through in her escape from the humiliation of the assault. Someone opened the door of the flat as she came towards it.

You alright, love?

She blundered into him on her way through, unable to apologise, intent only on keeping going. Once out on the walkway, she felt disorientated before seeing the stairs and heading for them. The ring of light within her head grew brighter with every move she made.

At the top of the stairs, she hesitated, her right arm waving in the air trying to locate the hand rail.

They were on her before she could avoid them. She'd heard what sounded like an animal stampede from somewhere behind her: thunderous footsteps, shrieking and baying. Stevo Wright and his little gang of feral children were out on their nightly rampage through Block B on the Grenadier Estate, shoving each other out of the way in their race down the stairs. Kim's legs buckled as they jostled her from their path, whooping with excess energy and excitement.

There is no doubt they saw her fall. One of them stopped, albeit briefly, a boy of ten who lived three doors down from Stevo. He heard the siren of the ambulance later when he was lying in bed. He'd noticed the blood dripping down from one of her eyebrows, like globules of wax on a candle. His step Dad had come looking for him, clipping him around the head when he found him –

You're grounded, you little shit.

He'd wanted to tell him about the lady but he didn't fancy another slap, or something worse. When he passed Stevo the next morning, asking him where he was going as he was walking in the opposite direction to the bus stop, no reference was made to the previous night's escapade.

No-one seemed to care about the woman with the bloody face who'd been pushed out of the way and fallen down the stairs.

~ THE END ~